the Wonder of All Things

Also by Jason Mott

THE RETURNED

jason mott

the Wonder of All Things

MIRA®

Recycling programs
for this product may
not exist in your area.

Printed in U.S.A.

First printing: October 2014
10 9 8 7 6 5 4 3 2 1

To those who pull us through the impossible.

the Wonder of All Things

ONE

FOR ONCE, DEATH took pity.

That is what the people of Stone Temple would say in the time that came after. It was late autumn and the townspeople were preparing for an early winter. The clouds were heavy in the days before the Fall Festival and that always meant hard, cold months ahead. The festival was their way of saying goodbye to short sleeves and tourist season, cicadas and apple brandy on the front porch at sunset.

The highlight would be Matt Cooper, who would come and entertain them with stunts in his airplane. He was one of only two people to venture out from Stone Temple and return with the world knowing his name. He had become a pilot for a traveling air show troop and, when he could, he came to town with his red-white-and-blue-painted biplane to show the people of this small town that he had not forgotten them. He would land it in the open field where the town held festivals and barbecues, and the townspeople loved him not only for his stunts, but because of how he had defied the fates of so many others who left the town, were broken by the world and returned with their hats in hand.

So on the day of the festival, the Ferris wheel was set up along with the tents for games and vendors and places where sweet foods could be cooked and there was a competition for blue-ribbon vegetables and a competition for the best gingerbread recipe. The entire town came out and the air was sweet and thick for miles when the day got late and Matt Cooper finally climbed into his airplane and buzzed above the earth. The townspeople took seats in makeshift bleachers and the old concrete grain silo was converted into an announcing booth. A pair of men sat atop it calling out all of Matt Cooper's tricks and techniques. They frequently remarked on both the inherent danger and, whenever they could, on the fact that he was a native of Stone Temple who had "done good." Folks craned their necks and held their breaths.

The plane ascended—straight up, the propeller chopping air, the engine buzzing, the sound of it softening as it stretched the rubber band of gravity, lifting into the heavens. Mountains could be stacked between man and earth just then. Finally, the crowd could hold their breaths no longer. They exhaled and, even though they knew full well that Matt Cooper could not hear them, they applauded.

It was when the tide of their applause was receding that they heard the sound of the engine sputter. The drone was broken, then restarted, then broken again. It went this way three times before only silence fell from the sky above. The silence remained. Because the plane was so far above them, it took a moment for the crowd to understand that it was falling. For so very long it seemed to be stationary—a dim, red star burning in the distance. Then the silence washed away and there came the long, dark aria of a man—who the town of Stone Temple believed was the best of them— falling to earth.

It was difficult to measure the space of time between when Matt Cooper's plane began falling and when it finally crashed into the earth. Some would later say it was all too fast to understand. Others that they had never known horror could last so long.

Then the waiting ended.

Matt Cooper was dead and there was a fire burning and the grain silo upon which the announcers had been seated lay broken, with the fragments of Matt Cooper's airplane scattered around it like dropped leaves. Everything was panic.

But for whatever reason that such things sometimes come to pass, fortune was kind. Debris from the plane washed over the crowd like sea foam. It left them bloodied and, in some cases, with broken bones, but Death stayed its hand. As people took stock of one another—still trying to douse the fire, still sifting through the rubble of the grain silo— the only death anyone could count was that of Matt Cooper, who died instantly when his plane hit the silo. Even the announcers, perched atop it like a bird, had somehow come out alive. The more time that came and went, the more people waited for bodies to be found—for the number of the living in this world to be lessened. But it was a day of miracles.

So it was with nervousness that the boy and girl were found buried in a pocket of concrete and steel beneath the grain silo. It was built with an infrastructure of steel pip-ing that, when felled by the plane, created small pockets. Macon Campbell, the town sheriff—a dark-skinned, over-worked man who had made it through the lion's share of his thirties with only a handful of things he wished he'd done differently—could just make out the pair of children held within the rubble. For a moment they were only shapes in dim lighting. Then he understood that one of them was his daughter, Ava. The other, her best friend, a boy named Wash.

The fear that came over him was like swallowed lightning.

"Ava!" he called out. "Ava! Wash! Can you hear me?"

His daughter responded by moving her hand. Her body was bent at an awkward angle—fetal, pulled in on itself like a ribbon—and she was half buried by debris. But she was alive. "Thank God," Macon said. "It's going to be okay. I'm going to get you out."

She looked up at him with fear and tears in her eyes. Her lip quivered and she looked around, as if trying to under-stand how all of this had happened, as if the world had bro-ken some promise she had always believed in. There was concrete and steel around her—sharp and waiting to come crashing down.

"Can you move?" Macon asked.

She answered by moving. First her hand—slowly, ten-tatively. Then, little by little, the other parts of her body. There was concrete atop her legs but, after some maneuver-ing, she freed herself.

"Don't move too much," Macon said. He spoke through a small, narrow breach in the rubble. He could fit his arm and part of his shoulder through it, but that was all. It would take help and time to move the rubble and safely get to the children. He called to the crowd behind him for help. "There are children here," he shouted.

It was after she had gotten her legs free that Ava saw the boy, Wash. He was unconscious and buried up to his chest in rubble. "Wash?" she said. He did not answer and she could not tell if he was breathing. "Wash?" she called again. His face was streaked with dust and there was a small bruise on his brow. By nature, the boy was pale—something that Ava teased him about as often as she could manage—but, just now, there was something different in his pallor. He looked blanched, like a photograph left too long in the sun. It was then that she saw the steel rod jutting out of his side, and the blood seeping from the wound. "Wash!" Ava yelled, and she started crawling toward him.

"Ava, don't move," Macon yelled. Again he tried to fit through the small gap in the rubble. Again only his arm and shoulder fit. "Ava, be still," he said. "This thing isn't stable."

She did not stop. She only kept her eyes on Wash, and continued crawling toward him. When she reached the boy she whispered his name. When he did not reply she put her hands on his face and hoped to feel something that might indicate that he was alive. Then she leaned close to his face, just above his open mouth, and tried to feel his breath. But it was difficult to tell what she was feeling. She was bruised and scratched from the fallen silo. She was frightened. Every nerve of her body seemed to be speaking to her at once. It drowned out any breathing she might have felt slide from Wash's lips.

"Is he alive?" Macon called.

"I don't know," Ava replied. "He's hurt." She placed her hand on his neck and hoped for a pulse, but her hands were shaking and the only heartbeat she could feel was the frightened thundering of her own.

"How is he hurt?" Macon asked. Finally help was arriving—firemen and volunteers. But they were only in the beginning stages of solving the riddle of how to stabilize the debris and get to the children.

Ava heard her father barking orders. She heard people shouting replies. There was talk of two-by-fours, steel rods, floor jacks, cranes. It soon became simply a choir of garbled voices. For Ava, there was only the wound in Wash's side, the sight of his blood spilling into the dust.

"I've got to do something," Ava said. She gripped him beneath his shoulders.

"No," Macon yelled. "Don't move him. Don't touch him."

But it was too late. She tugged at his shoulders and, as soon as she did, the debris that was covering him shifted in one great, awful lurch. The steel rod that was protruding into his side came free. His blood flowed faster.

Macon called out for more help.

Ava cried. She said, over and over again in a terrified voice, "I'm sorry...I'm sorry..." Her hands leaped nervously in front of her. She did not know where to put them. She was torn between her desire to help the boy and the truth that what she had just done made things worse.

"Ava!" Macon called. Eventually, his daughter heard him.

"I'm sorry," she said.

"Don't think about it," Macon replied. "Just put your hands over the wound. Put your hands over it to help slow the bleeding. Just hold on." For a third time, even though he knew it was pointless, he tried to maneuver his way through the small opening in the rubble. For a third time he failed. "Just put your hands on his side and press down, baby," he said.

Slowly, Ava pressed her hands over Wash's side. She felt the pulse of his blood as it spilled over her hands. She closed her eyes and cried. She hoped. She prayed. She called out to a god that, being only thirteen, she did not know that she understood or even believed in. But, just now, at this moment, she would believe in anything or anyone. She would give anything for her best friend to live, to be healed.

And then there was something akin to cold in her hands. A numbness in her palms and a feeling of needles racing up the length of her arms. The sound of her father calling for her faded away. The sound of everything receded and the darkness of her closed eyes was darker than any she had ever experienced before.

In the darkness, she saw him. Wash. He stood in the center of the darkness, the pale hue of his skin almost glowing. He was bruised and there was a cut on his brow. His clothes were covered with dirt from the fallen grain silo. The right side of his shirt was torn and there was blood pouring from the wound. But the boy did not seem to notice any of this. He only looked at Ava with a face that betrayed nothing.

"It's okay," Wash said. But, somehow, his words were in the voice of Ava's mother—dead for five years now. "It's going to be okay." He smiled—the small freckles dotting his face looked like cinnamon sprinkled over cloth. When he laughed, he laughed in the voice of Ava's mother.

Then Ava's eyes were open. Her father was still shouting her name. Her body was still bruised and sore. She still kneeled beside Wash with her hands covering his side—her fingers sticky with blood. She heard ambulances. She heard

yelling. She heard people crying—crying out of fear, crying at the loss of Matt Cooper, crying because they could
not understand how the day had turned so harsh so quickly.

Then she heard the sound of Wash's voice.

"Ava?" Wash said, opening his eyes. "Ava? What did you
do?" He reached across his stomach and placed his left hand
atop hers.

"No, Wash!" she said quickly. "I have to keep my hands
over it! You're bleeding! I've got to stop the bleeding!" But
there was no strength in her. She felt light-headed and could
not resist as Wash took her hands away.

Beneath where her hands had been—where, once, there
was a steel rod protruding into the boy, puncturing organs
and promising that even the lives of children were not guaranteed in this world—there was only the boy's skin, perfect
and unharmed.

"What did you do?" Wash asked again, looking up at her.

Then, for Ava, the world began to slide, as if the hinges
that kept the earth level were broken. The sight of Wash
became a glimmering dimness. Then the dimness faded, replaced by an empty, unbounded darkness.

The news of her healing the boy spread like wildfire.
Someone had been there with the camera of their cell phone
running. The video was uploaded and shared and transmit-
ted around the world. It leaped from screens to eyes to lips
to ears, fanned by the flame of imagination of a planet that
had been too long harboring a secret hope for some type of
confirmation of the miraculous.

For the next few days in the hospital, Ava's father sat by
her side and held her hand. He would talk to her, though

she was not always aware enough to recognize him. She existed in a haze, but she could tell by her father's face that she was not well. He seemed worried and afraid and reluctant, but he also wore a look of purpose. It was the way he had looked at her when, once, she and Wash were playing in the forest behind the house and she fell upon a shard of wood that stabbed nearly an inch and a half into her thigh.

Macon had brought her into the house and sat her at the kitchen table, looking at the wound and the splint of wood protruding from it like a crude arrow. He had the same expression he wore at her bedside now, an expression that told her there was a hard task to be done before the healing could begin.

Around the room Ava could see other people standing, waiting. Most of them were doctors, but there were others, too. People with cameras and microphones. Everyone in the room, including Macon, wore security badges. Each time someone opened the door to enter the room, the sound of shouting and the flashing of camera lights poured in from the hallway. Ava could see a trio of policemen standing outside.

"Ava?" Macon called out. She did not realize it, but she had drifted off to sleep again. Her body felt far away and floating, like a balloon resting on the surface of a lake, and she struggled to keep her eyes open. "Ava, can you hear me?" Macon said. "I'm going to ask you a couple of questions for these nice people, okay? You just look at me and pretend it's just the two of us. I promise it'll be quick."

A man that had been standing nearby with a video camera stepped forward and made an adjustment to a microphone that was sitting on the edge of Ava's bed between her and her father. He checked something on his equipment and gave Macon a nod of affirmation. Another man snapped photographs. He moved around the bed, alternating between squatting and standing, sometimes photographing Ava, sometimes Macon and, in turn, the two of them together.

Macon squeezed Ava's hand again to get her attention. "Has this ever happened before?" he asked. The photographer's camera shutter clicked. Then Macon asked another question, and Ava was not certain whether or not she had answered the first. Time was not linear for her. It bubbled up like air through water. She was never sure of her depth in it. "How long have you been able to do this?" Macon asked. "When was the first time?"

Again there was a foggy, confusing passage of time and then everyone in the room was suddenly talking at once, shouting questions at Macon, yelling for better answers. "You had to have known," Ava heard someone shout. The accusation was followed by several flashes from the photographer's camera, capturing the expression on Macon's face for posterity.

Macon withstood it as best he could, Ava could see. He was wearing the only suit he owned—charcoal-gray with a light blue shirt. The suit was frayed in places and there was a stain on the back of it from the time he'd attended a funeral and, on the way back, caught a ride with a friend who owned a pickup truck with greasy seats. But in spite of all that, Ava always loved the sight of her father in that suit.

"That's enough for now," Macon said to everyone. His voice was deep and booming. It was the voice of a man who was not only a father, but also the sheriff. "She's barely conscious and I won't keep harassing my daughter just because you want answers. You and everyone else will just have to wait."

"Ask her more," one of the doctors said. His name was Eldrich—Ava often heard her father yelling the man's name as they argued—and he was a thin, short man with a poor comb-over. His face was red with frustration. "We haven't learned anything yet," he barked. "Nothing about how all of this started, about how long she's been able to do it, about how she does it. And you, Sheriff, you've known about this all along. We have to do more tests." There was resentment in his voice. "Why did you think you could keep something like this, something like her, from the rest of the world? What made you think you had that right?"

Again the photographer snapped his photos. Again the man behind the video camera adjusted the audio on his microphone, recording it all, readying himself for the time when he would cut and edit and, finally, transmit it to the rest of the world. It was important that everyone see that here, in this small North Carolina town, there was a sheriff who had kept from the world a daughter who could do the impossible.

There was more yelling and arguing to follow, but Ava was not awake for it. Everything began to feel distant again. Darkness returned. Time jumped forward.

When she next opened her eyes she saw only the off-white tiles of the hospital ceiling. The smell of antiseptic was like a cloth draped across her face. She was cold, very cold. Somewhere, someone was talking. She began to panic and tried to sit up in the bed, but she felt a pain in her head that radiated outward in waves so sharp they halted her breath. She could not have screamed if she wanted.

And then the pain was lessened, like lightning arcing in the night, leaving only the shudder of thunder behind. Still, somewhere, someone was talking. The voice was low, garbled, like a song played underwater. She wondered if this was how deafness began. The sound of the voice stretched out, held a single, long note, then rose and fell slowly. It wasn't someone talking; it was a voice singing. Ava caught words and the tone and timbre of the voice behind them. And then, as if a switch were thrown, she knew the voice and she could hear it clearly, and the comfort of it helped her push the pain away.

"Wash?" she called, raising her head from the pillow.

The boy sat in a small metal-framed chair next to the wall at the foot of her bed with his eyes closed. He had one hand suspended in the air before him—with his thumb and forefinger touching, making an "okay" sign. It was the position his body always took when he was struggling with the pitch of a song…which was nearly always. Wash didn't have a voice especially suited to singing, and he was well aware of it. His voice was better suited to reading aloud, something he often did for Ava.

When Ava spoke, Wash stopped singing and smiled widely. "I knew it," he said.

"You knew what?" Ava replied. Her voice was thin and raspy. She sat forward, trying to ease up onto her elbows so that she could see him better, but her body was not ready for that. So she settled back down onto the bed, keeping her eyes on Wash. He was still the gangly thirteen-year-old bookworm he had always been. There was comfort in that for Ava.

"I knew you'd wake up if I sang to you," Wash said.

"What are you talking about?" Ava asked. Her voice was a hollow cone.

"It was 'Banks of the Ohio,'" Wash said. He straightened his back—sitting erect and looking both confident and proud of himself. "It's a fact that people can hear things when they're asleep, even if they're in a coma. I don't know that you were in a coma—at least, the doctors never really called it that—but I knew that if I sang something, you'd wake up." He reached around awkwardly and patted himself on the back. Then he pointed at Ava and said, "You're welcome!"

"I hate that song," Ava said. Everything was sore and she was freezing. Her bones felt like they were filled with concrete. When she lifted her arm, it responded slowly and clumsily, doing only half of what she told it to. She closed her eyes and focused on breathing deeply and slowly. It helped, but only slightly. "I really hate that song," she managed finally.

"I know," Wash said. "But if I picked one you liked, you'd never want to wake up and tell me to shut up."

In spite of the pain, Ava laughed.

"How do you feel?" Wash asked.

"Usually with my hands," Ava said.

"Jerk," Wash replied in a low voice. He got out of his chair and walked over to Ava's side. "Really," he said, "how do you feel?"

"I'm cold," Ava replied. "I'm cold and everything hurts." The boy went to a large cabinet in the corner of the hospital room and came back with a blanket. Ava watched him closely as he walked. There was something important she needed to remember, something that had happened. But when she tried to recall whatever it was, there was only grayness in her mind, like a fog that hugs a lake under moonlight.

He placed the blanket over her. "I'm not sure what I can do about the rest," Wash said, "but I can help with the cold."

"You're okay," Ava replied, finally managing to sit up on her elbows. Wash's smile faded and deep wrinkles formed on his brow. "Uh-oh," Ava said slowly. "Your thought trenches are showing, which means you're thinking. That's not a good sign."

"I'm fine," he said, and he rubbed his forehead. He stood beside her bed. "Are you ready for all this?" he asked, and Ava could not quite make out the tone of his voice. There was excitement in it, but also uncertainty.

"Am I ready for what?" Ava asked.

Next to the bed, Wash fumbled with his shirt for a moment—untucking it from his jeans with clumsiness. He adjusted the upper waistband of his underwear so that they did not show, then lifted his shirt up and turned to the side.

"Can you believe it?" he asked, smiling awkwardly, awaiting judgment.

Ava looked at the long stretch of skin from his waist to his ribs. The boy was thin and gangly and pale. "Believe what?" Ava asked. "That you're skinnier than a cereal box and pale enough to get sunburn from a book light? I've known that for a while now, Wash." She laughed, but the laughter rolled into a cough that made her eyes water.

Wash let the joke pass. He turned back and forth slightly to be sure that Ava was able to see the full scope of how he was not injured. Not bruised. Not scarred. "You did this," Wash said. He lowered his shirt and reached for the television remote, then pointed it at the screen that sat high up on the wall above the foot of Ava's bed.

He flipped through the channels on the television, scanning each one only for a moment. He knew what he was looking for and grew more and more frustrated by the fact that he could not find it. "Just give me a second," he said. "Don't go remembering anything just yet. It'll be so much better if I can just show you. You're not going to believe it."

"You're freaking me out, Wash."

"Shush!" he interrupted. Finally he stopped changing channels. On the television was a news program with a woman in a well-cut suit standing in front of a large screen with a picture of Ava on it. Across the bottom of the screen was the banner The Miracle Child. For the next few minutes Ava lay back in her hospital bed and watched as video from the Fall Festival filled the screen. She saw Matt Cooper's airplane rising and falling through the sky. There were images of families and children and people enjoying the booths and rides and the food, and everything seemed perfect and everything was bathed in sunlight.

All of this, Ava could remember.

Then she watched as the airplane rose into the sky—she just could make out the low drone of the plane's engine over the sound of the oohs and ahhs of the person shooting the video—and then the sound of the engine fell silent.

Then the video broke off and the news anchor returned. She looked into the camera and talked about the potential number of lives that could have been lost, the horror and tragedy that might have been. And then there was a photograph of Ava on the screen. It was taken from her yearbook.

Her smile was wide and slightly awkward, like a person who doesn't like the way their clothes are fitted.

"In a yet unexplained turn of events," the news anchor continued after explaining how Wash and Ava were trapped beneath the rubble, "this young girl, Ava Campbell, somehow healed her friend of his injuries." On-screen there was a photo of Wash being pulled from the debris. His clothes were torn and attention was given to the side of his stomach where, only a little while before, there had been a horrible injury. "The boy was utterly and completely healed," the reporter said again, repeating her words slowly and with faultless elocution.

"Look!" Wash said excitedly, pointing at the television. He looked back at Ava and he lifted his shirt again, as if to verify that what she saw on television and what she saw now, in real life, were both equally true. "You really did that," he said. "You really did this!" His smile was wide and bright again, filled with wonder and awe.

"It's not true," Ava said. She closed her eyes and shook her head. "It's a joke, right?"

The excitement faded from his face. "Sit up," he said softly. He lowered his shirt and reached over and put his arms beneath her back to help her sit up in the bed.

"What are you doing?" she asked.

"Just trust me," he said. He helped her swing her feet over to the side of the bed. She inhaled sharply with each movement. Wash grimaced with her. "This will be quick," he said. "I promise. You have to see this for yourself."

The two of them made their way across the room with her arm draped across his shoulders and his arms around her waist. When they reached the window, he helped her sit upon the wide sill. "Where's my dad?" she asked. "Why isn't he here?"

"It's okay," Wash said. He looked into her eyes. "My guess is that he's out taking care of what I'm trying to show you."

"What do you mean?"

"Look," the boy said, nodding toward the window.

Finally she turned and gazed out the window, which overlooked a parking lot that was crowded with cars and vans and people and banners and cameras. There was cheering and shouting and people waving signs. Along the front of the hospital was a row of policemen, standing in uniform, keeping the crowd from coming inside.

"What's happening?" Ava asked. "What do they want?"

"You," the boy said softly. "They're all here because of you. Can you believe that? You won't believe how famous Stone Temple is right now—how famous *you* are right now. People are coming from all over to see you. Hundreds of them—thousands, maybe."

The crowd below her was like an ocean. There were waves of movement, rivulets of cheering, of signs flagging back and forth.

"It's just amazing," Wash said.

"Help me back to bed, Wash," Ava said. There was the lightning of pain inside her again suddenly, and an emptiness in the pit of her stomach that throbbed like a heartbeat. It made her feel as though the center of her did not exist, as though her body wasn't completely formed. Then her stomach clenched and there was no more strength in her legs. Wash was not fast enough to catch her as she tumbled to her knees. Ava coughed. It was a hard, rattling cough, and there were flecks of blood on the floor beneath her mouth. More came with each cough.

"Nurse! Nurse!" Wash yelled. "Somebody help!" He struggled to lift Ava from the floor and put her back in the bed. Still he called for help.

"It's okay," Ava said as he maneuvered her awkwardly into the bed. She did not see the blood that was in the vomit she left behind on the floor. Only Wash saw that.

"It's going to be okay," Wash said softly. In the hallway there was the sound of footsteps approaching.

Ava closed her eyes.

"Before they get here," Wash said, "I just want to say thank you. Thank you for...well...for whatever happened. For whatever you did."

"I want to go home," Ava said. Drowsiness and fatigue was a tide rising inside of her. "When I go home everything will be okay," she said. In her mind there was the image of her father's small gray house in Stone Temple. The paint was faded and the wood was worn and broken in places, but home is always a thing of beauty to a child. "I don't want any of this," Ava said softly. "I just want to go home."

"Everything's different now," Wash said. "Home isn't quite home anymore."

By the time the girl is five years old her mother has found the rhythm of things. The two of them have established a pattern where Ava is never far from her mother's heels and her mother is always smiling when her daughter comes to be with her. Oftentimes, in the warm hours of the afternoon, when the work is done for the day and her husband is still away at the station, it is possible for them both to believe that they are the only ones left in this world. At these times they will disappear into the mountains for the sake of disappearing.

Heather walks out in front, checking the ground for snakes and pitfalls like a concerned parent, and Ava, for her part, does the job of running up ahead and causing her mother to worry just enough. As Heather walks she thinks about how their lives might change in the years to come. She foresees the day when her daughter will not need her. The day when her child will not be a child but will become a woman who runs ahead into the world and, perhaps, does not look back. What will become of her then?

"Come on, Mom!" Ava calls.

"I'm coming," Heather replies.

The sun is high and the wind is still and the earth is buzzing with the sound of life. The birds sing. The insects hum.

"Mom?" Ava calls. She has flitted around a bend in the trail, and there is something different in her voice now, as she stands in this place where her mother cannot see her. A knot of fear rises in Heather's throat.

"What is it?"

"Mom!" Ava screams.

Heather rushes through the brush. It is inescapable, the fear she feels now, the fear she did not know was possible. But she has always been afraid; she simply lacked a location to affix to it. Now she has that: she has a child.

By the time Heather rounds the corner she can hear her daughter crying. It is a wet, choking sound, a soft shudder like the sound of ice breaking. "What is it?" Heather asks, just as she sees that her daughter is unharmed. Sprawled in the thick green grass is a deer. It is a female, its pelt the color of the late evening. There is an arrow rising out of its chest. The animal wheezes, slowly.

"Mom..." Ava says. Her face is streaked with tears. "Mom," the child repeats. The word is a mantra. Heather looks around, hoping to find the hunter, hoping that things might be brought to a quick and less painful end for the animal. But there is no one. "Is it going to die?" Ava asks.

"It's not your fault," Heather replies, though she does not quite know why.

Ava weeps. She tries to understand. "How long is it going to take? What happens after? Is anyone going to bury it?" On and on, she gives voice to the questions that dance in her head.

Her mother does not have the answers. And so the two of them sit in silence, sharing this moment of time, this small plot of a large cruel world, with an animal in its last breaths of life. The deer watches them without fear and it does not flinch, does not withdraw when the child reaches out a trembling hand and places it on the animal's neck. The deer's hide is smooth.

Heather kisses the top of Ava's head. They are both crying now.

The animal's breathing slows. Without asking, Ava reaches up and grasps the arrow that has pierced the animal's lung. She pulls it and, after a moment of resistance, it comes free. The deer trembles. It releases a sound like the bleating of sheep. Ava tosses the arrow away.

"Ava," Heather says, "it's too late."

Heather can see in the child's face that all she wants is for the creature to be better. All she wants is for the blood to stop. All she wants is for death to turn away, just this once. Ava places her hands over the wound. The deer's blood flows in pulses, like a heartbeat. Ava closes her eyes and wants for nothing other than for the deer to be better.

What comes next is a trembling of her hands, like the spark of electricity placed beneath her palms. Then the deer is up, on its feet. It is still bleeding, but it is able to walk, ever so slowly.

Heather takes Ava in her arms and scuttles backward in the grass. Ava is limp. "Ava!" Heather calls. "Ava!"

Heather watches as the deer walks slowly away—still wheezing, the blood still flowing from its pierced lung, though not as vigorously as it had been. Step after step, the animal disappears into the forest, leaving a trail of blood.

"Ava?" Heather continues, again and again. "Please wake up," *she pleads. The minutes grow into one another like vines until, at last, Ava stirs.*

"It's okay," Ava says in a voice so low that her mother can barely understand.

Heather weeps with joy at the sound of her daughter's voice.

"The deer," Ava whispers. "It's okay? I wished for it to be okay."

Heather looks at the trail of blood leading into the forest, but she does not understand anything of what has happened.

TWO

"**THAT GIRL OF** yours really started something, didn't she, Sheriff?" John Mitchell put his hands akimbo and tightened his mouth into a querulous frown. He had been the sheriff of Stone Temple before Macon, and had not retired the cynicism acquired from a lifetime of upholding the law. He was a wiry man made of hard corners: sharp elbows and pointed shoulders, a long nose and deep wrinkles at the corners of his eyes that made him seem to scowl even when he was happy. He cast the type of bitter appearance that made children uneasy around him, even though he was a kind man who loved children.

Since passing the ornaments and instruments of sheriff on to Macon, he came by the station every Wednesday afternoon to check in on Macon and to get a general sense of what he'd left behind. Most days there was little to talk

about other than missing farm animals—usually just animals
that had walked off of their own accord—and where the best
fishing or hunting spots were, depending on the weather and
the time of year. But today John had come by and there was
much more to talk about than fishing and runaway animals.
"Looks like all hell's done broke loose," John said.

"Can't argue with that," Macon replied. The two men
were standing in Macon's office, peeking out through the
window blinds. Outside there was a mob of reporters and
cameras and people with signs. Macon sipped from a cup of
coffee and watched and considered it all.

Macon was wrapping up work in the sheriff's office of
Stone Temple and doing the best he could to ignore the
crowds of people surrounding the building, preparing to pick
up his daughter from the hospital in Asheville. He didn't like
looking at the crowds outside the station, but looking away
was a challenge, as well. He wanted to understand it all, and
the road to understanding is always paved with hours spent
doing something that it would be easier not to do. Still, all
watching the crowds did for him was remind him that the
world around him was getting out of control.

He'd been to the hospital every day since the incident
and, each day, the process of getting there was more and
more complicated—traffic, people, reporters. And once he
was there, he was forced to sit and watch test after test after
test run on his daughter. The doctors and nurses came like
clockwork. They poked, they prodded. They took Ava's
blood. They took Macon's blood. There were theories that
whatever Ava had done might be rooted in her genetics. And
with her mother deceased, Macon became the pincushion
through which they hoped to explore their theories. They

took bone marrow, DNA samples. And then, like old-world oracles, they came back for more blood, saying that the answers had to be hidden within.

Macon's arm was still sore from a young nurse who didn't quite seem to have yet perfected her craft. Time and again, she missed his vein. It was somewhere around the sixth error that he decided he'd had enough. "It's time to stop this," was all he said. And, from that point forward, he limited the doctors' access to his daughter and he told them, in no uncertain terms, that he would be taking her home.

Today was the day he would bring her home. And the entire world seemed to be watching. He had always been a private man, and nothing that was happening in his life right now sat well with him. The earth was falling away beneath his feet.

"Never would have thought it," John said.

"What's that?"

"That all of this could fit into a town like ours."

"I suppose nobody ever thinks something like this will fit," Macon replied, taking another sip of his coffee. Finally he closed the blinds and returned to sitting at his desk. "But there it is," he said, motioning at the window and the crowd beyond it.

"I still can't quite see why you wouldn't want to stay in Asheville," John said. He leaned back on his heels a bit and thought. "Then again," he said, "I suppose that if I were you and Ava was well enough that she didn't have to be there, I reckon I'd want to have the home field advantage, too. Up there in Asheville, it's just a city of people you don't know. At least here, you know who you can trust. And, if you really, really want to, there are enough mountains and backwoods paths that you could sneak away from all of the cameras, even if only for a little while."

Macon's office, much like the town of Stone Temple, was small and old. The sheriff's office building had been rebuilt in the late sixties after having burned down—something to do with lightning. And from that rebuilding onward, little had changed—apart from wiring the place for internet a few years back.

"Any actual crimes going on?" John asked, returning from the window. "I expect not, but I like to ask."

"Crimes? No," Macon said. "Mostly it's just people. Too damned many of them. And everybody's got their own agenda. You been out there on the mountain road lately?"

"Not if I can help it," John said. "I try to stay in town most these days."

"You couldn't get over the mountain now if you wanted to," Macon said. "At least not without burning three or four hours. It's a parking lot. Just full of people. People in cars, people in vans, people in buses, people on bicycles, people walking. I don't know where they're planning on staying. Folks have already started renting out their houses and their property to anybody with enough money, but even with all that, I don't think Stone Temple is big enough to hold all of this. It's like watching floodwaters rise. Except I feel like we didn't get the part where it started at our ankles and crept up slowly. All of this—" he made a motion with his hand to indicate the mass of people outside his window "—all of this makes me feel like the waters are already up to our necks."

John nodded to show that he understood and agreed. He walked to the opened door of Macon's office and looked out at the rest of the station. "Got a few new faces out there," he said.

"State police loaned us a few bodies, just to help keep a handle on things," Macon replied. He leaned back in his chair and scratched his chin. "A lot of people in town now with a lot of different opinions. Some folks think it's all just some kind of hoax. And I can't say I'd believe too much differently if it was me. All they saw was some video on the web. And there isn't much in the world these days easier to disbelieve than what you see. So the skeptics have come and so have the people who think Ava's the Second Coming. Put those two together, and you've got a recipe for shenanigans. At least somebody had the good sense to decide that maybe we could use a little help."

"On whose dime?" John asked.

"Not sure if they're getting paid overtime or what," Macon said. "I think most of it is coming from the state— damned sure ain't coming from us. But..."

"But what?" John asked.

"Honestly," Macon said, "I think some of them might be volunteering for all this."

John grunted disapprovingly. He closed the door to Macon's office. "Can't say I'm surprised by that. Keep an eye on them."

"On who? The volunteers?"

"Yep," John said. "Nobody volunteers for any damned thing. Not in this lifetime. They got mouths to feed, just like you do. If they're here, and if they're working, they're getting paid. Likely as not they're working for those reporters out there." He motioned toward the window through which he and Macon had been looking. There was disgust in his gesture. "Chances are they're getting paid for information. Little tidbits they can sell to the tabloids or whatever. They show up here, work, listen, watch and then when their shift is over they head out there and debrief." John sighed. "Oldest trick in the book," he said.

Macon thought for a moment. "Suppose I knew that, but I hadn't really paid any attention to it."

"Got any of them volunteering to work close to your house?"

"A couple," Macon said.

"Yeah," John replied. "Those are the ones getting paid the most."

"Think I should be worried?"

John waved his hand dismissively. "I wouldn't. Yeah, they're out to make a buck off you, but I don't think a single person out there would do it at the expense of your family. They'll keep you safe, but they'll make a little gravy if they can. I'd just be careful who I talked to," he said.

Macon watched John as he spoke. The old sheriff shifted in his seat and licked his lips as he glanced around the office. "Are we going to get down to business anytime soon?" Macon asked. "I know that, as Southern folks, we've made taking the long road in conversation into an art form, but my world is too crazy right now to spend much more time on whatever it is you're trying to bring up, John. I gotta make the drive up to Asheville and, like I said, with the road the way it is, it's going to take hours."

John squinted and leaned in toward Macon. "How did she do it?" he asked. "How did she heal that boy, really?"

"I don't know," Macon said. "Just like I told the reporters, the doctors, all those biologists they brought in, the twenty different preachers that have called me, the bloggers who keep emailing me. My story hasn't changed, John. I don't know anything about what's going on here."

"Bullshit," John said gruffly. "We both know that you can bury a dead body in the distance between what a person knows and what a person pretends not to know. And I have a hard time getting my mind around the notion that you didn't have any kind of inkling about any of this." He shook his head. "No, I think you knew and you wanted to keep her...it...this thing that she's able to do, you wanted to keep it under the radar."

Macon sighed. "Everybody on this planet seems to think that, even if it's not true."

"You were wrong to keep it secret," John said. "My wife," he began. His fingers picked at a nonexistent piece of lint on his pants. "I loved my wife," John said. "She was a good woman, a kind woman. Better than this world deserved, if you ask me. She was in that hospital a week before the end. Doctors did everything they could to save her. At least, that's what I thought." When he finally looked up from his fidgeting hand and into Macon's eyes, there was a dark mixture of blame and bitterness in his eyes.

"I'm not going to have this conversation with you, John," Macon said.

"It's just that you could have helped," John replied, and this time he was no longer the hard-nosed sheriff; he was simply a man who had lost his wife two years ago and now, very suddenly, believed it could have happened another way.

"John..." Macon said.

John snorted. "Let me guess," he said. "You don't know how she did it. You didn't know anything about her being able to heal people, right?" Before Macon could answer, John continued. "Whatever story you stick to, you're going to have to answer that question a hell of a lot more. You might not believe it, but those reporters out there paid me five hundred dollars just for walking in here," he said. "I told them I wouldn't have anything to tell them when I came out, and that's still true. But I'm not the only person in this world who, now that they know what you've been hiding, will ask questions about what right you have to keep something like this to yourself."

"They're already asking those questions, John," Macon replied. "As for them paying you to come in here, well, do what you feel you need to do. I know how much your pension is, and it's not enough. Everyone's got to make a living."

John nodded emphatically. "They do," he said. "Each and every one of us, from the day we're born to the day we die, we've got to live. And we've got to make a living. Times been tough lately."

Macon leaned back in his chair. "What else is there, John?" he asked. There was less patience in Macon's voice now. He respected the old man, thought of him as a good friend, but he saw in John's eyes that a shade of resentment still remained there. He was still thinking of his wife, Mabel, still imagining what might have been, still imagining what he believed Ava could have done.

John stared at him across the table briefly. The old sheriff's expression shifted from surprise to acceptance to anger to something akin to embarrassment. John took a deep breath. When he let it go, the words that followed slid out of him like an apology. "There's this preacher coming to town."

"We got bushels of them already," Macon replied. "Could

sell preachers by the pound if we wanted right now. Preachers and reporters, whole churches trying to set up camp out there. You name it, we got it."

"No," John said. "This one is different. Bigger. If I can talk you into sitting with him for a while..." His voice trailed off.

"Who is he?"

"Reverend Isaiah Brown. You've probably seen him on TV."

"Can't say I've heard of him. But I don't really keep up with reverends and I haven't really watched TV since they canceled *Seinfeld*."

"I'm not the type to ask for favors," John said, not pausing for the joke. "And I damned sure don't beg anyone for anything—"

Macon held up a hand to stop him. "I'm not going to make you say the words," he said. "I'll think about it. How much will he give you for that?"

At last, the fidgeting and nervousness stopped. "Don't know," he said. "But I figure that's got to be worth something."

"Good," Macon said.

John stood. "I'll let him know," he said. Then: "Just tell me, Macon. Promise me. Promise me you didn't know. That she couldn't have helped my wife. If you say it one more time, I'll believe it, and I'll be able to sleep tonight."

The hardness and intimidation was stripped away from him. He was a man trapped between the solace that he had done everything in his power to save his wife's life, and the possibility that, even though he didn't know it at the time, he could have done more. Every brick of self-forgiveness that he had placed around his heart since his wife's death was loosened, and all it would take was a word from Macon for it come to crashing down, leaving John to hate not only Macon but, most of all, himself.

"I promise," Macon said. There was exasperation and confusion in his voice. He had known John for nearly all of his life, and yet here the man stood, ready to test the bounds of their friendship, ready to lay the blame for the death of his wife at Macon's feet, all because of what Ava had done. But even through his frustration, Macon wondered if he would have behaved any differently. "This is all just as new to me as it is to everyone else, John," Macon said. "If there was anything that I could have done to help your wife, anything at all, I would have done it. People have a duty to help one another, a responsibility. That's one thing we've always agreed on."

"All right," John said finally. He made an awkward motion with his hand, something between a wave goodbye and a gesture of dismissiveness. "I believe you," he said. "But there's going to be people who won't. Your daughter has started something. Something big. People in this world are looking for something to believe in, and they're going to ask for help. When they do, if you say no—regardless of the reasons—they're not going to like it."

He turned and opened the door and finally left, leaving Macon to think about the future of things.

"Good news, kiddo. You're getting paroled today." Macon stood in the doorway of Ava's hospital room with a small bouquet of flowers in one hand and a gym bag in the other.

Floating above the flowers was a pair of balloons. One read Get Well Soon. The other It's a Girl.

"See what I did there?" Macon asked with a grin, pointing up at the balloons.

"Carmen's idea?" Ava asked. She sat up in the bed. Her father had never been the type to give flowers.

"Why wouldn't they be my idea?" he asked Ava as he entered the room.

"Where's Carmen?"

Macon placed the flowers on the windowsill. Outside the hospital the sun was high and bright. There were still reporters and people waving signs and banners in front of the hospital. "She's at home," he said. "She wanted to come, but it was just simpler if she stayed. Leaving the house is a little like heading out into a hurricane. People everywhere. Holding up signs. Shouting. Cheering. You name it. She and the baby don't need to be a part of all that if it can be helped."

"She just didn't come," Ava replied.

"It's more complicated than that and you know it," Macon said, dropping the gym bag on the foot of the bed. "I brought you some clothes to go home in. Go ahead and get dressed. We're not in a rush, but I'd rather get this circus started." He sat on the windowsill next to the flowers and folded his arms. "How are you feeling?"

"Fair to middling," she said.

"Haven't heard that in a while," Macon replied. "Your mom used to say it."

"I know," Ava said. "She would have come to pick me up, no matter how many people were outside the house." She sat up on the side of the bed and placed her feet on the floor. The cold ran up from the soles of her feet and tracked all the way up her spine. She still had trouble keeping warm since what had happened at the air show. She told the doctors about it, but they all assured her that it would be okay. They were always assuring her of the "okayness" of things, which did nothing more than convey to her that things were very far removed from okay. They saw her as a child, someone to keep the truth of things from, even if they did not know what the truth of things was. So they went on and on about how much they understood what had happened, and the more they said they understood, the more frightened Ava became. Though she was only thirteen, she knew that the bigger the lie, the more terrible the truth.

"How bad is this going to be?" she asked Macon as she took her clothes from the gym bag.

"We'll get through it," he said gently. "Go get dressed."

Ava took her clothes and went into the bathroom to change. When she came out Macon was standing in front of the television—his neck craned upward at an awkward angle to watch. On the screen there was an image of the front of the hospital. The banner across the bottom of the screen read Miracle Child to Be Released. He switched it off.

"What happened to your hair?" he asked. Ava's hair was a frizzy black mass atop her head. She had always had exceptionally thick hair—dark as molasses—and she was just enough of a tomboy that she gave it the least amount of attention that she felt she could manage. "Bring me a comb and come sit down," Macon said, standing beside the bed.

Ava did as she was told. In the years between Heather's death and the time when Carmen came into his life, Macon had become a very well-rounded single father. While he had never considered himself the type of man who believed in "women's roles" or "men's roles," he had always been willing to concede that, simply from having split the duties of parenthood along the typical gender lines, he had a lot to learn raising a daughter.

And of all the things he had learned on the path of fatherhood, of all the moments he and his daughter shared, it was the simple act of combing her hair that was the most soothing to them both. For Macon, it was the stillness of it. She was thirteen now, and soon she would reach the age when a daughter drifts away from her father in lieu of other men of the world. He knew that these moments, when nothing was said between them and he could treat her like less of a woman and more a child, would become fewer and fewer as time marched forward.

"How sick am I?" Ava asked. Her voice was assertive—not like that of a thirteen-year-old girl, but like that of a woman deserving answers.

Macon was almost finished with her hair. He had combed it and smoothed it and fixed it into a very neat ponytail. He took pride in how well he had learned to manage his daughter's hair. "I don't know, Ava," he said. "And that's the truth. The fact is, nobody really knows what the hell happened. Nobody knows how Wash got better. Nobody knows how you made him better." He sat on the foot of the bed, as if a great weight were being loaded upon his shoulders, word by word. "Wash seems okay, but they're doing all kinds of tests to be sure—not quite as many as you've been through or as many as they've still got up their sleeve for you, but they're definitely putting him through his paces. They kept him here for observation for a couple of days after everything happened, but then Brenda made a fuss and let her take him home. Brenda says he's feeling fine. But I think there's still something weird going on with him." He laughed stiffly. "As if all of this doesn't qualify as weird enough." She rested her head against his shoulder.

"As for you, Miracle Child, you're just a whirlwind of questions," Macon continued. "Hell, the only reason they're letting you go home is because I've had enough of you being trapped in here. And as much as I hate to admit it, I'm learning how to maneuver through all of this attention. You'd be surprised how much clout you get when you can threaten to hold a press conference if people don't let you take your daughter home."

"Do they want me to stay?" Ava asked.

"Some do," Macon replied, "but not because they're afraid for your life, just because they want to poke and prod you. And I've got nothing against tests, but they just want to do things they've already done. They all agree that you're out of danger and, for me, that's enough." He took her face in his hand and kissed her forehead. "I won't let them have you permanently," he said.

"What's wrong with me?" Ava asked.

"They're saying there's something going on with your blood cells. There's some type of anemia, which is the reason you're so cold all the time. Or maybe it's the iron deficiency. At least, that's what they think. Nobody is really willing to say with certainty what's going on. If you don't like what one doctor is telling you, just wait five minutes." He cleared his throat. "But the one thing they can all seem to agree on is that you're on the mend, and that's enough for me to get you the hell out of this place. I've spent too much time in hospitals over the years. Both of my parents died in this very hospital. But I'll get you out of here."

There was a knock at the door and, before Macon or Ava could answer, the door was flung open and a pair of men entered in a rush. They were both dressed in scrubs like doctors, but something was wrong. They were too young to be doctors and, even more than that, they were wild-eyed. Macon and Ava leaped up from the bed.

"You're her!" one of the men said. He had brown hair and a wide, bumpy nose. "We just need help," the man said quickly. "Our dad, he's sick. He had a stroke a few weeks ago and he's not getting any better."

The second man was shorter, with long blond hair and a sweaty upper lip. He only looked at Ava as the first man spoke. There was both fear and need in his eyes.

"He can't move his right side," the first man added. He huffed as he spoke, his words running together. It was obvious that they had used the doctors' outfits to get past security. Macon pulled Ava behind him. He placed his hand on his hip—out of habit as sheriff. He had expected to find his pistol there, but he'd left it locked in the glove compartment of the squad car when he arrived in the hospital. He took another step back, keeping Ava behind him and opening the distance between her and the men.

Ava peered over his shoulder, frightened. Even with everything Wash and her father had told her about how things had changed since the incident, she hadn't truly believed them. Perhaps she had not wanted to understand. There is always comfort in pretending that change has not happened in life, even when we know full well that nothing will ever again be the way it was.

From outside came the sound of footfalls running though the hallway toward the room. The second man looked back over his shoulder. "Shit," the man said. He tugged his brother's arm, as if to prompt the man to run. Then he stopped, realizing that they would not get far and, more importantly, that they had come to plead their case. So he stepped past his brother and toward Macon and Ava. "We just want our dad to get better," the man said. His voice was full of sadness and insistence. He pointed at Ava. "She can do for our dad what she did for that boy," he said. "That's all we wa—"

His words were cut off as a pair of policemen came racing into the room. They tackled the two men to the floor. The man with the bumpy nose hit hard against the linoleum. Blood trickled from his mouth. But never, not even when another police officer stuck a knee in his back as he was handcuffed, never did he take his eyes off Ava. Never did he stop asking her to help his father.

Coming out of the hospital was as terrifying as Ava had expected it to be. It was a blur of yelling and lights and cameras and people calling her name. The policemen formed a wall between her and the crowd, leaving enough room for her and Macon to make it to their car. Parked in front and behind the car were state policemen, their lights flashing.

The sea of faces called her name again and again, and she could not help but look at them. Each time she turned to see who was calling her name, a wall of light flashed before her eyes. She could not count how many reporters there were, how many cameras, how many people holding up signs that read Ava's Real and It's a Miracle. Her eyes landed on a woman waving a banner that read Help My Child, Please.

She had frizzled blond hair and heavy lines around her eyes and she looked worn down by the world around her. She did not chant or cheer like the others. She only looked at Ava pleadingly.

Then they were inside the car and the wall of policemen surrounded them.

"Not so bad," Macon said. He'd driven his squad car. It was one of two the small town of Stone Temple owned. When he switched on the lights atop the car, the police cars in front and behind did the same. And then the car in front started off and Macon followed as they slowly made their way out of the hospital parking lot, past the crowds, through the streets of Asheville toward the highway.

"I don't know what to do with all this," Ava said as the crowds disappeared behind them.

"Do the best you can," Macon said. "Just don't get lost in it."

Just as Wash had promised, home was not home anymore. The town of Stone Temple had always been a town that the world did not care to bother itself knowing. It was named after the Masonic temple that once stood in its center. But it was well over eighty years ago that the temple burned to the ground, along with a good portion of the town itself. The population, on average, was counted somewhere around fifteen hundred, and for the most part, it was the kind of place that people didn't even pass through on their way to better locations—not since the building of the bypass almost twenty years ago. But there were still businesses that made life possible. And there were still people being born, living and dying here.

Stone Temple was an odd beauty. The town lived in a

cradle of old trees and older mountains. The main road in and out of town rested on the shoulders of the mountain. In places, it promised to cast a driver off, to send them tumbling down the slopes that were covered in oak and pine and birch or, in some sections, covered in nothing but the unforgiving and constant rock.

But Stone Temple was peaceful, quiet. It was a place that slept.

All that was changed now.

It took hours to drive the length of the winding mountain road. Even before they'd entered the city, Ava could see how different it all was. In the fields along the outskirts, Ava could make out tents and vans, RVs and cars, all spaced in a field that had been harvested and sat bare and waiting for the next planting season.

"What do they all want?" Ava asked her father.

Macon grimaced, trying to keep his eyes on the road ahead. The state police had done a decent job of clearing the path into Stone Temple, but they could not remove everyone from the small road. People stood on foot—sometimes on the narrow edge of the road, other times in the oncoming lane, even though doing so meant they would have little place to go if someone came along the road out of Stone Temple.

"Turns out," Macon finally said when he felt that he could split his attention enough to reply to his daughter, "all of that stuff people used to talk about, all that stuff about wanting to keep the world out, about wanting to keep Stone Temple a secret. Well, it went right out the door when folks started opening up their checkbooks." He glanced at one of the fields brimming with people as they passed. "Gotta make a living, though, I suppose."

The closer they got to town, the busier things became. The road leading into Stone Temple was two lanes, climbing and falling through the mountains, full of blind curves and steep drop-offs. It was generally a quiet road, but now it was inundated with vehicles, the traffic thicker than Ava had ever seen it. The police escort slowed to a crawl as they came up behind the wall of cars. Those passing in the opposite direction stared at Ava like rubberneckers watching a horrific accident.

When they finally arrived to Stone Temple proper, there were people gathered in the narrow streets. They had been waiting for Ava to arrive and were filled with a fervor that was typically reserved for presidents and celebrities—though neither a president nor a celebrity had ever come to Stone Temple.

Ava didn't recognize any of the people standing along the streets, cheering and yelling and holding up their signs. And she couldn't exactly say why she felt the need to look for familiar faces among the mass of people. Perhaps she simply hoped that if she saw someone she knew, it would help to lower the scope of everything that was happening, everything she did not understand.

"They won't be at the house, will they?" Ava asked her father. He was concentrating on the road. Thus far the people around them were not encroaching on the car, but he couldn't help but feel that it was only a matter of time before someone jumped out into the road—maybe even onto the car itself—the way they did on television.

"No, no," he said. He answered quickly and confidently, as though he had been expecting the question. "They've got everything cleared off once we get through the town," he continued. "I tried to tell these guys that it would have been better to come up from the other side. You know, swing up along Blacksmith Road, through the forest. But it rained pretty hard the other day, so they didn't want to risk it." He motioned to a man standing along the street with a sign held above his head that read Help Me, Too.

Ava and Macon stared at the man as they passed.

"Just take it as it is, Ava," Macon said. "It'll get better. Things will be strange for a little while, but they'll calm down. You, this whole thing, it's just the flavor of the month, you know? People get excited, but eventually the excitement cools and people go back to living the lives they know. These things don't last."

"Everything lasts forever," Ava said quietly as though she were making the statement to herself rather than to her father. "Older people always think that things like this can't last. But that's not the way it is anymore. Things can last forever and ever now because of the internet. Everything is saved somewhere. Everything is permanent. Nothing dies anymore."

"That's...insightful," Macon said. He'd wanted to use another adjective, but he had become distracted. They were almost out of town now, almost to the point where the small buildings and few streets that comprised the town would fall away and give rise to the fields and trees surrounding the town. Not long after that, they would take the narrow, winding road up the mountain to their home.

"Wash'll be at the house when we get home," Macon said with more than a little playful accusation in his tone.

"Who said I was thinking about Wash?"

"You two have been Bonnie and Clyde since the day you

met," Macon said. "I have no doubt that you've been won-dering why he wasn't there at the hospital when I came to pick you up. I know I'd be upset if I were a young girl and my boyfriend wasn't there to greet me when I came out of the hospital."

"He's not my boyfriend," Ava said with a flash of embar-rassment.

"Do you prefer paramour, then? Is that the language all of the cool kids are using these days? Keeping it a little retro, you know?" He stretched across the front seat and elbowed her playfully. "I mean, you know, I'm old and everything so I can't really be expected to keep up with all this stuff. You little whippersnappers are so dabgum..." He paused, and then he laughed. "Hell," he said finally. "I can't really think of the word I'm looking for to finish that joke."

"Do you know why?" Ava asked, smiling a little.

"Why?" Macon replied.

"Because you're old," she jabbed, and they both smiled.

When they were properly outside the city, the crowds that had been in the streets were gone and there was only the countryside and the mountains and the trees and the sky above transitioning from the bright blue of afternoon into the softer hues of evening, promising a languid sunset.

"Ava!" Wash called as she stepped out of the car. He, his grandmother, Brenda, and Carmen were standing in the doorway of the house, the light from inside washing over their shoulders. He waved at her as if he had not seen her in months. He seemed to be holding back the urge to run over and hug her.

"Hey, Wash," she said softly, resisting her own urge to

rush to him. Being home, seeing Wash, it was like opening the windows of a house in the wake of a spring rain.

But it was Carmen, Ava's stepmother, who came out of the doorway and walked over and hugged her first. She was pregnant, very pregnant, and so her walk was a slow, awkward waddle. Carmen was of average height, with sharp, bright features. She smiled often, in spite of the tension between her and Ava that sometimes filled the house and made it seem as though the walls were not strong enough to hold the entirety of their family. She had been born to Cuban parents living in Florida and had grown up bouncing from state to state as her father sought work. Eventually her father settled in the Midwest and opened a garage and, when Carmen was out of high school, she went to college in North Carolina and, after college, decided to stay. She was working as a teacher in Asheville when she met Macon—a dark-skinned widower sheriff with an unrelenting optimism and a smile that made promises she could not ignore.

The two of them became a part of each other's life quickly, despite Ava's resentment over the fact that Carmen was not her mother. Now she and Macon were married and all of them were trying to make the best of things.

"It's so good to have you home," Carmen said, holding Ava tightly. The swell of her belly was pressed between them. No sooner than Carmen's arms were around her, Ava broke the hug. "We've got such a great night planned," Carmen said. She had grown accustomed to Ava's resentment. "Brenda brought pie, and you know she never cooks anything unless you hold a gun to her head."

"I'm not cooking again unless somebody's dead," Brenda said, walking over. She was tall and willowy and with a crown of red hair. She was a strong woman who, in spite of her thin frame, exuded a regal and authoritative air. Macon sometimes called her the "Vengeful Peacock," though he was smart enough never to call her that while she was within earshot. "How are you feeling, child?" Brenda said, stepping in to hug Ava just as Carmen pulled away. She smelled of cinnamon.

"Why does everyone keep asking me that?"

"Because it's what people do when they don't know what else to say," Brenda said matter-of-factly.

"She's doing fine," Macon said, walking up beside them. "And she's going to be even better with each and every day," he added.

She hugged Ava again and said, "Well, whatever the hell it is, we'll sort it out. Don't worry any more than you have to."

"Yes, ma'am," Ava said, peeking around the woman.

"I suppose you want to say hello to Wash," she said as she released Ava and stepped aside.

Ava and Wash met each other just beneath the eaves of the porch. He was still pale, Ava thought, but he seemed to be doing well enough.

"Hey," the boy said softly.

"You're not going to show me your stomach again, are you? Because you really don't have anything worth showing," Ava said. "You know that giant marshmallow guy at the end of the *Ghostbusters* movie? That's totally what you reminded me of."

"Shut up," Wash said, grinning.

"I've had nightmares about it," Ava continued.

"Shut up!" he said, and finally he stepped forward and hugged her. He smelled like pines and grass and the river.

"Okay, okay," Macon said, walking over. "Break it up. We've got a dinner to eat. And I'm starving."

Dinner was a blur of sweet and fried foods and conversations about the hospital, about what was going on in the town, about what the internet was saying about the air show, how far the videos had spread.

The subject no one discussed, the subject they all talked around, was what exactly had happened that day. What exactly did Ava do, and how? And why couldn't she remember it? Would it truly fix itself? And what of Wash? Was he really healed? Like some rare breed of sword swallowers, they swallowed their curiosity that night.

After dinner, Wash and Ava sat alone on the front porch, looking up at the stars and listening to Macon, Carmen and Brenda in the kitchen telling stories about how Stone Temple used to be—conversations sparked by the news reports of how the town had been taken over by people in the recent days.

"Does it hurt?" Wash asked.

"Does what hurt?"

He shrugged his shoulders. "Anything, I guess. You don't really look like yourself," Wash said.

"For a person who reads as much as you do, you'd think you'd be a little better at describing things, Wash."

"Whatever," Wash said.

A small cricket made its way up onto the porch. It sat on the worn oak wood and looked at the two children. It did not sing for them.

"You know what I mean."

She did know what he meant, of course, even if she did not want to admit to it. She noticed it immediately in the days after she woke up in the hospital. It was on the day when she was well enough to get out of bed on her own and make it to the bathroom. Macon was there with her and tried to help her, but she had inherited stubbornness from her mother. She refused him and, very slowly, made her way to the bathroom as he watched her every step, ready to leap up to help her. "I'm fine," she told him when she finally reached the bathroom.

She closed the door and stood before the sink. She was so tired from those few steps that she'd almost forgotten her reason for coming into the bathroom to begin with. She leaned in against the edge of the sink, huffing. When she finally caught her breath she lifted her head and saw a different version of herself in the mirror.

The girl in the mirror had Ava's bones and skin, but the bones were too sharp, the skin pulled too tightly about the face. Her cheekbones, which were naturally sharp—another inheritance from her mother—looked like shards of stone reaching out from the side of a cliff. The color had drained from her usually dark skin, and it was dry and flaky, as though it might suddenly crack and bleed at any moment, worse than any winter windburn she'd ever known. It was mottled and spotted in places, though the appearance of it was so odd that she wondered if she might be imagining it.

This was the worst of it, she had thought that day.

Now she was out of the hospital and a part of her had hoped that the version of herself that she saw that day was gone. But now Wash, being of the honest nature that he was, had confirmed for her what she had known the entire time: nothing was healed, not really.

A cricket on the porch seemed to look up at them. Out

in the night, among the darkness and grass and trees and breadth of the world, other crickets sang a soft melody. It was always a mystery, how creatures so tiny were able to build such a large presence for themselves in the world. The sound of the insects rose and filled Wash's and Ava's ears and drowned out the conversation they were not having—the one they both knew they should have, the one about what really happened that day, beneath the rubble and debris of the fallen grain silo.

"It must be sick," Wash said, looking down at the silent insect. "Otherwise, it wouldn't just come up here this close to us like this." He leaned forward, but the insect did not retreat, as it should have. "Yeah," Wash said, "definitely sick. Or hurt. Did you know that you can always tell the males apart from the females because the males are the only ones that chirp?"

"You're rambling, Wash," Ava said. A chill swept over her and she folded her arms across her chest to keep warm.

"Sorry," Wash said. He reached down and gently picked up the cricket. It was a delicate black marble in his hand. It did not try to escape. It only positioned itself awkwardly in his hand. "Its leg is broken," Wash said. He showed it to Ava.

The silence that came and filled the space between them then was one of demand, one of curiosity, one that sought answers to a question so confounding that, between the two of them, they could not think of another way to answer it.

"Have you always been able to do it?" Wash asked.

Ava opened her palm.

Wash placed the wounded cricket inside.

"Does it matter?" Ava asked. "Does it make me different?"

"If you thought you had to keep it secret, even from me,"

Wash replied, "I guess that would make you different than I thought you were. That's all."

"I just wanted you to be better," Ava said.

For a moment, Ava only stared at the insect. It shined like a pebble, glossy and iridescent in the dim lighting from the porch. She did not know exactly what to do with the creature. She looked at Wash, as though he might have the answer, but the boy looked back at her blankly with his brown eyes and his mop of brown hair.

Ava closed her palm. The cricket wiggled about briefly, trying to maneuver away from her fingers. She was slow in her movements, being sure to keep a wide pocket in the pit of her hand so that the insect was not crushed.

"What now?" she asked.

Wash shrugged his shoulders.

Ava nodded. She closed her eyes and tried to imagine the thing she held in her hand. From the wall of darkness in her mind, the insect began to emerge. It was shiny and small and full of angles. She thought about its broken leg and how she wanted it to be better.

Then the cricket she saw inside her mind—which was large and the center of her focus—receded into darkness and, in its place, there came what looked like a Ferris wheel lit up at night. Ava smelled cotton candy and caramel apples. She was gripped by the sensation of being very small and being carried on someone's shoulders. The person that carried her smelled like her father—sweat and grease and earthiness. She soon understood that this was memory in which she now lingered. Something from the recesses of her mind having to do with a Fall Festival they had attended as a family before her mother's death.

In the time since the death of her mother, Ava had forgotten nearly all of the moments she shared with the woman. She could not say exactly how or when it began—this specific type of forgetting. But neither could she deny its reality. For Ava, there were only two versions of her mother: one was the woman in photographs. In the early months after Heather's death, when Macon was most at odds with accepting what had happened, the man took to collecting and archiving any photograph that contained his deceased wife. He kept them all in a box at the foot of his bed for that first year, and would spend late hours of lonely nights sifting through them, studying the woman's face, trying to understand why she had done it, why she had taken herself away from a husband and daughter that loved her so. He would cry some nights, and Ava would hear him. So she would get out of bed and come to his room and hug him and sit with him as he went through the photos. Some nights Macon would narrate the photographs, laying out all of the details of how and why a certain photo was snapped. If Heather was smiling in the photo, Macon went through great effort to explain to Ava the conditions that caused the smile. He recounted jokes, told stories of sunny afternoons and days at the beach. And Ava sat with him, listened, and pretended she could remember the moments her father described for her.

The smiling woman in the photographs was one version of her mother. It was the easiest to see, the easiest to believe. But that was not who Ava remembered. The only memory of her mother that lingered, intact and undiminished, in Ava's mind was the sight of her swinging from the rafters of the barn.

But now, on the porch with Wash, with the broken insect

in her hand, she could remember something more: she and her parents together at the Fall Festival, happy.

And then her eyes were open and she was on the porch again and there was something rising up inside her throat. She turned her head away from the porch and heaved until she vomited and, even in the dim light of the night, they could both see the blood mingled with the bile.

"Oh, God," Wash said. He stood and turned to go into the house, his eyes wide.

"No!" Ava managed. "I'm okay. Don't tell. Please."

"What?"

Ava spat the last of the bile from her mouth. Her head ached and her bones felt hollow once again.

"I don't want to go back to the hospital, Wash," Ava said. She sat up, huffing, and looked Wash in the eyes. "Just keep this between us. I'll be fine." She smiled a fast, apologetic smile. "You've never seen a person vomit before? It's no reason to call the ambulance."

Wash sat again. He pulled his knees to his chest and folded his arms across them. "Okay," he said, and there was guilt in his words.

"I'll be fine," Ava said. "Really."

It was only later that the children remembered the cricket. When the vomiting began, Ava had opened her hand and the cricket had escaped. Neither of them, amid the darkness and the worry, saw the small black marble leaping away quietly into the night. Neither of them heard its song, vibrant and full of life.

Where there should have been crickets and the singing of owls in the deep darkness of the woods, there was only the sound of door hinges rattling. The sound of a low, snuffling growl. The sharp intake of air as a large dark snout sniffed at the bottom of the door.

Her father—tall and wide, with skin as dark as blindness—was there with the shotgun, easing up to the front window above the couch, craning his neck to get a better angle on the animal.

"You can't kill it," Ava's mother said. She appeared suddenly behind the child, like the ghost she would eventually become. She placed her arms around her daughter—the two of them standing in the center of the living room like small trees, both of them thin as rails, their nightgowns displaying all of their bony angles. Ava's mother squatted beside her and placed one hand on her head and said, in a voice that seemed like a command rather than a reassurance, "He won't kill it. I promise."

"I suppose I've got to reason with it, Heather?" Macon said. "Dear Mr. Bear," he said in a stern voice. "Please cease and desist your activities on these premises and return to your home. Have a beer."

"You can't kill it, Macon," Heather replied, holding back a smile.

"I'm open to other ideas," he said. "But I don't think they make an Idiot's Guide to Speaking Bear, so I believe my options are limited."

"You can't kill it," Ava parroted. Very suddenly her concern over the life of the bear was greater than her fear of it. After all, she was only five years old. "You can't kill it, Daddy," she said.

Still Macon was at the window—shotgun in hand—twisting his neck and squinting his eyes, peering out and seeing little more than darkness. But the pounding on the door and the bellowing confirmed that nothing had changed. There was still a bear trying to get into their home.

"It just wants food," Heather said.

"It's just hungry," Ava said, supporting the case for the bear.

Macon stepped away from the window and walked to the door. He lingered there, looking at the hinges and listening as the bear growled and moaned and banged against the door.

Macon moved away from the door and returned to the window above the couch. There was darkness and the broken silhouette of a mountain covered in trees beneath a thin salting of stars. But he could not see the bear. He would not be able to take aim at it from here. If he were to kill it, he would have to open the door. A thought came to him then. "Ava," he called, "did you feed this bear?"

"No!" Ava said loudly, and the bear responded with a bellow—whether it was confirming or condemning the girl's story was uncertain. The yelling of the bear was so loud and well-timed that, for an instant, the family couldn't help but laugh. They knew then that all of the dark sharp-tooth things that existed in the world would not enter into their household. At least not tonight.

Macon sighed and, with resignation, said, "Okay." Then he opened the breach on the gun and removed the shells and leaned it near the door and, in the loudest, deepest, most policelike voice he could muster, yelled, "Dear Mr. Bear! As sheriff of Stone Temple, I hereby demand that you vacate these premises. If you do not comply I will be forced to issue a warrant for your arrest. We do not entertain visitors at this late an hour."

The bear fell silent.

Macon chuckled to himself. "I can't believe I'm doing this," he said, turning to his wife and daughter. But in their faces he saw something akin to gratitude. Come what may, he would spare the animal's life, and they loved him for it.

"Go away, Mr. Bear!" Ava shouted, looking at her father as she spoke. He seemed pleased, happy even. "No visitors this time of night," she said.

"The diner doesn't open until seven," Heather shouted. And then they all laughed. "I'll cook you eggs in the morning," she yelled. "Eggs and bacon and maybe pancakes, whatever you want. But you'd better be a good tipper!"

"No bad checks," Ava inserted, her face bright.

The small family could hardly breathe for laughing. It was a loud, hearty laugh that reverberated around their small, drafty home in the heart of the mountains. "Come with me," Heather said. She took Ava's hand and led her into the kitchen. When they returned Ava and Heather both carried cooking pots and metal spoons and they began banging and stomping in circles, half danc-

*ing, half marching, with Ava chanting, "Diner opens at seven,"
in rhythm with her stomping and banging.*

Macon held his sides with laughter.

*"You hear that, Mr. Bear?" Ava called. "You'll get eggs and
ham in the morning. The diner opens at seven. But go away now,
people are trying to sleep!"*

*Then, after a few more moments of silliness, Heather and Ava
stopped and all three of them listened. They heard only silence.
The bear was gone.*

*The family sat up together for the rest of the night, giggling and
talking of nothing in particular. And when the sun rose it found
them crumpled in a heap on the couch—Ava's mother holding her
in her arms, Ava's father holding them both. Then, without word
or explanation, the three of them cooked breakfast and, true to their
word, set aside some eggs and ham. They set off into the woods,
far enough away from the house so that the bear would not begin to
think of their home as a place to be frequented in the hopes of food.*

"We shouldn't be doing this," is all that Macon would say.

*As a family, they cleared a place and left the eggs and ham and,
just to properly complete the scene, Ava picked a flower and gar-
nished the ham with it. "Do you think he'll like it?" Ava asked.*

*"I'm sure," her mother said, smiling. The sun crested the moun-
tains and it filtered down through her dark hair and lit a halo
around her head so that, when Ava looked up at her, she seemed
to be floating above the earth, unattached to anything and yet connected to everything. She reached into her pocket and took out a
small slip of paper. On it was written "Diner Hours: 7:00 a.m.–
5:00 p.m. Closed Sundays."*

*"The world doesn't have to be cruel," Heather said as she took
her daughter's hand. "Sometimes it can be whatever we want it
to be."*

THREE

WASH'S GRANDMOTHER, BRENDA, had always had a way with animals—dogs in particular. She garnered the nickname "the Dog Lady" and, for the most part, didn't think it was something worth getting worked up over, so long as people chose discretion over valor and never said it to her face. If there was a dog that didn't have a home, or one that had a home and simply needed a place to mend, it was brought to her. And sometimes the animals were left for years and simply became a part of the household, with no questions asked and no complaints offered by the commanding old woman.

So when the years had stacked up around her and life unfolded in its unpredictable way—taking from her a husband and a daughter—cancer for one; a car crash for the other—and she found herself with a grandson named Wash, who needed everything a child needed, the notion of turning her home into a dog shelter and clinic was as good a way as any to help the ends stay met.

And because she was an old-fashioned woman appreciative of her solitude, she liked the way the dogs always let her know when someone came calling. This morning they were at full tilt.

Wash heard what sounded like a car door closing outside, followed by the slow *swish-swish* sound of his grandmother's house shoes sliding across the floor as she approached his bedroom. "I'll handle it," she said, looking in at the boy. "Likely as not it's some damned reporter. Most of them got the hint, but there's a hardheaded one in every bunch. And sometimes you just got to give them both barrels."

Wash hoped his grandmother was speaking metaphorically, but he couldn't really be sure. She kept an unloaded shotgun by the front door—a habit that, as legend went, she learned from an ornery cousin who lived on the other side of the state. She kept the shells for the gun in the pockets of the flowered apron she wore around the house because, as she once told Wash, "The world likes to sneak up on you, so you may as well be as ready as you can."

"Just go back to sleep and get your rest," she said, leaving Wash's doorway and heading down the hall. "I'll get this situated."

"Yes, ma'am," Wash said. He pulled the covers over his head and listened to the sound of the barking dogs out back as his grandmother moved to the front of the house. He heard the curtain in the living room slide back gently as she peeked out to see who had come so early in the morning. Then the knock came at the front door.

"Hell," Brenda said, but Wash couldn't discern exactly which "Hell" it was. She had a "Hell" for every occasion.

He heard the door open.

"Hell," she said again.

"Hello, Brenda," the voice said. It was a man's voice, deep and even.

"I guess the creek done rose that high, huh?" Brenda said. "High enough to bring you back this way. Can't say I expected otherwise. Not really."

"How have you been, Brenda?" the man asked.

"Rose petals and beef Wellington," Brenda replied. "I suppose the polite thing for me to do is to ask how you've been."

Wash got out of bed and walked softly to the doorway of his bedroom.

"You stay right there," Brenda said loudly.

Wash froze. "Yes, ma'am," he answered. He'd lived with his grandmother all of his life, and he knew which commands to obey and which were elective.

"Well…" the man at the door said.

"Well…" Brenda replied.

"You're not going to make this easy, are you, Brenda?"

"Give me one good reason why I should?"

The man sighed. It was then that Wash recognized his voice. Perhaps it had been the sound of the dogs barking that had made it take so long, or perhaps it was the early hour—the sun had only just broken the sky and the world was still gold and amber and sluggish in the new day—or perhaps it was simply that he had not heard the man's voice in nearly six years.

"Dad?" Wash called, stepping out of his bedroom.

"Hell," Brenda said.

Wash's father was a tall man, tall and thin and with more wrinkles than Wash remembered. The scar on the side of his face—a memento from the car accident that took Wash's mother—was still there, a stark and off-putting wound that seemed to twist and contort into a new version of itself whenever the man smiled.

"Hey there, son," Wash's father said as the boy entered the living room.

"What are you doing back here, Tom?" Brenda said. There was a mixture of civility and hardness in her voice, like snow draped over a wall of ice. "I suppose I could take a guess and, likely as not, that guess would be right, but I'd much rather hear you say it. I'd rather hear how you frame it, as folks say."

"Don't do this, Brenda," Tom said. He shifted his stance, and continued to look past the woman and at Wash.

"How have you been?" Wash asked.

"Good," Tom said. "Boy...you've gotten so big. Handsome, too. You're thirteen now." He declared the fact, as if to prove that he had kept proper count in the years since he had last seen his son. "I imagine you've got a girlfriend. And if you don't, then you're not far off."

"No," Wash replied, blushing.

"Keeping your options open, then?" Tom asked. He laughed awkwardly in the silence that fell between them. "You got your whole life ahead of you, son. A long time to find out about women."

"I guess," Wash said.

"You watch the news much, Tom?" Brenda asked. "Is that why you're asking about Wash's love life?" The smile on the man's face receded.

"I suppose there was never any hope of this going smooth, was there, Brenda?"

"Can't rightly say," Brenda said. "I suppose it's got to go the way you've set it up to go. This is the way you've made things."

"Grandma…" Wash said.

"I'm trying," Tom said.

"Of course you're trying now," Brenda replied, her voice rising. "There's something to be gained."

"It's not like that."

"How the hell else is it, then? You ain't had time for him in years, and now you do. Can't you see how I might find that just a little suspicious?"

"I'm trying," Tom said again, his voice harder.

"Grandma," Wash said.

"You should have stayed away," Brenda said. "When's the last time you had a drink?"

"He's my son," Tom replied. "Dammit, Brenda, he almost died."

"That's right," she replied. "Your son almost died, Tom. And you weren't there."

"Grandma!"

The room went silent, and Wash felt a palpable heat between the three of them, as if the door to a furnace, long kept shut, had finally been opened. His grandmother stood tall and still. She scowled at Wash's father, as if she could make the earth open up and swallow him.

But Tom remained there at her door, waiting, with an echo of Wash's face hidden in the architecture of his own.

It took a little more time and arguing but, in the end, Brenda conceded to letting Wash and Tom spend the afternoon alone together, just so long as they didn't stray too far from the house and so long as they didn't take Tom's car. "No farther than you can limp off," Brenda had said to the pair. "Doctors say he's okay, but I'm not convinced. And the last thing I need is for him to have an episode and for me not to be there." When Tom asked what she was afraid might happen to the boy, Brenda would only reply, "If a person could predict the unexpected, it wouldn't be the unexpected, now would it?"

"I suppose not," Tom said.

"And don't be gone long," Brenda added before they left. "He's got somewhere to be."

She stood out back near the dog kennels and watched with disapproval as Wash and Tom made their way up into the mountain. There was a faint path that had been worn into the mountain over the years and the man and boy marched single file through the tall grass. Tom walked in front as Wash trailed behind, and before they reached the ridgeline, where they would disappear from sight, Wash looked back over his shoulder to see if his grandmother was still watching. She was. She stood like a lighthouse, tall and stoic and full of warning as, behind her, the dogs barked and pawed at their kennels, waiting to be fed.

Then Wash and his father reached the top of the mountain and Brenda disappeared.

"Pretty day," Tom said, turning his eyes upward and breaking the silence between them. The sky was blue. The sun was bright.

"Yes, sir," Wash said.

"I hate to say this," Tom said, "but I'm not totally sure what to do now. I'd hoped to take you to a movie or something. Or, at the very least, to grab a bite to eat somewhere." He huffed. "But, well, your grandmother...she's..."

"Protective," Wash said.

"Yeah," Tom replied. "That's the word I was looking for." He turned and looked back at Wash. "So now I guess we just go for a walk through the woods."

"That's fine," Wash said.

They marched in silence for a few minutes.

"Do you still sing?" Wash asked. He could scarcely remember a thing about the man, but his memory was full of his father singing. There was a collection of moments that clouded his head, moments in which his father was holding a banjo or guitar in his hands, his face contorted awkwardly as the passion of the song overtook him. In those brief years when Tom was a part of Wash's life, the man always filled the air with the tinny sound of bluegrass and folk songs. And when he went from Wash's life, the music stayed.

"I've been learning a lot of murder ballads," Wash continued. "Ava says they're morbid, but she actually likes them."

"You're singing now?" Tom asked.

"I try," Wash replied. "But my voice...well, I don't think I'm any good."

"Stop singing," Tom said sharply. "Just let it go. It won't get you anywhere. If you ask me, you should give up music altogether." Tom's steps seemed to fall more heavily, as though he were treading upon his own regrets. Then he asked, "You do any camping?"

"A little bit," Wash replied. The sun was growing warmer and he was beginning to sweat. "Ava and I have camped up here a few times."

"You spend a lot of time with her, don't you?"

"I suppose," Wash said.

"You like her?"

"I guess so."

"No," Tom said, smiling. "I mean, do you *like* her. You're too old to pretend you don't know what I mean when I ask that kind of a question."

Wash didn't answer.

"You a virgin?" Tom asked.

"I'm thirteen."

"That's not what I asked," Tom said. "You wouldn't be the first thirteen-year-old to have sex, and you wouldn't be the last. I'm not accusing you of anything, I'm just asking."

Wash looked down at the ground and marched forward behind his father. "I'm thirteen," he repeated.

"I'll take that as a yes," Tom said. "But if you ever want to talk about it, I'm here for you. Okay? This is the kind of stuff boys are supposed to be able to talk to their dads about. My dad and I, we didn't really talk much. But that doesn't mean that's how it's got to be between you and me." Tom scratched the top of his head and sighed. "Did she really do what they said?" he asked, looking back over his shoulder. "Did she really heal you? I mean, really and truly. It's not just some scam, some hoax or something?" When his son did not reply to his questions, Tom scratched the top of his head again. "Wish I had a beer," he said nervously. "I'm a little out of practice with all this. I'm not sure if I'm doing anything right."

They walked for a little while longer and eventually came to a clearing beneath the shade of a large patch of pine trees. Tom paced in a circle, as though looking for something. "How are you at making a fire?" he asked.

"What do you mean?" Wash said. He sat on the ground and folded his legs. He was more tired than he expected and the coolness of the shade from the pine trees felt good against his skin. "I should have worn sunblock," he said.

Tom laughed. "You'll be okay," he said. "So, can you start a fire?"

"With matches."

"No," Tom said. "I mean, can you start a fire from scratch? Without matches or a lighter."

Wash thought for a moment. "Probably," he said. "I've read books that tell you how to do it. Do you like Jack London?"

"I've heard of him," Tom replied. He was on his knees in the edges of the tall grass surrounding the clearing. He picked up dried pine needles and some dried pieces of wood. "That's what we'll do," Tom said as if finishing a thought. He rose to his feet and came to the center of the clearing and placed the pine needles and wood into a pile. Tom walked around the clearing, kicking rocks, examining them as he did. "The good thing about being up here is that it's never really too difficult to find what you need to start a fire," he said. "That won't be the case everywhere, of course. I've started fires in places where there probably should have never been a fire." He kicked more stones, and there was a slight bit of frustration in his movements. "I really don't want to have to do this with a pair of sticks," he said, a hint of laughter at the end of his sentence. "Takes forever and, while I won't say it's not worth the effort—because if you ever get into a situation where you really need a fire, any amount of effort is worth it—today's just one of those days where I don't really think it'll give us what we're looking for. You know?"

"Yes, sir," Wash replied.

"Aha!" Tom shouted, squatting into a pile of brush. "Here's what the doctor ordered." He stood holding a pair of small rocks. He brushed the dirt from them. "Yes," he said, "these will work just fine." He came back into the center of the clearing and kneeled and began stacking the bits of wood and grass together. He stretched out on his belly. "It's difficult," Tom said. "More difficult than people ever really understand. Everybody thinks that, if they had to, they could start a fire. But the truth of it is that there are few people who could really do it. Not many folks understand the amount of nurturing and care it takes. Every moment it's on the verge of dying on you. Every single moment."

"Yes, sir," Wash said. He found a stick and traced absentminded patterns back and forth in the dirt.

When Tom had arranged the pine needles and grass in a satisfactory pile he held up the two rocks for Wash. "Come here," he said. "Come and look at what I've done."

Reluctantly, Wash went over and kneeled across from his father.

"The key is to think upward," Tom said. "The fire has to start at the bottom so you put your thinnest, driest stuff at the bottom." He struck the two rocks together. A small spark danced in the air, and then disappeared. "If the wind is high," Tom continued, "you've got to be sure that you're out of it. Block it with something, or pick a better place. You wouldn't try to start a fire like this out here in the open if it were windy. Wouldn't ever work."

"You can also use glasses," Wash said.

"What's that?" Tom answered, striking the stones together, his attention focused squarely on the dry grass at the bottom of the pile.

"If you wear glasses, and if they're thick enough, you can use them to focus the sunlight," Wash said, an ember of excitement in his voice. "It'll focus the sunlight enough so that it heats it, just like a magnifying glass, and that'll start the fire."

"That sounds like something you read in a book somewhere," Tom said. "I don't know which one, but I guess it's true enough. Just be careful of believing what you read in books. Books are okay enough, I suppose, but too many people forget that there's a real world out there and that they can touch it, feel it, smell it." He continued striking the stones together and, slowly, a small thread of smoke began to rise from the pile of brush. "There it is," he said. He began blowing gently into the base of the fire. "There we go," he whispered.

But Wash did not see. He looked off into the distance and thought of all the books he had read, all the places he had visited in his mind, all the stories that swirled around inside of him each and every day, like an ocean he had been building up inside himself over the years, page by page, word by word. The ocean was vast and limitless, filled with joy and sadness, terror and betrayal, the deaths of friends and the final fate of enemies. And it was at this moment, as his father lay on the ground, making a fire, as he kneeled across from him, watching the man huff and puff gently into the growing fire, not looking up, not looking around at the world, but only looking into the fire, into the immediate obstacle before him, this was when Wash understood both who his father was and who his father was not.

"There we go," Tom said, smiling. The small thread of smoke had grown into a long, silver chain rising up out of the air. Tom took more small pine needles and placed them on the growing flame. The fire sizzled and the flame leaped up. "Now we're making something happen," he said. "Now we're building a future."

For the rest of the day Wash did not ask his father about singing or about books. He gave up talk of folk songs and he did not make any more references of characters he'd read about or scenes he had enjoyed. He only listened as his father talked about fire and all the different ways to build and maintain it. He answered "Yes, sir," at the proper intervals. He smiled when he felt it was what is father wanted. He spent the afternoon watching the dream of who he thought his father would be if he ever came back to him die, piece by piece, in the firelight.

Yet he could not deny the way that being with the father who had been gone for so long made him remember the family they once were. He remembered the small things: the lavender scent of his mother's hair, the roughness of his father's hands as the man lifted him into the air and spun him the way fathers sometimes did. He remembered the sugared strawberries his mother used to make. He remembered the way his father argued with sports announcers while watching football games. And he remembered how it all ended.

They were in the car together, rumbling over the highway with Tom behind the wheel. He was a construct of muscles and brown hair staring out through the windshield and chatting, now again, with Wash's mother about what she picked out for dinner. Wash was buckled into the backseat, barely tall enough to look out of the window. He lolled back in the seat and watched the clouds as they passed in their predictable patterns, punctuated now and then by the upper quarters of buildings that he remembered from previous shopping trips. His mother turned on the radio and sang along with it and he sang along when he could. There was the sound of their voices mingled with the music and the sound of cars passing from time to time as the blue sky swept along silently, stretching out over the entirety of the world.

And then there was a squeal of the tires and Tom cursed and the sky turned at an awkward angle. The angle steepened until the boy could understand that the car was rolling, over and over. The car trembled and Wash was thrown back and forth in his seat belt and he was frightened. And then, as quickly as it started, everything came to a silent stop. The car was on its side and Wash was crying and calling for his mother. She hung from her seat belt at an awkward angle with her arms swinging limply like pendulums back and forth above the earth.

"Mama! Mama!" Wash called.

"Stay still, Wash," Tom said. He was on the side of the car that was on the ground and he wrestled with his seat belt until it unfastened. Wash cried and rubbed his eyes and grappled with his own seat belt. "Just stay where you are for a second, son," Tom continued. There was a tremble in his voice, a wince of pain. It was then that Wash saw the blood.

The glass of the car window had broken and there was a large open wound stretching across the side of his father's face. Tom reached up with one hand and touched it and grimaced and the blood was beginning to flow. Wash had never seen his father bleed. It felt like a broken promise.

Wash's mother still hung limply in her seat belt. Tom put

his arms around her unconscious body and carefully cradled her neck and, after some effort, released the seat belt. She fell like a marionette doll into his arms. He collapsed beneath the weight of her, barely able to stand. Wash cried harder. "It's okay, son," Tom said. "I'm coming to get you. Let me just get Mommy squared away." He placed her gently at his feet—he was standing on the passenger's side door, still getting his bearings in the sideways car. Then he maneuvered his way back over the front seat and unbuckled the boy's seat belt and caught him when he fell. "We're going to be okay," he said.

But everything was not okay. It was not until she was completely out of the car that Wash and Tom saw the wound on the side of her head. The medical examiner would eventually tell them that she had hit her head against the frame of the car as the car rolled down the side of the mountain. Death was instantaneous.

Nothing much worked for Tom after that. He took to drinking and lying in bed for the whole of the day. In the late hours of the night Wash would waken and hear his father crying behind the closed door of his bedroom. When he knocked on the door and asked his father what was wrong, the man did not answer. He did not yell for the child to go back to bed. He did not try to hide his tears. He only continued wailing and calling his wife's name while his son sat on the other side of the door, small and powerless.

Wash began spending the weekends at his grandmother's after that. And then the weekends spilled over into weekdays until, finally, Tom arrived one day and sat on the couch beside his son and said, in a flat and hollow tone, "I'm leaving for a little while." The gash Tom sustained during the car crash had healed over, leaving the scar that would remain for the rest of his days. It was long and garish and impossible to ignore, like the emptiness death leaves in its wake.

That was nearly six years ago. Now Wash was alone in the mountains with a man that looked very much like the father he used to know, but who was not that man. And neither was Wash the boy he once was. They were both strangers living in the bodies of people who used to love each other.

"Five more minutes," Carmen called through the house.

"I heard you five minutes ago," Ava replied.

The two of them were on opposite ends of the house—Carmen in her bathroom, using it for the third time in the past fifteen minutes. Meanwhile Ava was on the other end of the house in the other bathroom, wrestling with her hair so that the two of them could leave for Dr. Arnold's.

They had been spending more and more time together now that their world had gotten so far out of hand. It was too dangerous for Ava—and even for Wash—to attend school, and since the episode at the hospital when the two men broke into Ava's room, it felt safer to stay inside. There were more policemen stationed around the house and, thus far, they had managed to keep people out. But because Macon's job as the town sheriff still demanded that he leave the house, Carmen took on the role of staying with Ava, even if the girl didn't particularly care for her. Ava felt like a prisoner in her own home.

It was enough to make a person fear the world.

They grated upon each other, hour after hour, day after day. Ava fought Carmen at every turn, picking fights over things as simple as what television program to watch and why Carmen had chosen to hang a certain color curtain in the kitchen. They were petty, small skirmishes, but most battles of family are.

But all the while Carmen smiled, offering any olive branches she could manage.

Now Carmen needed to go to the doctor for her standard checkup and Macon was tied up at work and could not go along with her. He tried his best to be with her for everything having to do with the baby, but just as he was about to leave the station to meet her at Dr. Arnold's, a call came in about business that needed tending to across town. There was a church coming into town. There were already a few religious organizations that had set up shop in the wake of this event, but this one was larger, more organized. They brought dozens of people with them and were going about the business of erecting a large tent in the center of the park. So massive was the project and there were so many people being displaced that Macon had to be there, if only to remind everyone that there was still a sheriff in town. People oftentimes needed to be reminded of things like that, Macon knew.

Plus there was the simple annoyance of bureaucracy that demanded his being there, as well. There was paperwork that came with the job, and he was still the town's sheriff.

So it would be just Ava and Carmen at the checkup. It was the first that Macon had missed, and he promised that it would not happen again. But even though he wanted to be there himself, he wasn't particularly opposed to the fact that it was to be Carmen and Ava without him. Over the past few years he was constantly engineering ways to put them alone together. If there was an errand that required a long drive he would invoke responsibilities of work or the potential onset of illness. Then he would stand in the doorway and watch them as they pulled out of the driveway in the car together. He would wave until they were out of sight, as if the image of him standing there would be enough of a glue to keep them from drifting apart in their time alone. And while he could not swear to its efficacy, the two women in his life got along well enough, he felt. Small victories were still something to celebrate, after all.

More and more, since Carmen's pregnancy began, Macon pinned his hopes to the baby. If all other efforts failed, the new life that entered the household would be the common bond between Carmen and Ava. He sometimes imagined Carmen and Ava sitting at the kitchen table together, feeding the baby, laughing as the child refused some vegetable-flavored paste. In his mind, he'd see the three of them—Ava, Carmen and the baby—walking up the driveway together, Ava's arm linked with Carmen's as she pushed the baby along in a stroller, coming toward him as he stood in the doorway, waving at them, waiting to wrap his arms around them all. These were the visions he held in the most hidden parts of himself. These hopes of his were too fragile to share.

Unbeknownst to Macon, Ava quickly confounded his plans. When she got word that her father wouldn't be coming, she asked Carmen, "What about Wash?"

Carmen didn't mind the idea of having Wash there to act as an intermediary between her and Ava. "Wash can come," was all she said.

Ava and Carmen left the house these days under police escort. The state trooper who had been camped out at the end of the driveway knocked on the door and, when they were ready, he got into his car and led the way. Another police car slotted in behind Carmen. No sooner than they got out of the driveway was there a line of people standing along the edge of the road, yelling and shouting at the car as it passed, lobbing questions like confetti. They yelled for Ava to tell them how she had done what she had done. They called out to Carmen and asked why she and Macon had "kept it all secret."

"People never cease to amaze me," Carmen said to Ava as the car finally got up to speed and the crowds were left behind. They swung by and picked up Wash from his grandmother's. There were no crowds at Brenda's house. The lens of scrutiny was upon Ava, not the boy she had helped. They would encounter more people once they neared Dr. Arnold's and made their way into the town proper, but neither of them commented on it. It was slowly becoming something they could pretend to ignore.

Dr. Arnold was one of the dying breed of rural doctors who was necessity-bound to be a specialist in everything. There were painfully few illnesses or health-related circumstances he couldn't fix or, at the very least, alleviate. He had treated women with pregnancies worse than Carmen's and brought their children into the world healthy. More than that, he wasn't afraid to admit when he was in over his head. And, thus far, he reassured Carmen that he wasn't and that both she and her child would survive.

Dr. Arnold's wife was named Delores and she greeted Carmen, Ava and Wash at the front door carrying a pitcher of iced tea and a smile as wide as the sunrise. "Come in," she said excitedly. She was blushing. She was a woman in her late sixties who walked with a slight limp and who al-

ways cooked food for her husband's patients—whether they'd
come in for a simple checkup or if they'd be staying for a
few days of observation. Delores Arnold believed food was
the best help for healing, and so she did her part for anyone who walked through the door. "Come on in and I'll
get you all squared away." She presented the pitcher of tea.
"I've got orange juice, too, if you'd like that," she said. "I
know that, for some folks, it's still a little early for tea. But
I don't believe it's ever early enough." There was an exuberance in her, an excitement that removed the sediment of
time from her bones. Still holding the pitcher, she hugged
Carmen, Ava and Wash in turn. "I just still can't believe any
of this," she said.

The children returned her hug and nodded politely.

"I'll start cooking a little something once you're settled in.
I sat up all night last night, just waiting for you to get here.
You'd think I would have used that time to go ahead and get
some food ready." She laughed. She was trying her best not
to make Ava uncomfortable. Her husband had treated the
girl in that house since she was barely old enough to walk,
but things were different now. Her hand lingered upon Ava's
shoulder. "I'm just so excited," she added.

"You don't have to cook anything," Carmen said, remov-
ing her coat and hanging it by the door. Delores only waved
the comment away and led them to the examining room.

The examining room had once been a bedroom for one
of Dr. Arnold's seven children, all of whom had long ago
marched off into the distances of the world. The small room
had the charm that comes with age and use. There were
small nicks in the floor and along the molding of the walls,
and a papier-mâché snowman perched atop the mantel, the

feeling that, within the silent recesses of the house, laughter might arise at any moment.

Carmen perched herself on the edge of the examining table. Ava and Wash sat in a pair of small chairs by the far wall.

"My husband will be in shortly," Delores said. "He's in his office on the phone." Then she looked at Ava and winked proudly. "You just can't understand how proud I am that you're standing here in my house. A true healer! I still can't believe it. You're a walking miracle, Ava!" The woman's eyes danced as she watched Ava and waited for the girl to say something.

"I taught her everything she knows," Wash said. And then he leaned back in his chair and returned the wink Delores had given Ava.

"It's okay," Delores said, undeterred. "You don't have to say anything. I can only imagine what your life is now, how much it's changed." She paused and let the image fill her mind. Then: "Is there anything I can get you?"

"No, thank you," Ava said.

"I'll take a glass of tea," Carmen said.

"Of course," Delores replied, reaching for the pitcher she'd placed on a table near the door.

"Do you have any bourbon?" Wash asked. "Single malt." He winked at the woman for a second time and, finally, she acknowledged his joke.

"I'll see what I can come up with," Delores replied. She left the room with the pitcher in her hand and came back shortly with two tall glasses of iced tea. But the pause to gather drinks had done nothing to redirect her interest. "So how does it feel to have all of this attention, Ava?" she asked. "Was that a police escort I saw outside?"

"We're all keeping up with it," Carmen answered quickly.

"Oh, I can only imagine," Delores replied, crossing her hands in front of her. She glanced around the room, but always her eyes returned to Ava.

"She's not going to float away," Carmen said, nodding in Ava's direction. Delores and Ava both looked at her, each of them taking something different from the comment.

"I know that," Delores replied, a pang of hurt in her voice. "I'm just fascinated, is all. It's just a marvel, isn't it?"

"Yes, it is," Carmen replied. "I'm sorry. I shouldn't have said it like that." She exhaled. "I guess all of us are still trying to figure out how to behave now."

Carmen finished off the glass of tea and handed it back to Delores. She placed her hands on her stomach. "Could you excuse us for just a moment, Delores? The baby's acting up and I'd like to talk to Ava and Wash for just a second alone if that's okay."

"Oh, of course," Delores added. "Just look at me, standing here harassing you all." She turned to leave the room. When she was at the door she paused. "It's just a splendor," she said. "Just such an impossible blessing. All of it. I hope you understand that." Then she left.

Ava, Carmen and Wash sat silently. They heard the sound of Delores's footfalls as she went back into the kitchen. They heard the gentle cracking of the ice cubes as they floated in the tea.

"It won't be like this forever," Carmen said. Ava had been looking out the window, watching a large bank of gray clouds roll by. "This will all blow over," Carmen continued. "There will be a few things that have to get sorted out first, but it'll get better." She reclined on the examining table with her hands on her stomach.

"She's right," Wash added. He gulped down his tea and placed the glass on the floor beside his chair. "People are just weird right now. But they'll get less weird, I think." He scratched the top of his head, not unlike the way his father sometimes did. "Yeah," he said confidently. "It'll get less weird."

"It already has if you ask me," Carmen said. "Or maybe we're just all starting to get acclimated." She tightened her lip and thought for a moment. "It's like when Macon brought you home from the hospital. You remember how wild that was. Looking back on that now, I see it differently. I don't think it's gotten any better. Every day more and more people are showing up in town. I never would have thought getting a routine checkup would take a police escort." She shook her head. "But I think we're doing okay."

"You didn't come with Dad to get me from the hospital," Ava said, taking her eyes from the window. "My mom would have."

Wash started to speak, but stopped. He looked at Carmen.

"It's okay," Carmen said to him. Then she leaned back on the table with a sigh. "And if I had come, Ava," she said, "you would have told me how your mother would have stayed at home and had dinner ready for you when you got there. Wouldn't you?"

"She would have come," Ava said flatly. "She would have wanted to be there with me."

"I *was* there with you, Ava," Carmen said. "I slept there, right beside Macon, both of us propped up in those damned uncomfortable chairs. But you were unconscious for that, so I guess I don't get credit for it." She adjusted her position on the examining table. "And I knew I wouldn't get credit for it the whole time I was doing it, but I did it, anyway. Because that's what a mother does. Even a stepmother." She spoke without malice or hardness in her voice. Then she inhaled quickly and exhaled slowly, looking down at her stomach. "The baby's kicking," she said.

"Can I feel it?" Wash asked.

"Sure," Carmen said.

Wash was already out of his chair and halfway to the examining table. When he was close enough, he reached toward Carmen's stomach. He hesitated as his hand neared her. She had let him feel the kicking baby before, but his fascination and sense of reverence was never diminished by repetition. He always waited for her to guide his hand the rest of the way.

Carmen took the boy's hand and placed it atop her stomach. The seconds passed slowly until, at last, there was dull thump of the child's kick.

"So cool," Wash said goofily, taking his hand away. "You've got to feel this, Ava." He walked over and took Ava's hand and led her to the examining table.

Ava hesitated.

"Here," Carmen said, taking Ava's hand and placing it on her stomach. "Wait for it." And then the two of them held their breath and waited. When it came, the kick was soft, like a greeting.

Carmen laughed. "Did you feel it?" she asked.

"Yeah," Ava said. The anger was gone from her voice, replaced by fascination. "There really is a person in there," she said. "It's kinda hard to believe. It's…it's so much."

"It's everything," Carmen replied. "You feel fuller than you've ever felt in your entire life. Full in a way that you never imagined possible, like everything—the earth, the trees, the sky, the stars, everything—is inside of you."

Ava held her hand on Carmen's stomach, and the universe inside of Carmen kicked again. All three of them giggled at the magic of it.

"Ava," Carmen said, still holding the girl's hand on her stomach.

"Yes?"

"You'd tell me," Carmen began. She took a deep breath and looked up into Ava's eyes. "You'd tell me if something was wrong, wouldn't you? With the baby, I mean. If you could tell something about it like that."

Ava said nothing.

"I'm sorry," Carmen said, still pressing the girl's hand to her stomach. "But I'm not sorry, too. I don't know if it's even how your gift—or whatever it is—works. But you'd help, wouldn't you? Like you did with Wash. If you knew the baby was sick, you'd help it, wouldn't you?"

In Carmen's face, Ava saw a thousand other people like her. People wanting help. People wanting hope. People hurt and afraid and looking to mend the broken things in their lives. People simply wanting to be reassured that the horrors they imagined in the late hours of the night would not come to pass.

"Is that why you're being nice to me?" Ava asked. She flinched and took her hand from Carmen's stomach.

"Please, Ava," Carmen whispered, her voice thick with fear. "You don't understand. You can't understand."

"I should have known," Ava replied. "You're just like everyone else."

Carmen reached for the girl's hand, trying to get it back, but Ava had already taken a step away.

"I don't think she meant anything, Ava," Wash said.

"She just wanted something," Ava replied to the boy. "Just like everyone else."

"I lost a baby once," Carmen said. "It was born in the night and never lived to see the sunrise. I try not to think about it. I try to block out the memory of it. It was a hard pregnancy, just like this one, and the doctors had to medicate me pretty heavily after the baby was born. I woke up in the afternoon, expecting to see my baby. But there was my mother, sitting in a chair at the foot of the bed. She started crying as soon as I opened my eyes. Never said a word." Carmen wiped her eyes. "It breaks a person, losing a child. No matter what someone says, no matter how much they may smile, no matter how long ago it happened...it's a break that never heals. And I'm not sure I can survive that again." She sighed, as if she had finally given up holding on to a secret.

Ava and Carmen stood watching each other, both expecting, both anticipating. Then, without a word, Ava turned and left the room. Wash followed after her.

"I'll get her," he said to Carmen on the way out the door. Then the two children were gone.

Not long after, Dr. Arnold came into the room and Carmen quickly wiped away her tears and placed the fear back into the small box inside of her. "How have you been feeling?" Dr. Arnold asked Carmen once the examination was over. He was balding and overweight, but full of energy and almost always smiling. He reminded Carmen of an Irish Bill Cosby, and that image alone was enough to make her feel better most days.

"About the same," Carmen replied, sitting up on the table.

"Well, your vitals all look perfectly healthy. Yours and the baby's. There's a small indication of some placental abruption, but if it was anything to worry about, I'd let you know."

"That's the same thing you said the last time I came in for an examination."

"Because it was true the last time, as well," he replied. He smiled. "Face the facts, Carmen. You're healthy and you've got a healthy baby inside of you."

"I just feel pain some days," Carmen said. She rubbed her stomach rhythmically. "Everything hurts. Everything except the baby. Sometimes it feels like I'm the weak link here…if that makes any sense."

"How's your diet?"

"Good. Eating everything I'm supposed to."

"Good," Dr. Arnold said, nodding heavily. "Have you talked with Macon about all of this?"

"Of course," Carmen said. "But he's not the doctor, now is he?" She grinned, but her tone was serious.

"Listen," Dr. Arnold said. He shifted his weight on the rolling stool he was sitting on and folded his arms in front of him. "I'll do anything I can to reassure you that everything is okay. If you'd like another opinion, I know someone up in Virginia who I trust. He'll give you a thorough examination and, when it's all over, you can come back here and we'll talk. But you really will be fine. Few are capable of more worry than expectant parents."

His expression was full of warmth and comfort and trust and confidence, and Carmen could not help but believe him, as she always did. He had been the town's doctor for almost all of his life. He had delivered more children than the town could hold—something he was fond of saying at parties when people asked him if he was staying busy.

"You're going to be okay," Dr. Arnold said.

"You're sure?" Carmen replied. Her voice trembled a little.

"I'm sure," Dr. Arnold replied. "You've got to believe that you're going to be okay, because you are. And that's my professional opinion. You've just got to have faith," he said.

It was the height of summer and the air was electric with the in-sect songs and the humidity that pressed down upon everyone like an anvil, but still Heather stood beneath the summer sun on the far side of the yard with a shovel in her hand, digging a hole. Ava stood at the window of the house watching her mother dig. The ground was hard at times and she would gouge the earth with the shovel and the streams of sweat dripped down from her mother's brow so much that it looked like rain.

Ava listened to the noise made by her mother's digging—the heavy chuff, chuff, chuff of the shovel entering the earth rhythmi-cally. She could not understand why her mother was digging a hole in the ground, but because it was hot outside and her mother looked exhausted Ava decided that the best thing she could do was help. So she climbed down from the window and went to the kitchen and fixed a large glass of iced tea and walked out of the house and carried it to her mother.

"Mom?"

"Yes," Heather answered. She looked up, huffing, sweat dripping from the end of her nose, and saw her daughter with the glass of tea. "Thank you," she said, taking the glass.

"Are you okay, Mom?" Ava asked as Heather gulped at the drink.

"It's hot," the woman said eventually.

"Can I help?" Ava replied.

"Grab a shovel."

Her mother never said exactly why they were digging this hole on the far edge of the yard and Ava did not ask. Her mother was full of magic, and that was not something a child questioned.

They dug through the hottest part of the day with Heather sending the girl back and forth to the house now and again for more water and tea. She took more care about the temperature now that her daughter was with her. When the afternoon had stretched on late she sent the girl in and asked her to make a meal for them. Ava returned with bologna and cheese and peanut butter and jelly sandwiches and more tall glasses of tea. The two of them took a break for nearly an hour in which they stretched out on their backs beneath the sun, stared up at the sky and said nothing. The sun did not seem quite as hot as it had been. There was a coolness radiating out from the hole that they had dug—it had filled partly with water and Ava couldn't be certain just how far down they had dug, but the hole was above both her and her mother's head and that felt like a feat that few people in this world could ever hope to achieve.

When they had eaten and rested they slipped back down into the unfinished hole and they went back to digging and Ava's mother began to tell her daughter stories. She told her about a man several counties away that, according to legend, had lived to be over one hundred and fifty years old. It was only because of a farming accident that he finally met his maker, just two years ago. "If it wasn't for that," Heather said, "he'd still be alive and kicking."

And then Heather spoke about two men who were digging a root cellar and came upon a large mound of ice, like an iceberg hidden inside the earth. The men dug and dug and dug and, as they went farther down and more of the ice was exposed to the sun, the ice began to melt and so they took to covering it with tarps and shades and blankets in the hopes of keeping it intact. And then one morning, on the third day of digging, the men came out and found the ice melted and there was a great, gaping chasm left in the earth large enough to fit a house into. "And then it all collapsed," Heather concluded.

The two worked until after sunset and then—sore and tired and aching—they went into the house and bathed and they were too tired to eat and so they both stretched out on the floor of the living room and fell asleep. When Ava awoke the next morning she found that a blanket had been placed over her and her mother and, in that moment, she could believe all of the stories her mother had ever told her.

The world was grand and sometimes prone to unexplained acts, and that was the beauty of it.

FOUR

THE ARNOLD HOUSE was at the end of a large, wooded lot of land on Highland Street. It was the area of town where most of the wealthy northerners who migrated to Stone Temple built their houses. Dr. Arnold, though he hadn't actually made himself wealthy working as the general practitioner of a small town, had built a house here before all of the new money came. And over the years he'd gotten by well enough that, even though his house was visibly more fatigued than the rest standing along the street, he'd kept it up enough that it did not seem out of place among all of the newness.

Privacy fences wrapped each of the yards along the street, including the doctor's, but Ava had been to Dr. Arnold's enough times over the years to know which of the boards in his fencing were loose enough to be pushed aside and slipped past. Every six months, like clockwork, Macon came to Dr. Arnold for a general checkup. He had always been a man that believed in the power of preventative medicine. And while he underwent the checkup, Ava, when she had answered all of Delores's questions and eaten her fill of the woman's food, would come into the backyard, slide through the loose board in the fencing and explore the large expensive houses of Highland Street.

Now, after leaving Carmen in Dr. Arnold's examining room, and with Wash racing after her, Ava came out of the house, crossed the yard at a lope, wriggled through the loose board in the fencing and started up a narrow, wooded path that, eventually, emptied out again on Highland Street several houses down. It was a discreet enough path that anyone unfamiliar with the town, such as reporters, would not have been able to see her, and yet it afforded her the safety of having a way to get back to Dr. Arnold's if someone did find her and she needed to get away from them.

She was hot with anger and the coolness of the day did nothing to detract from it. Only the sound of Wash, stumbling and panting as he struggled to catch up to her, did anything to relax the girl. "Ava," Wash called out. "What are you doing? Where are you going?" he barked in pain as a tree limb Ava pushed aside suddenly snapped back and slapped him across the face. "That was straight out of the *Three Stooges,*" he said, and there was a strange pride in his voice. In spite of the gravitas and bedlam swirling in the world around them, it was only the comedy of the moment that the boy cared to acknowledge.

She did not want to go far—with all of the people that had come to town, she was afraid of what might happen if she strayed too far away from the Arnold house. But she needed air. She needed to be away from things. She needed to be alone...or as close to alone as she could get. And Wash had the uncanny ability to make her feel like she was away from everyone, but not alone in this world.

So it was with some degree of comfort that she made her way through the wooded path, around the back of the houses, and returned to the openness of Highland Avenue.

"Jeez," Wash said, coming out of the bramble behind her. There was a large red mark on his cheek where the tree branch had smacked him. He rubbed it with the palm of his hand to soothe it. "Is it as bad as I think it is?" he asked, presenting his face to Ava.

Ava held back her laugh. "It looks like you got punched by a feather duster."

"Funny," Wash said, but there was lightness in his reply. He rubbed his cheek a little more, then looked back and forth along Highland Street. It was empty and quiet. Ava turned on her heel, and began slowly walking up the street.

"You do realize," Wash began, falling into step beside her, "we shouldn't be out here. You know how everyone is. There's no telling what kind of people we might run into. There's a reason you have police escorts now."

Ava tucked her hands into her jacket pockets. The cold that lingered within her since waking up in the hospital tightened its grip on her. She straightened her back and tensed her jaw to keep her teeth from chattering. Then she walked and looked at the large houses lining the street.

They were grand and majestic. They had swimming pools—empty now in preparation for the winter—wrought-iron gates, sweeping, pristine lawns and statues. Ava imagined that everything inside those houses smelled new. She hated the houses as much as she loved them.

"What are you going to be?" Ava asked Wash.

"Excuse me?" he replied, caught off guard by the question. Then he immediately understood what he was being asked. "I don't really know," he said. "A teacher, maybe. I like reading enough for it. I'd have a class where people sat and read to one another. That's the only thing I never really liked about reading at school—we do all of it at home. We should do it more in groups. Make a really big deal out of it. That way everyone gets to hear the story at the same time, you know? It turns into something we share instead of something we just do by ourselves."

"But what if someone doesn't read well?" Ava asked.

"Then the class teaches them to get better at it. Next silly question?"

Ava bumped him with her shoulder playfully. She was getting used to the cold. "What about you?" Wash asked. "What do you want to do one day? If that was your house," he said, pointing to a large multigabled estate tucked behind a wrought-iron gate. "What would you do for a living? What kind of person would you be?"

The two of them stood before the house as if its gates might suddenly open and beckon them to enter and take up the lives of their imaginings. "I'd live alone," Ava said finally. "Away from everybody. I'm not sure what my job would be, but if I could, I'd have a gate just like this and I wouldn't let anybody come and visit me."

Wash laughed. "I'm not sure I like that idea," he said. "It can go one of two ways—Master Yoda did it, and he came out okay. But Gollum from *Lord of the Rings* did it, too, and that didn't turn out okay. But, now that I think about it, in both cases they came out green and weird looking. So…if that's what you're shooting for…" He shrugged his shoulders comically.

He waited for Ava to smile, but when it did not come, he continued. "People don't really live like that," he said. "Not really."

"Yes, they do," Ava replied.

"No, they don't," Wash replied. And then he bent down and lifted a small pebble from the street and, with a grunt, tossed it over the fencing. "And, even if they did, why would you want to? People live with people. That's just the way it works. Everybody needs someone." He paused for a moment, as if grasping an idea in his mind but then immediately losing his handhold on it. "Or something like that. And I know you feel like everybody wants something from you right now, like everybody expects something. But that still doesn't change the fact that you've got to have people. You can't build a wall in front of the world."

"Maybe I'll have dogs," Ava said. She started walking away from the house and Wash hurried to catch up to her. "Maybe I'll do what your grandmother does and just have dogs."

"But she doesn't just have dogs," Wash said. "She's got me."

"You're not much smarter," Ava said, and she smiled.

"I'm smarter than the average Pomeranian."

"What about a dachshund?"

"I figure I could hold my own in a game of chess against a wiener dog," Wash said. On his forehead, his thought trenches had sprung up, denoting the seriousness of his thinking.

"You don't play chess," Ava said.

"I get the idea of it, though."

"You're an idiot."

"But I'm cute, though," Wash said, and he laughed.

Ava paused and took in the image of the boy. "Maybe," she said finally. Then she tugged his ear and continued walking.

But in their playfulness and conversation, neither of them saw the man walking down the street behind them. It wasn't until he spoke, standing less than twenty yards away, that they spun, startled, and saw him. "Hi," the man said. He stood on the far side of the street with his arms at his sides and a look of pleasant excitement across his face. "My name's Sam," the man said, his face beaming. He was tall and very large, with the frame of a man who had been an athlete in his youth and whose body, though it was in its forties now, had not relinquished its hold on its former glory. Beneath the dark crown of hair on his head—parted awkwardly on one side—Sam's face was clean-shaven and with a tinge of childishness about it. "You're really her, aren't you?" Sam said.

Ava's stomach tightened. Macon had told her that there would be people who wanted to meet her, people who would go to great lengths to do so. "The world is full of strange types," he had said, his face full of conflict, as if he would not allow himself to say what he really wanted to. "Be careful of those kinds of people," he said.

"We should go," Wash said quickly. He took Ava by the elbow and stepped back.

"Don't be afraid," the man said, holding up his hands passively. He took a step backward almost as quickly as the children did, furthering the distance between them. "You shouldn't talk to strangers," Sam said. His voice was full of innocence. "I'm just, well, I'm just excited to meet you. My name's Sam," the man said again. He waved at Ava as if they were recognizing each other across a crowded room.

"We heard you the first time," Wash said. He tugged Ava's arm. "Let's go," he said, never taking his eyes off Sam. The two of them began walking back down the street, headed to where there was the path that would lead them back to Dr. Arnold's. Ava walked with her eyes forward, the way she had learned to walk when there were reporters snapping her picture. Wash walked beside her, on the side facing the street and Sam.

"You're that boy, aren't you?" Sam called out to Wash. He remained on the far side of the street, but matched their pace as they walked. "You're the one she healed!"

"Just keep walking," Wash whispered to Ava.

"No, please," Sam said, his voice quavered. "Please, I just want to talk to you. Please."

Perhaps it was the apologetic tone of his voice. Perhaps it was the childishness in his face. Or perhaps it was the infinite courage of youth, with its inability to understand the harshness that the world is capable of. Whatever the reason, Ava stopped walking away.

"What are you doing?" Wash asked her.

"What do you want?" Ava asked, turning to Sam.

"Ava…" Wash whispered.

"Nothing," Sam said. "I just wanted to meet you." Sam still remained on the far side of the street, doing nothing to try and close the distance. His arms still rested at his sides, and there was something awkward about the way they did.

There was something awkward and off about everything Sam did, Ava thought.

"I've got to go," Ava said.

"Wait," Sam replied. "Please." He lifted his hands in a show of submission. He looked down at his feet for a second, and then he eased down onto the ground and sat with his legs folded. He tucked his hands beneath his, so that he was sitting on them. "Is this better?" he asked.

Ava and Wash both stared at the man. The size and width of him, which has been intimidating at first, was diminished now that he was sitting on the ground with his hands beneath him. Even Wash felt that, perhaps, the man really did only come to talk. And maybe he wasn't as bad as first expected.

"Why did you come here?" Wash asked Sam.

"To meet her," Sam replied. "Because you're something amazing." The smile he wore widened just a little. "I've followed all of this since the very beginning. Since the very first story, my brother and I both." His voice rose and his body rocked and swayed with the energy of his excitement. "You're amazing. You really did something!"

Ava studied Sam. She watched him as if she were watching an envoy of the entire world.

"How long have you been able to do it?" Sam asked.

"Can we go, Ava?" Wash said. He tugged Ava's arm, but still she remained. "I don't like this guy," he said. "He's...I don't think he's a hundred percent."

"My brother is like you," Sam said. "He's a healer." Then Sam's smile cracked for a moment, as though an unpleasant memory were intruding upon the moment. "He does what he can to help me," Sam said, and his voice was full of apology, "but I'm still not better."

"I should go," Ava said. The air was suddenly colder than it had been. A tremble ran through her body and she stuffed her hands into the pockets of her coat. "I should get back," she said.

"Finally," Wash added. But, still, Ava did not move.

"I understand. I'm sure that there are people worried about you." Sam lifted one of his hands from beneath his body. It was pale from lack of circulation. He waved it to see the blood flow. "Do you mind if I stop sitting on my hands?" he asked, and offered his discolored hand as evidence of need.

He liberated his other hand and rubbed them together. "This is weird," he said, looking at his hand, but perhaps talking to Ava. He shook his head. "Do you mind if I stand up?" He stood and brushed the back of his pants and put his hands into the pockets of his coat. He shifted his body weight from one leg to the other and stamped his feet, smiling all the while. "Cold," he said. Then he offered his hand to Ava and took two steps forward. "Can I just shake your hand?" he asked. He looked down at his hand, then at the girl.

"No," Wash answered.

"It's okay, Wash," Ava said. "I'm tired of being scared of everything. It's just a handshake." Before Wash could step in, in spite of everything inside of her that told her she should not be doing so, she walked forward across the street and shook Sam's hand. "It's good to meet you, Sam," she said.

Sam gave Ava a two-handed handshake. "Thank you," he said softly. "Thank you." The handshake continued into awkwardness. It continued until Ava realized that, for her, it had already ended. Sam was clutching her hand. "You'll help me, won't you?" Sam said softly. There were tears in the corners of his eyes. "I'm not well," he said. "I haven't been well for a very long time. But you'll change that, won't you? You'll help me." Ava tried to withdraw her hand, but Sam seemed made of concrete. "I just need you to do for me what you did for your friend," he said. "I just need you to help me. And then I'll leave and you'll never see me again. I promise."

"Let me go," Ava said. She was afraid. Truly and genuinely afraid. She struggled to pull away, but Sam matched her efforts. He overcame them, pulled her in like a sinkhole. Wash raced across the street and tried to pry the man's grip from Ava's, but to no avail. All of the size and muscle the man had previously exuded returned to him.

"You just have to help me," Sam said.

"Let go!" Wash shouted, still struggling.

"Please," Sam said. "Please heal me. Please fix me." She struggled, but Sam's arms were everywhere. He pulled her body against his. Finally, he had both arms wrapped around her and had lifted her—still kicking and yelling—from the ground. "You have to do it," he said. Still his face was like a child's, as if he truly meant her no harm.

He got down onto his knees and pulled Ava down to kneel with him. Wash punched the man, but it made little impression upon him. Sam grabbed Ava's wrists and placed her hands on both sides of his face. "Do it," he said. His cheeks were wet with tears. "Help me," he pleaded. "Help me so he'll be proud of me."

And then Sam was silent. He closed his eyes and held Ava's hands to his face and he wept softly. His lips moved soundlessly, as if uttering a prayer. Ava was still afraid, still terrified, by what was happening, but she felt sorry for the man. Even Wash was caught unprepared by the man's reaction. Where the boy had expected violence, there was only a man—whose intellect seemed somewhat childish—asking for help.

"Please," Sam said, sobbing, but still not letting go of her wrists.

"Okay," Ava said softly. "But I need you to let go of my hands."

"You'll really help me?"

"Yes," Ava said.

"What are you doing, Ava?" Wash asked.

"You promise?" Sam asked.

"Yes," Ava replied.

After a deep breath, he let her go. "Okay," he said, his voice trembling. He still wept. "I'm ready," he said. And then he waited. Ava waited, too—for what, she wasn't sure. The man continued to kneel and to wait. Ava stood and watched him—her hands still cradling his face. "I'm ready," the man repeated, again and again, in a low voice. "I'm ready...I'm ready..."

Ava looked down at her hands as they cradled Sam's face. They were small and darkly colored, as they always had been. They reminded her of her mother's hands. She could almost hear her mother's voice, just then. It was in the wind that rustled the bare branches of the oak trees lining the street. It was in the low shaking of the underbrush of the forest. And it made her angry. Her mother was dead. And she always would be. And there was nothing in her hands that could change that.

When Sam finally tired of waiting for God and opened his eyes, he found himself alone, mumbling prayers to an empty street.

"Macon," the deputy called as he opened the office door. He was young—barely twenty—and had grown up in Stone Temple. He was one of the few people working at the station who was there because he wanted to be and not for the money he could make selling info to reporters.

"Yeah?" Macon answered. He'd just finished taking care of the business with the church. Now he'd finally made it back to the office and was hoping to find a way to plow through a small mountain of paperwork that sat on his desk waiting for him.

"There's a preacher out here who wants to talk to you," he said.

"Tell him to get in line with the rest of the preachers," Macon replied, still not lifting his head from the paperwork. "In fact," he continued, "have the preachers and the UFO people line up in alternating order."

"It's a pleasure to meet you, too, Sheriff," a deep voice replied.

Macon looked up from his papers to see a tall, broad-chested man entering the room at a lope. He patted the deputy gently on the shoulder as he passed him, as one might thank a bellman for holding the door. "Thank you, son," the man said.

Macon put his pen down and sat back in his chair. He waved the deputy away. "I got it," he said. The deputy nodded and left.

The man walked over and sat in the chair on the other

side of the desk. From the way he carried himself, he seemed to be a man accustomed to getting his way in the world. "Reverend Isaiah Brown," the man said, offering a hand to Macon. "John Mitchell must have told you I'd be coming by."

"Nice to meet you," Macon replied, standing to shake the man's hand.

"First of all," Reverend Brown said, "I want to apologize for my intrusion here today. I can only imagine how much you've got going on in your life right now. It must all be chaos and bedlam."

"It's something like that," Macon replied. The man seemed familiar, Macon thought. He looked to be in his mid-fifties, with a smooth-shaved face and a roof of thick black hair. He wore a well-tailored suit and there was confidence and assuredness in his demeanor. "What can I do for you, reverend?"

"For today, nothing," Reverend Brown replied. "I just wanted to come by and introduce myself properly and, if possible, to offer you any help you or your family might need."

Finally Macon recognized the man. He had seen him preaching on the television to a congregation that measured in the tens of thousands. He was a phenomenon, a man who had started with a small church up north and, slowly, built it up to be something of an institution in its own right.

"You've got a lovely town here," Reverend Brown said. "Filled with wonderful people."

"We do okay," Macon said politely. "You know, I recognize you now. It's an honor to meet you." He stood and offered another handshake, one slightly less reserved than the previous one now that he had a better sense of who he was dealing with. "Sorry if I seemed a little standoffish before," Macon said. "There are lots of types coming and going these days. So, do you need help with permits or something?"

"Not at all," the reverend said. "It's all been taken care of. I came here merely to meet you face-to-face. To speak with you. And I completely understand what you mean when you say 'lots of types.' I understand who you're referring to. And I can also understand if you think I'm just another one of those types, just someone else who has come to town in the hopes of gaining some greater notoriety by using you and your daughter as leverage."

"Then you won't take offense when I say that the thought had crossed my mind," Macon said. "Nothing personal, but I'm sure you can understand that I need to be, shall we say, reserved when it comes to people."

"I'll definitely excuse you." Reverend Brown sat forward in his chair with his elbows on his knees. "I like to be sincere whenever I can," he began, "so I'm going to get straight to the point. I'm not here to take advantage of you or your daughter, but I am here to be a part of this moment, this event, whatever it may finally turn out to be. I won't ask about your personal stance on all of this—not just yet, at least. I'll admit to being curious, but I can respect the idea that your religious beliefs are your own and I'm not here to make you believe the same things I believe." He smiled, and there was sincerity in it. "I'm here because, whether you're religious or not, you've got something happening here that is steeped in religious connotations and implications. Your daughter healed someone. She touched him and his wounds disappeared. That's a *miracle*—even if that might not be the word you would use for it." He paused. "Am I making any sense at all?" Reverend Brown asked. "There's a part of me that feels like the more I say the more you'll think I'm trying to con you."

Macon thought for a moment. He tried to remember what he knew about Reverend Brown. He remembered images of the man on television: tall, pacing across a stage with a Bible in one hand, a microphone in the other. He was always imposing on the television, and now that Macon was sitting across from him, he seemed smaller. "I think I understand what you're saying," Macon replied. "You just want to be sure that your side of the argument is represented here. Does that sound about right?"

"Something along those lines," Reverend Brown said, and there was a look of relief about him, as if he was thankful that Macon had, in fact, understood his intentions. "It's easy to be leery of people, and for some in this modern world, it's easiest of all to be leery of religious figures. But we're not all, as I once heard a colleague accused, 'wearing suits only to hide our tails.' Some of us are just trying to help. And if I can help, then I invite you to let me know."

Macon wasn't sure exactly what his opinion on the reverend's words was, but he was leaning in favor of the man. Macon's views on religion and God had oscillated heavily over the years, and they had yet to settle one way or another. Now, with the whole world looking at him and his daughter, with everyone—on all sides of the religious aisle—laying claim to Ava and what she had done, Macon had to admit to himself that he liked the idea of having a preacher he could lean on.

The world, and what was happening in his life right now,

was bigger than the small-town sheriff, and he knew it. As much as he hated to admit it, he wanted help.

"Thanks for coming in," Macon said. He stood and shook the reverend's hand. "I'll think about what you've said. And, well, maybe we can sit down together another time."

"I'm delighted to hear that," Reverend Brown said. He turned to leave the office. When he reached the door he looked back at Macon. "Whatever you think about all of this, about what your daughter did and what it means," the reverend said, "you're allowed to believe it. Don't forget that, and don't let anyone else, not even me, make you feel otherwise."

Macon and Ava made their way over the mountain in silence. It was a couple of days after his meeting with Reverend Brown and he was still trying to puzzle it all out. They'd managed to sneak away from the house unnoticed thanks to the darkness of the predawn forest and the bitter cold of the night that had sent nearly all of the people camped out at the base of their driveway home. Carmen wasn't happy with the idea of the two of them heading off into the woods, but Macon assured her that there were still places in this world where, even among chaos, it was possible for people to slip away safely. It was one of the reasons why he hadn't wanted to stay in Asheville when Ava came out of the hospital. He'd had offers from people who insisted that Ava should be kept close and examined more. But he felt safer having his daughter home. These were their mountains, the part of the world the two of them had learned to navigate together over the years. How could he take his daughter away from that at a time like this?

The wind was cold and it swept down off the mountain like an arm trying to dislodge them. They'd started out before sunup—slinking off into the forest like thieves, escaping the photographers and reporters and fanatics under cover of darkness—and the frost that would disappear in the early part of the day was still on the ground as their feet crunched a little in the grass as they walked. Sound traveled deeply and the world seemed empty.

They would spend the day hunting near a cabin upon a mountain on the north side of town. Once upon a time, Old Man Rutger and his wife had lived there. But then the woman died from pneumonia and, not long after, Old Man Rutger died. Most folks said it was from not knowing how to live alone. Now that both the man and his wife were gone, it made a good place to camp and, if you were hunting, it was an even better place on account of how the deer liked to come near the cabin and eat from the remnants of the vegetable garden Rutger's wife left behind—a garden which was overgrown and wild, but alive every year.

"Cold," Macon said when they had almost reached the place where they would ascend into the tree stands and wait for the deer to come. He had placed the tree stands here years ago and they had hunted from them and been successful many times. He hoped today would be no different.

"It'll warm up," Ava said stoically. She stopped walking briefly and stood in the low light and looked around. "We're almost there."

"I'm glad you wanted to do this," Macon said.

"We don't get to hang out anymore."

"I know," he replied. He clenched and released his hands

to get the blood flowing and to evacuate the cold from his fingers. "Things are a bit strange right now."

"That's one way to put it."

She continued down the slope of the mountain. The wind came down again and pushed at their backs and almost made them lose their balance, but they continued on, certain that soon the sun would rise and the day would brighten and they would be warmer. When they reached the bottom of the mountain Ava looked across the field and listened. There was only the wind and the rustle of the leaves and branches.

"Good to be away from it all," Macon said.

"We should get to the tree stands," Ava replied.

"We've got a little time still," Macon replied.

"Sun's already up," Ava said. "Just hasn't cleared the mountain."

"So what," Macon said. "That doesn't mean we can't stop and talk for a while."

"I thought you wanted to hunt," she said, and then she walked off toward the edge of the tree line to where the tree stands were.

Macon followed, slowly, feeling the missed opportunity.

The tree stands were placed closely together, too closely. But he had placed them that way out of a parental instinct when Ava was younger. He'd wanted to be near her in case she needed him. As consequence, this had become the place where their secrets could be passed back and forth in the calm and quiet of the forest, the place where there was no one to stumble upon them, the place where there could be a father and daughter alone in this world.

Ava had already ascended into the stand by the time Macon got there. She pulled her bow up to where she sat using a length of rope and placed it in her lap and began looking out over the forest just as the rays of the sun broke the tops of the trees.

Macon thought for a moment, then he ascended the tree beside hers and climbed into the tree stand and pulled his bow up just as she had done and he sat and looked through the dense forest.

"Do you think about her sometimes?" Ava asked in a soft voice.

"Your mom?" he replied, and then he immediately nodded an affirmation.

"What do you think about?"

"Depends," Macon began. "Usually I think about her around the holidays. On your birthday. Things like that. I wish she was here to see you."

"Do you dream about her?"

"Sometimes," Macon replied. "How often do you dream about her?"

"A lot."

"How long has this been happening?"

"Sometimes I can go for a long time and not dream about her—even though I think about her every day. Do you?"

"Do I think about her every day? No, Ava. I think about her. But I'll admit that it isn't every day. It was at first, but not now."

"Is that going to happen to me, too? Will I stop thinking about her? Will I forget her?"

"Never."

"How do you know?"

"Because you loved her. Because you still love her. And you don't forget people you love. That's just how it works.

So, no, you won't ever forget her." In the distance of the forest, they heard the sound of a twig breaking. "But you have to let her go."

"And what if I can't?"

"You have to."

"But if I can't, will I kill myself like she did? Is that why she killed herself? Was there something she couldn't let go of?"

"Truthfully, Ava," Macon began, "I don't know. Maybe. I never really thought of your mother as a sad woman, but then, in the end, maybe that's when I found out I didn't really understand her." He cleared his throat. "That's something I think about a lot."

Ava was silent. In spite of their talking, there was a deer approaching through the dense forest. The sun had reached the halfway point in the trees and the deer came tentatively through the underbrush. Ava raised her bow and notched the arrow.

The deer came closer still. It tested the air with its nose but Ava and Macon were downwind and so it did not find them when it searched. It was a male deer, full and old. Its antlers stretched wide and dangerous, like the branches of a great tree reaching up from it. Then, not far behind, came the doe and her fawn. They walked through the forest without hesitation, the buck having searched for predators in the dim light and heavy wind of the morning. But it was the same wind that was leading them into Ava's arrow. The wind was heavy enough that it rustled the trees in such a way that Ava could not be heard when she shifted slightly in her position in order to better get the buck in her sights.

She watched them walk closer.

"How are you doing with everything else?" Macon asked softly.

Ava kept her eyes on the deer.

"The world has gotten so big so quickly," Macon said. "I can hardly keep up with it. So I can only imagine what it must be like for you." He wanted to stop talking, but he could not. There was a question he wanted to ask. "People are going to want you to do it again. That damned Eldrich keeps calling, saying that he wants to do more tests. He keeps talking about 'controlled conditions.' He says maybe it'll help them understand why you're not feeling right. Like maybe if you do it while they're watching, while they're monitoring everything, then maybe they can learn what's actually happening." Everything inside of Macon was conflicted. "Do you think you could do it again, Ava? Just once? Maybe then they'll leave us alone."

"What does everyone want?" Ava asked.

"It's a little different for each one, I think," Macon replied. He thought for a moment. "What do *you* want, Ava?"

"I want to know if I could have saved Mom," Ava said. She said it in a voice so small it could have been birdsong. Then she loosed her arrow. She fired wide, missing the deer. She exhaled and watched the family of animals bound into the bracken, trembling with life for another day.

For Carmen, the morning came on the heels of another night of sleeplessness and pain. She had spent most of the hours in the bed taking shallow breaths and trying not to wake Macon, trying to convince herself that everything would be okay. Her doctor told her that everything was fine and that the baby was developing just fine and that, in the end, everything would be fine. *Fine* was one of Dr. Arnold's favorite words. He even hinted that much of what was bothering Carmen, much of her pain, might be rooted in her mind rather than her body. And she had, eventually, been willing to admit that perhaps that was true.

Macon told her not to think about it. He gave her daily reassurances that everything was going to be okay, that she was doing everything correctly and that she had done everything correctly the last time. He tried his best to take away from her the guilt of losing her child. And, sometimes, it worked. There were days when she could believe that she had not caused the death of her first child. She would find her steps lighter than they had been the day before, and she would not be so irritated by the way people drove or by the rude things they said. And on those days, she could spend the day seeing other children in the world and she could be genuinely happy for them and for their parents. She could look upon them and smile and think to herself that the world was not such an unbearable place.

But then those days would pass—as they always did—and she would once again rise in the morning and think to herself the name of the child who did not live to see a single sunrise on this earth: Jeremy.

He'd been born early in the evening and spent the late hours of the night in an incubator while Carmen faded in and out of consciousness, always asking about him every time she woke. Again and again, the nurses told her that everything was okay and they smiled at her and squeezed her hand gently and told her not to worry. And then one time she was greeted by the sight of her mother crying and she knew then that her child was dead.

She wanted to cry. She wanted to scream. But instead she only closed her eyes and stopped clinging to the waking world and the medicine in her veins took her into a deep, dark sleep.

When she awoke it was to the sound of soft crying as her mother sat in the far corner of the room watching her through puffy eyes and with trembling lips. "He went before sunup," was the first thing Carmen's mother said.

Then she went back to dabbing the corners of her eyes gently with handkerchief and watching her daughter. Carmen wept, as well, but it was a strange type of weeping. She felt numb and empty, as if she were outside her body seeing herself mourning the loss of her child. She did not know how long the weeping went on. The next thing she remembered was her husband coming into the room and standing next to her bedside. He looked down at her with a face made of stone and he squeezed her hand. "It's okay," he said.

"No, it isn't," she replied.

"We'll get through this," he said.

"No, we won't," she replied.

And that was the truth. It all came apart in less than a year. One day he came home from work and stood in the center of the kitchen while she sat in the living room, watching him, and he looked over at her and said, "I'm going to my mother's." He looked down at his feet like a child. "I feel like I should say more," he added.

"You don't have to," said Carmen.

"It's not your fault."

"I know."

"It's just...it's just too much to carry around. It's too much to hold on to all the time. I just don't have it in me."

2

"So you're going to leave it here with me?"

"No," he said. "But maybe, if I leave, there'll be less of it."

"There won't," she said.

And that was the end of that.

The next several years were composed of drifting from one city to the next. She was a teacher and managed a year in a school before the faces of the children she taught would come to her dreams and then she would have to move again. And then she found a town called Stone Temple with something that could barely call itself a school and a sheriff named Macon and his daughter, Ava. And, for a little while, the hurt that she had been feeling was lessened and she could smile and wonder.

But now she was pregnant again and her body was always in pain, and even though the doctors told her she was fine, she knew better. There was a child within her that could be lost at any moment. It had happened before, after all.

The autumn came on quickly and without warning. The town of Stone Temple awoke one Thursday morning to find the trees ablaze with gold and red leaves and the temperature hovering above freezing. Ava saw it as a splendid thing. She'd never much cared for the summertime. There was a quietness that came with the autumn and the winter that could not be found in any other time of the year, so when the temperatures fell and the leaves changed and the migratory birds took to the air, she went to school each day with a smile upon her face and a spring in her step.

The autumn also brought with it the county fair. She was only six and she had never been to the fair, but she'd heard enough about it that she knew it would be a magical and breathtaking event. And when her father told her that the entire family would attend the fair that weekend, it was all the girl could do to sleep at night. She tossed and turned in her bed, and when she closed her eyes there were lights from Ferris wheels shining and the sound of men in elaborate hats standing atop boxes yelling for her to "Take a chance! Test your luck! Win it all!" And she saw strange and mysterious animals in her mind. She saw a lion with a snake for a tail and she saw a monkey that wore a suit and sat at a table sipping tea like a person. And then there was the scent of foods— sweet and salty and chocolaty. It was like a song given substance and placed upon her tongue.

When the Friday evening of the fair finally came, the girl could not sit still. From the time she came home from school, she raced around the house, doing chores that were not even assigned to her. She did not ask how long it would be before they left because she knew that would do nothing but frustrate her parents. So she simply cleaned and swept and made her bed and picked up stray items lying around the house and tried to find their proper place until, finally, Macon said, in a playful voice, "Well, I suppose I can't deny you forever, can I?"

The drive to the fair was one of excited babbling. She asked her mother about fairs that she had been to when she was young and, in return, Ava was regaled with stories of bearded women and men with crocodile scales for skin and contortionists that could fold themselves into suitcases. "This world can be amazing sometimes," her mother said. But, as she spoke, there was a hollowness in her words. It happened to Ava's mother sometimes—a type of sadness that her daughter could hear in the folds of a laugh or see in the edges of the woman's smile.

"Are you okay, Mom?" Ava asked as they rode.

"Of course I am," her mother replied.

Not long after sunset Ava could make out the glow of the fair just over the mountains. Her stomach fluttered and she sat forward in her seat with her mouth agape. "There it is!" she shouted, the

excitement of things pushing from her mind the uncertainty that
had been there.

"Yes, it is," Heather said with a smile.

Ava could hear the music—a tinny, high-pitched sound of
revelry—and she rolled down the windows to better let the sound
in. A wall of cold autumn air filled the car and raised chill bumps
on her flesh and she expected her mother or father to tell her to roll
the window up, but they never did. There was a genuine excitement among all of them.

When they arrived, Ava raced from the car, shouting and calling for everyone to come after her. Her heart beat between her ears
at the sight of the lights and the rides and the men spitting fire—
just as she imagined them—and the men standing above the crowd
wearing strangely ornate hats, shouting that there was a wonderful show to be seen. "Step right this way!" they called, and Ava
could not be stopped from following.

She rode every ride. She ate until her stomach could hold no
more. She played every game of chance and, even when she did
not win, she came away smiling.

The hours came and went. When the night was late Heather
took her daughter's hand and said simply, "That's enough."

"Do we have to go?" Ava protested, rubbing the drowsiness
from her eyes.

Heather reached down and took from Ava a large bag of cotton
candy and passed it to Macon, who took the bag and sampled the
candy and smiled.

"Can we come back?" Ava asked. And then she felt her body
being lifted from the ground and suddenly she was resting on her
father's shoulder. She could smell that Macon was wearing cologne,
another indication of how special the night had been.

"We'll see," Macon said.

"We're not coming back," Ava said.

"We didn't say that," Heather replied.

"You didn't have to," Ava said. She was half-asleep now, lulled by the gentle up-and-down rocking as her father carried her across the parking lot toward the waiting car. Through her drowsiness, through her fatigue and the burgeoning sadness inside her, Ava looked back once more at the fair.

Lights and rides and fire jugglers and contortionists and bearded women and giraffes and animals she could not name. She saw her mother, tired and walking slowly, but smiling. She saw the back of her father's shoulder. She felt the texture of his hair against her face, the strength of the man beneath her, as solid as the earth.

Before the darkness of sleep took her, Ava caught one more glimpse of her mother. Walking behind her husband and daughter, Heather turned for a moment, like Lot's wife, for one final glimpse. And when she had taken it in she started back after Macon and Ava, but her face was hard and dim. Her brow—normally smooth—was furrowed. Everything that had been there before—the joy, the excitement, the bright sense of adventure that her mother had worn all evening—was gone, consumed as quickly as a room in a house in the depths of a moonless night, when the last flickering candle is extinguished.

"Mom?" Ava called.

Her mother's smile came back, as if it had never left. "Yes, Ava?"

"It's not necessarily a bad thing," Ava said drowsily. She was still in her father's arms, her head resting on his shoulder.

"What isn't?" Heather replied.

"When things come to an end. Sometimes, they're just supposed to. You don't have to be sad." Ava closed her eyes and, in the way it does, sleep took quickly and completely.

She did not see the way her mother suddenly began to cry. She did not hear how, when Macon asked what was wrong, Heather's only reply was, "I smile, but I'm never sure if I mean it."

FIVE

"I WISH WASH were here," Ava said.

"Try saying that three times fast," Macon said. He leaned forward and kissed her brow.

The two of them sat at the kitchen table. It took two days for Macon, Ava and Carmen to all agree to Eldrich's proposal. Their decision came with the stipulation that they did it here, at home, and not in Asheville. Macon was tired of seeing his daughter in hospitals.

There were electrodes placed all over her body that monitored everything from her blood pressure to her heart rate, and atop her head was a rubbery helmet laden with wires and more electrodes. The man hooking up the device told her it was designed to monitor her brain waves, her thought patterns, "the how and why of everything," he said proudly.

"I'm just going to be in the next room," Macon said to Ava.

"If there's anything you need, if there's anything about this that you don't like, all you have to do is say the word. Okay?"

Ava smiled faintly.

Macon left the room and did not look back over his shoulder. He passed the team of doctors and technicians and videographers who were all waiting for him to leave. They glanced at him as he passed, the way one looks at a squatter who has been too long clinging to a property that was never his to begin with. He passed Carmen and Dr. Eldrich in the living room and did not speak. Carmen had been grilling Eldrich about the test, about Ava's safety, about what Eldrich would do if something went wrong.

Macon left the house and walked into the front yard. It was a chilly day—another early blow of the hard winter that was promising to come—and the sun was high. Around the yard there were cars and vans and trucks and an ambulance sent down from Asheville just in case things should happen to take a turn for the worse. At the sight of the van a knot formed in Macon's stomach. He remembered the sight of Ava and Wash at the air show. He remembered the blood on her hands, the fear in her eyes, the sight of her falling unconscious.

He had thought she was dead in that moment. He didn't know what he would do if he lost her, and suddenly he felt himself start to panic. He wanted to throw out all of the doctors and technicians and cameramen—the crowds of people who were the cause of the fear he now felt, who represented the rest of the world that was waiting and watching, each and every day, to know more about Ava. To know her secrets, her truths, to put her on display.

He was losing his child to the world.

He stood in the center of the yard looking at the house. He took in the sight of its worn and withered clapboard. The faded paint. The holes chewed through its eaves by wood-peckers and wood bees and perhaps even mice. For the first time in a great many years, he was able to see everything that his house was, pure and unfiltered by the familiarity of seeing a thing day in and day out.

He saw the house as it was and, consequently, he saw the life of his family. And the sight of it all made his stomach tighten. If he were driving along the highway and hap-pened to come across a house like this, a house like the one in which he was trying to raise a family, he would think it was abandoned. He would cast judgments about the people who lived within it. He would wonder how they had al-lowed their lives to fall so far. He would wonder how they lived that way, how they did not see the desperate state they existed in. Few things breed contempt like a life viewed in passing.

Still Macon's legs would not carry him forward, to kick out the doctors, the cameras, to return their lives to what they had always been. "Please," he whispered to himself. "Let this be the right decision." He stood and waited, as if there might come an answer from someone else, as if there would be a sign that would vouchsafe his decision, reassure him that, after all, he was doing the correct thing and, in the end, his family would endure unharmed.

He waited and waited and waited.

Ava sat up straight in her chair as the group of doctors en-tered the room. They formed a half circle around the other side of the table at which she sat.

"Do you understand what will happen now?" Eldrich asked. His thick comb-over was out of sorts, but there was excitement in his face.

"I think so," Ava said.

"We'll bring in the animal," Eldrich began. "There will be cameras to document all of this, obviously. We'll hand the animal over to you and, well, you'll do whatever it is that you do, or did, or allegedly did." He chuckled gently to himself, as though he had made a joke.

"And then what?" Ava asked.

"Well," the dark-haired man replied, "then we'll see what we'll see, won't we?"

The people behind the cameras pressed buttons and the red lights came on, one by one. There were three cameras placed around their living room: one in front, and one on each side of Ava, angled just a little behind her, as well. She assumed it was so that they could tell if she was doing something behind her back. It was very much like they were attempting to catch a magician in the act, she thought.

"We're ready," Dr. Eldrich said. The front door of the house opened and a young woman in a lab coat came in with a small dog in her arms. The dog was furry and it had a face that seemed specifically bred for viral internet videos.

"It's okay," the woman said, speaking to the animal, stroking it gently.

"What's the matter with him?" Ava asked softly. The animal eyed her skeptically.

"For the sake of the experiment," the woman said, "I think it's best that I give you as little information as possible about exactly what the condition of this animal is." Then she turned and faced the cameras. She stated her name and the date. She referred to what was about to happen as "Experiment Number One."

As the animal trembled gently in her lap, Ava did not need the woman to tell her what was wrong with it. Its right front leg was broken. The animal kept the leg pulled close to its body and tried not to lie down in her lap, even though it seemed very tired and in need of sleep. Ava gently stroked the animal, which licked her face and trembled just a little bit less.

"Do you need anything else before we get started?" the woman asked, turning from the cameras back to Ava.

Ava thought for a moment, still looking down at the small dog with the broken leg. "I don't suppose so," she said.

The woman nodded and left the room without any reaction to being interrupted. She seemed eager to leave, eager to get things under way. And then Ava was alone. There was only the sound of the refrigerator running in the other room. The sound of the small dog huffing gently in her lap. It shifted its position every few seconds, almost like a cat, as it tried to find a way of sitting that reduced the pain in its broken leg. Now and again it whined softly and Ava would stroke it and shush it like a child.

The moments came and filled the room, one by one.

Somewhere in the house someone cleared their throat. Ava figured it was one of the doctors. She had almost forgotten that they were there, waiting for her like ghosts. She imagined them pressed against the walls, listening, watching through computer monitors—their breaths held, their mouths wet with anticipation, all of them hoping for something they could not quite name.

"Okay," she said softly.

She wondered about herself as much as everyone else did, she realized now.

Gently, she took the dog's paw between her hands. The animal flinched, but did not draw away. "This won't hurt," Ava said. "At least, I don't think it will." She smiled. The dog lowered its snout and licked the back of her hand.

Ava closed her eyes and squeezed gently on the animal's leg. She breathed in and out slowly and, in her mind, the dog appeared. It was just as scruffy and rough-looking as the real thing. She saw the animal's leg and she focused on the thought of the animal's leg not being injured. She built a type of dream in her mind. She saw the animal uninjured, tail wagging, able to bounce around playfully. She thought more and more of the animal's leg until it was the only thing she could see in the dream in her mind. She wanted the dog to be healthy, to be happy and to not be hurt.

Then the dog was gone and, in its place, just as it had been before, there came another memory of her mother.

Waking was like pulling herself out of quicksand. Ava's eyes opened slowly. They were heavy, heavier than she had ever remembered them being. She saw only a dimness. She lifted her arm—which felt soft and slow to respond—and she rubbed her eyes, trying to remove what must have been gauze or cloth draped across her eyes. Try as she might, she could only see shades of unfocused light and blurry shapes.

"I can't see," Ava said. Her voice cracked. Her heart was like a small bird, trying to escape the cage of her chest.

Someone squeezed her hand. "Stay calm," a voice said. "Dad?"

"Yes," Macon answered. And then Ava felt the weight of

his body press down on the bed beside her. "I'm here, kiddo. You're in the hospital. In Asheville. How do you feel?"

"I can't see," Ava said again. Her heart had not stopped racing. She blinked over and over again. She reached up and rubbed her eyes with her hands—as if that might change the state of her blindness—until Macon had to take her hands away from her face. He shushed her.

"I know you're scared," he said. "It's going to be okay." Ava could hear the uncertainty in his voice.

"I'm here, too," Carmen said. And then Ava felt Carmen gently ease herself down onto the opposite side of the bed. Carmen clasped Ava's hand and squeezed it. "We're both here," Carmen said.

"You can't see anything at all?" Macon asked.

"Is it still just darkness?" Carmen said.

"I can't see," Ava repeated. Her breaths were fast and shallow, as though she had run too far too quickly, as though there were not enough air in the room to sustain her. "Dad, why can't I see? What's going on? I don't understand. I can't see anything!"

Then there was a gentle kiss applied to her forehead. A rough, heavy palm stroked her brow. All Ava could make out were shadows and light. "Deep breaths," Macon whispered. "Just focus on the sound of my voice if you need to. Take deep breaths. It's going to be okay."

"I'm scared."

"I know," Macon replied, and his voice wavered. "But I promise it's going to be okay."

"Just relax," Carmen said.

"Why can't I see? Why can't I see?"

She rattled off the sentence like an incantation. And her

father gave back an oath of his own. "I promise this will get better," he said, again and again, as if he could speak between the moments of her fear, as if he could balance out what she was feeling. "I promise, I promise, I promise."

"It's going to be okay," Carmen said again. She squeezed Ava's hand more tightly. "What do you see, Ava?"

"What?" Ava eventually replied, choking back tears. She could tell by Carmen's tone that it was not the first time she had asked the question. But it was the first time Ava heard it.

"What do you see?"

"Nothing! I don't see anything," she said. "Just light. Just bright light." She was still crying, still angry that the woman holding her hand at this moment was not her mother, and never would be. "I can't see anything," Ava said.

There was only blurry brightness before Ava's eyes. And then the light fluctuated, as did the darkness, like something passing back and forth before a flashlight.

"Did you see that?" Carmen asked. "Did you see a change in the light just then?"

"I didn't see anything!" Ava yelled. "Just shadows! I can't see anything!" She snatched her hand away from Carmen. Ava's tears stopped, replaced by anger and bitterness.

Then there was the sound of Carmen laughing. It was a high, proud laugh. And then Macon was laughing, as well, and the fear that had been in his voice was less than it had been.

"What?" Ava said. "What's so funny?"

"You're doing better," Carmen said. She kissed Ava's hand. "You're doing better! You couldn't see any changes in light before. The doctors said that, if you got better, that's how it would start—with changes in light. You're getting better." Her voice was bubbling with a joy that, in spite of the many grudges Ava held against Carmen, the child was comforted by.

"I don't understand," Ava said.

"It's okay," Macon said softly. He sat up on the bed, still holding Ava's hand. "What's the last thing you remember, kiddo?"

Ava thought for a moment. The racing of her heart was beginning to slow. "I remember the dog," she said.

"Okay," Macon said. "Anything else?"

"He's fine, by the way," Carmen added. "The dog. You really did heal his leg. You really did it!"

"You've been in and out of consciousness for the past few days," Macon said. "This is the third time you've woken up. The doctors said you might not remember. It was like watching someone in a fever dream—speaking and responding to questions, but you know they're too sick to really understand." He sighed. "Scared the hell out of us, kid."

"You woke up screaming the past two times," Carmen said. Her tone was almost cheerful, as if delivering a death letter in a gift envelope. "You woke up screaming that you couldn't see anything and calling for help." Ava could hear the smile on Carmen's face. "You said it was nothing but whiteness."

"But now, there are shadows, too," Macon added, a hint of cheerfulness in his voice, as well. "Which means you're on the mend."

"The doctors said that maybe that would happen," Carmen added. "They said that you might get better, that maybe your body had had some type of overload, or something—

they're not really sure what's going on—and that maybe you'd get better all on your own with enough time."

"I don't remember any of that," Ava said. She focused on her vision. There was still darkness, but the light she could see was like having bandages over her eyes. There were shapes that she could almost see, and the more she focused on them, the more they seemed to become more than simply a binary of light and dark, but a composite of angle and gradations.

"You were only conscious for a few moments. But we knew you'd be okay."

"Wash came by while you were sleeping," Carmen said. "He sat and read to you for a while. He seemed pretty sure that you'd wake up if he read to you."

"Where is he?"

"His father took him home," Carmen replied.

"We'll get him down here now that you're awake," Macon said. He squeezed Ava's hand with a hint of finality. "I'm going to go let the doctors know you're up. Okay, kiddo?"

"Yeah," Ava said.

"And I'll get word to Wash, too."

"Okay," Ava said.

He kissed her on the forehead once more. Then he stood and, after lingering for a moment, left the room. Then there was only Ava and Carmen together.

"You thirsty?" Carmen asked. "I imagine you've got to be."

"Yes," Ava said. She closed her eyes. There was an instinct within her to rest them. Maybe, she thought, the next time she opened them she would be able to see.

Carmen carefully rose from the bed and waddled over

to where the nurses had brought in a pitcher of water and a Styrofoam cup. "I knew you would start to get better," she said. "I'm not saying that nothing bad can ever happen to anyone—I know better than that—but I knew that you'd be okay. You're a kid who can chew glass." She pressed a button on the side of Ava's bed and it tilted upward. "Here," she said, pressing the cup up to Ava's lips.

Ava drank slowly. Now that she was no longer thinking about her loss of vision, she realized how dry and sharp her throat felt. More than that, she began to understand just how bad the rest of her body felt. Everything was sore and almost no part of her seemed as if it wanted to work. It was like a blanket of stones had been placed over her.

"More?" Carmen asked as Ava finished the cup.

"No," Ava said. "I mean, no, thank you."

"It's not quite so bad, is it?" Carmen asked, placing the cup back on the small food stand that had been wheeled into the room.

"It's good," Ava said.

"I mean, this," Carmen replied. "You and me. This."

Ava inhaled and held the breath. She thought of all the different ways she could reply. She thought of the snide remarks, the cold acquiescence, all the ways she usually protested Carmen's having married her father, come into her life. But the breath in her lungs was still uncertain, still laced with fear over her blindness and the pain racking her body and the general confusion of her world.

But, within that breath, there was the fact that she did not want to be alone. The fact that, in spite of everything she had said and done to Carmen, the woman had never resisted, never become angry, never fought back. She only endured the girl's attacks, one after the other, and did not leave, did not submit, did not become angry or resentful. She behaved like a mother.

Ava did not answer, which, in its own way, was a type of admission that, even in the worst of wars, there can be moments when both sides are willing to have a moment of peace.

Macon was proud of the security the hospital was managing. It was much better than it had been the first time around, but he hoped this wouldn't be frequent enough that they might yet improve. The entire floor where Ava was held was guarded by policemen stationed at the elevators and stairwells. Everyone had to have ID just to get out of the elevators, regardless of how much the families of other people on the floor disapproved of it.

It was all necessary, especially now. The doctors had done everything they'd promised to protect Ava, and now that the experiment was over, they took the video and the dog and studied them both, finding that everything they were skeptical to believe—the fact that the girl did, in fact, have the ability to heal injuries—all of it was true. And no sooner than they'd finished analyzing the data did they place the video online, and let the fire spread as quickly and wildly as it wanted.

"Macon? Macon?" a voice called. It was Dr. Eldrich. "You got a second?" He took Macon by the arm and led him into a small, empty office at the far end of the floor. "I wanted to talk to you about Ava. About how the experiment went."

When they were inside the office Eldrich closed the door. Macon sat at a small desk littered with papers and notes.

There was a photograph of a smiling woman and child on the far corner. "What is it?"

There was an excitement in Eldrich's eyes. "As you know, your daughter healed the subject, the dog. Fully and completely healed its broken leg."

"That's what you've been telling me for days now," Macon said.

"Well, we've been able to do more in-depth tests," Eldrich said. "It's very exciting, really. She healed it better than healed actually."

"What do you mean?"

"I won't go into too much of the details, but the short version of it is that there's no scar tissue. Normally, when a broken bone heals, there's a mark left. You can always tell, through X-rays or autopsy, that it's been broken. Well, that's not the case here." His hands began to move as he spoke. He made imaginary bones and broke them and put them back together again. "It's really, really amazing."

Macon thought for a moment. He got the impression that he should be more interested in all of this, more fascinated by it the way Eldrich was, but he wasn't. "What about Ava? What happened to her? The whole reason I agreed to do any of this was because you said that it would help you find out more about what's going on with her body, why she's cold and tired all the time. I want to know what this is doing to my daughter."

The excitement in Eldrich waned. "Well," he began, "we've got a few theories on that."

Eldrich paused. He almost spoke, then stopped himself. Then he sighed and said, "Honestly, we don't know much. All we know is what's happening to her after she does these...

things, whatever we want to call them. Her red and white blood cells are dropping dramatically. This latest effect, the blindness, we honestly don't know what caused that. From everything we've been able to test, she should be fine. We can't really spot anything physically that's causing her to go blind. But, again, her blood isn't normal right now, so the baseline we would normally use to find out about her eyes is, well, skewed."

"But she's getting better," Macon said. "She just woke up. She can see light now."

"Really?" Eldrich said, his eyes going wide. "That's terrific. We'd hoped that might happen."

"So you can't tell me much of anything, can you?" Macon asked.

Eldrich paused. "I can't tell you the things you would want me to tell you," he said. "I don't know the why of any of this. I don't know the how. Hell, I'm even having a hard time telling you the what."

"Would it offend you terribly if I told you that you're giving me a headache the size of Russia? That wouldn't upset you, would it?" Macon rubbed his temples. "Is there a point here? Anywhere on the horizon?"

"I'm sorry," Eldrich said quickly. "It's just so exciting. During the autopsy—"

"Autopsy?" Macon interrupted. "What autopsy?"

"The dog's," Eldrich said. "It's dead."

At last, there was silence.

"What are you talking about?" Macon asked after a moment.

"Heartworms."

"Wait…what? I thought it had a broken leg?"

"It did," Eldrich said. His voice was solid and calm now that he was again doing what he knew very well how to do: talk about science and research and not about people and daughters and feelings. "It had a very bad fracture, which—"

"Which Ava fixed," Macon interrupted, almost yelling. He stood and walked closer to Eldrich with his thumbs hooked in his belt. Very suddenly, he was the sheriff again. "Ava fixed that. She healed it. You told me that as soon as it happened."

"Yes, she did," Eldrich answered, his voice beginning to waver again.

"So what the hell are you talking about the dog's dead?" Macon poked the man in the chest with a finger. "Did you kill it?"

"What?"

"Did you all kill it? Wanted to dissect it, maybe? Try to see what happened from the inside out."

"You've been watching a lot of television, haven't you?" Eldrich quipped.

"Answer the question," Macon demanded. "Why is the dog dead?"

"Heartworms," Eldrich said again. Then, before Macon could interrupt, he continued. "It had heartworms the entire time. I promise you. Had them the whole time." He held up his hands to keep Macon from speaking. "Yes, the animal had a broken leg, but that was just one of its problems. It also had heartworms. Well beyond the point of medicine doing anything for it. It was only a matter of time before the animal died. That was part of the reason we chose it for the experiment."

Macon's jaw clenched. "Okay," he said slowly, finally beginning to believe Eldrich's version of things. "But what about Ava—what Ava did?"

"Yes," Eldrich replied. "She fixed its leg, but not the heartworms."

Finally, Macon took a step back from Eldrich. His head was swimming with questions. There was an image of the world—this new world in which his family lived—and the image was beginning to crack at its foundation.

"I don't understand," Macon said, even though he was beginning to understand perfectly well.

"Neither do we," Eldrich replied. "But it does explain the situation with Wash, doesn't it?"

"What situation with Wash?"

"His cancer," Eldrich said flatly. "Didn't anyone tell you?"

"Does Wash know?' Macon asked. He stood in the doorway of Brenda's house. He didn't bother to come inside or say hello before the question spilled from his mouth.

Brenda fidgeted, as though she had been expecting the question, and yet she was unable to escape the sting of it. She wore an old white-and-yellow flowered dress and an apron. Both were worn and tattered—she wore nothing for fashion, only for practicality or out of habit. Macon had seen her in this particular dress and apron more times than he could remember. But, today, they seemed more tired from use than before. There was a white stain on the bottom corner of her dress. The woman smelled of bleach and sweat.

"No," Brenda said flatly. "He doesn't. And I'd thank you to keep it that way." She turned and walked into the house.

"Dammit, Brenda," Macon said. Finally he crossed the threshold and came inside. The smell of bleach was overpowering. It stung his nostrils. "How long have you known?" he asked. There was little hospitality in his voice.

"A week now," Brenda said flatly, "more or less."

There was a scrub bucket filled with water on the floor next to the couch. The smell of bleach poured out of it. Brenda walked over to the bucket, drew a sponge from the tepid water, got down onto her hands and knees and began scrubbing the floor. "Mind that you don't track all that mud in here," she said to Macon over her shoulder. Then she added, "They told me over the phone. What kind of a thing is that to tell a person over the phone? You'd think they'd call us into the hospital for something like that, wouldn't you? Or maybe even come out here. But I don't suppose people do house calls anymore, do they? Not even for telling a woman her grandson has cancer."

"Jesus," Macon said. He stepped forward across her newly cleaned floor, tracking in dirt from outside and not noticing. "How did this happen? Were you going to tell us about it?"

"I asked you to mind my floor," Brenda said evenly.

Macon looked down at his feet, then at Brenda. "To hell with the floor, Brenda! Dammit. How could you keep something like this to yourself? How could you not tell us? Hell, never mind that, how could you not tell Wash? How serious is it?" Macon paced. His hands gesticulated with each new question. His mind shifted from thoughts of Wash to thoughts of Ava to thoughts of the both of them at once.

Since they were five years old they'd been inseparable. They were in every class together at school since kindergarten, and when school was over they spent the afternoons together. During summer break you couldn't find one without finding the other within arm's length. It was a bond that's hard to come across in the world these days, Macon had always mused. Nowadays, nothing lasted forever. People relocate. They move away. They die. The world comes and takes people from your life, year by year. But he had hoped for something different for Wash and Ava. He saw a childhood friendship that would eventually blossom into a young romance—if it hadn't already. Then maybe they'd marry, and on and on. It was a dream that he had never realized he believed in. And now it was all in question.

Wash was like a son to Macon. The sheriff had already lost a wife, his daughter's health was precarious, his new wife was struggling with a pregnancy that, as much as he tried to convince himself otherwise, was not guaranteed... and now Wash had cancer.

"Jesus, Brenda," he said finally. He spoke slowly and with exhaustion. His anger at the old woman was replaced by exasperation as the truth of the situation filled his head. Still ignoring her newly cleaned floor, he walked across the room and sat on the couch. "Let's talk this out, Brenda. How serious is it?" he asked again.

"How serious?" Brenda said, almost laughing. "Can you name a case when cancer in a child wasn't deadly serious?" She stopped scrubbing the floor and heaved a heavy, fatigued sigh. She stood and, after rubbing the soreness from her knees, walked over and sat on the other end of the couch. Her face was flushed and sweat beaded upon her brow. Her long red hair was pulled in a ponytail that had been coming undone from the exertion of her work. She rested her hands in her lap and began massaging them.

It was then that Macon noticed how red they were. Her hands looked as though she'd touched scalding water. They were raw. "You think I'm cruel, don't you?" Brenda asked. She straightened her back and faced him. "You ask your-self, 'What type of a person doesn't tell a child that they're sick?' You want me to make it make sense for you?" Her mouth tightened. "I've got my reasons. And it's not your child. You're not responsible for him. You don't have to look into his eyes when the time comes to tell him that he might be dying."

"He needs to know," Macon said softly.

"And he will know," Brenda replied. "I'm just not ready yet." She looked over at the scrub bucket waiting by the end of the couch. Then she looked at the dirt that had ridden in on Macon's shoes.

"But how long can he wait?" Macon asked. "How long can you let him go untreated? This is his life we're talking about here, Brenda."

Without a word, Brenda stood and crossed the room and retrieved a broom from the kitchen. She came back into the living room and began sweeping the dirt from the floor. "I'm going to have to scrub this again," she said.

"Brenda, stop," Macon said.

But she did not stop. She swept the dirt from his shoes over the threshold of the door and out into the world. Then she returned the broom to the kitchen and kneeled on the floor next to the bucket of bleach water. She dunked the sponge and returned to scrubbing the floor.

Macon watched. He had never seen the woman like this. Not even when her daughter died in the car crash with Tom, not even then had she behaved this way. She stood tall at her daughter's funeral, like a statue. She didn't even cry—at least, not that Macon saw. She only sat with her arm around her grandson as he wept. In the pew next to them both was Tom, blubbering and moaning, with both hands over his eyes, as if not looking at the body of his wife could make her death any less real than it was.

Macon had come over today expecting to find that same version of Brenda. But, instead, he found a woman hanging by a thread. Even stone crumbles after being hit enough times, he thought.

"I'm sorry," Macon said softly. He walked over and took Brenda's hands and helped her up from the floor. "Just stop that," he said. "I'm sorry for showing up here like this. I just…it just all caught me off guard." He led her back to the couch and sat beside her, still holding her hands.

"You want to know why I don't tell him?" Brenda began. "You want to know how I can let him walk around not knowing what's going on inside him?" She squeezed Macon's hands. "You want to know what the greatest thing in a lifetime is, Macon? What's better than climbing some damned mountain, better than falling in love, better than having a child, better than all of that?"

Macon watched the woman carefully. The fire that she had been missing was slowly returning to her. "Okay," he said. "What?"

"Believing that the world can't hurt you," Brenda said. And, at last, she looked at the blood flowing from her hand. She dabbed her knuckle with the cloth, and did not flinch when the antiseptic came in contact with the wound. "That's the most amazing thing a person can ever feel, can ever believe. And it only ever happens once in a lifetime, and it never lasts. The world always tells you the truth of things. People around you start dying, you get hurt—whatever happens—and eventually you start to understand that you're not invincible, that you're not special. That, just like everybody else in this world, your days are numbered." She shook her head. "Hell of a thing to lose," she said. Then she stood and continued trying to staunch the bleeding of her hand. "There's a word for that feeling, Macon," she said. "It's called childhood. And once it's gone, it's gone. And that sense that the world is this large magical thing gets taken away with it. In that moment, you become an adult, and you lose your ability to see the wonder of all things. All you see from that point forward is how broken everything will one day be."

"But he needs to know," Macon said softly. "Wash needs to know what's happening to him."

"He will," Brenda said. Finally, the tears flowed down her cheeks. "But is it so wrong of me to want to give him a couple more days? A few more moments of his childhood? Does it make me a bad person, Macon? Have I wronged the boy?" Her voice was filled with pleading and fear and the sadness of a grandmother who is afraid of outliving her grandson. Macon kneeled beside her and wrapped his arms around the woman. "I've already lost a daughter," she continued. "Parents don't bury children. That's not how it's supposed to be. And, every day, I wonder if it was my fault. I don't blame Tom. I don't even blame God. I blame myself, because that's just what you do when your child dies, regardless of how it happens. Every single day she's not here and every single day I wonder what part I played in that. And now there's a chance I might lose Wash, too, and I just want to let him have a little bit more of his childhood. Tell me," she said, "am I so wrong for that? Am I?"

The sound of her crying filled the house. And it was a terrible sound, not unlike the sad, lonely trill of a single harp string being plucked.

"No," Macon said, holding the woman. "You didn't do anything wrong. We'll find a way to make this better."

"Don't tell anyone," Brenda said. Then she looked into Macon's eyes. "Don't tell Ava. Promise me that."

The thought had been in Macon's mind before Brenda said it.

"Everything that's going on with her," Brenda continued. "It's enough. She's already done the impossible for Wash once. And she's still not fixed, not really. I know you see it as well as I do." Finally, she let go of Macon's hands. "Wash will be okay," she said. "The doctors will do what they do and they'll make him better. Your daughter can't save the whole world. Promise me you won't make her try."

"It'll be okay," was all that Macon said. He made no promises and he asked no more about Brenda's motivations. He only sat with her as the day rolled on and, somewhere in the time they were together, he tried to imagine if she could live without Wash. He wondered if Ava could.

They spent the afternoon in the mountains with a bucket and a small square of steel. They dug through rocks and rubble and Ava's mother would not tell them what they were looking for. "It'll be something you've never found before," was all that Heather would say, and Ava liked the hint of mystery it added to their expedition.

These were the mountains, after all, and even though she was young, Ava had heard stories of gold and diamonds and all manner of valuable things being found in mountains—even in these familiar mountains around Stone Temple. So she worked through the first half of the afternoon without complaint, finding excitement and strangeness in everything that she came across.

In just a few short hours she found an old bottle cap, a pocket knife, a stone shaped like a tooth, an actual tooth, a piece of wood shaped like the state of Texas—a state which she liked very much on account of the movies that came on television sometimes about the Wild West—a piece of rubber whose origin she could not explain and more.

For her part, Ava's mother focused on one specific area. Now and again she would take the small square of metal from her pocket and run it back and forth over the rocks as though it might show her something that she could not otherwise see.

"What is that?" Ava asked, pointing to the square of metal. It was late in the afternoon and Ava had not found anything particularly interesting in several hours and so the excitement of the day was beginning to wear off.

"It's a piece of steel."

"Why do you have it?"

"Because I need it."

"Why do you need it?"

"To find what I'm looking for."

Ava was tired and her attention was beginning to wane. She thought of Wash and the television back at home and her father who had not come with them and a dozen other things that had nothing to do with whatever it was that she and her mother had come to the mountain for that day.

There is a world beyond this, she thought.

"There it is," Heather said, a glimmer of excitement in her voice. She kneeled over a large, smooth stone with the pane of steel placed above it. When she lifted the steel, the rock rose with it.

"What's that?" Ava asked.

"It's a lodestone," Heather said. She pulled it away from the iron rod and placed it in her daughter's hand. The child responded by moving the stone back toward the metal. When it was close enough, it leaped from her hand and attached to the iron.

Ava smiled.

"It's yours," Heather said.

"I can have it?"

"Of course you can. It's been waiting here for you for all these years."

"What do you mean?"

"When I was young," Heather began, *"I used to come up to these mountains all the time. And one day I came up here and I found a stone just like this, in this exact place. And I took it home and I kept it for many, many years. And then, one day, I lost it. But I never forgot this place. And I promised that, one day, when I had a child, I would bring them up here and let them find one of these stones."*

Ava held the small stone in her hand. She squeezed it tightly, as if trying to understand it better by feeling the weight and heft of it in her hand.

"And now, years later, you've got it. It's been waiting for you for longer than I've been alive. Maybe longer than anyone has been alive. It's almost impossible to tell how long something like that, something that's destined for you, can sit and wait, counting days, holding on, waiting for you."

"Is that true?" Ava asked. She opened her palm and looked at the stone and tried to imagine all of the years that it had been waiting for her. She imagined rain and wind and clouds and the earth rolling on its axis and animals passing by and people coming and going and, all the while, the stone sat and waited in silence, knowing her name.

"It's all true," Heather said. *"Everything that you can believe in this life can be true."*

SIX

"HOW DO YOU FEEL?" Wash asked in a loud voice.

It was the second time Ava had woken to his voice in the hospital. Over the past few days her vision had been slowly returning to her. Wash, along with everyone else in Ava's life, had come by and sat with her and talked to her and been excited when, each day, she could make out shapes and images a little more. All of them could feel their own fear lessening.

"What?" Ava answered in a groggy voice. Her head hurt a bit—she imagined a large bell being struck in the front part of her brain and, usually, it got worse when she opened her eyes. But, overall, she felt that Wash was worth the headache. She opened her eyes slowly, blinking and looking around the room. "Wash," she said. "Is that you?"

"What's wrong?" he asked, hearing something different in her voice than he had heard in the previous days. There was a sliver of fear in it. He got up from the chair at the foot of her bed and came and stood beside her. When he looked into her eyes, they were clear, but she seemed to be looking past him. "Can you see me?" he asked nervously. "Those clouds that were there before are gone." He waved his hand back and forth. "You should be better," he said, and the thought trenches sprung up on his forehead. "Ava, can you see?"

Ava reached up from the bed and took his earlobe between her fingers and tugged it—not enough to hurt, but enough to get his attention. "Does that answer your question?" she asked, giggling. The sudden motion made her head hurt more, but it felt good to make Wash smile.

"You jerk!" he said, laughing. "That was mean."

"It was funny," Ava said. She sat up on her elbows, excited by the fact that, for the first time in many days, she could see clearly, as though nothing had ever been wrong. She coughed and the pain that came with it reminded her that she was very sick. She was still cold and there was an ache in her bones that persisted. The coughing continued and there was the coppery taste of blood in her mouth. Wash sat on the edge of the bed and filled a cup with water from a pitcher sitting beside the bed. He watched the girl endure the coughing, and he waited to help her. He looked to the door, about to call for help.

"No," Ava managed.

Wash held the breath that was in his throat. When the coughing finally ended she sipped the water and rolled onto her side, wheezing slightly, while Wash patted her back. He picked up a small cloth that was lying beside her bed and wiped the blood from her mouth.

"Thanks," Ava said when the pain was lessened and she could speak again.

"Why won't you tell anyone how badly it hurts?" Wash asked.

"It wouldn't stop anything," Ava replied. She shivered and Wash adjusted the blankets atop her, making sure that she had as many quilts upon her as he could find. When she was covered and the warmth was finally beginning to kindle within her, she reached up and pulled Wash's earlobe again. "You're not singing," she said. "I thought that was your secret weapon for annoying me until I got better."

The boy smiled. "I'm taking a break from it," he said. "Maybe I should try something else. I brought *Moby Dick*. I could read that for you."

"I'd rather hear you butcher a song right now," Ava said gently. "And when you're in the hospital people are supposed to do what you want them to. Anything but 'Banks of the Ohio.' No more songs about people killing their boyfriends."

"Maybe I shouldn't really sing anymore," Wash said. "My dad said I should stop."

"Wash…"

"Maybe he thinks I don't have the voice for it, you know?" He rubbed the top of his head. His shaggy brown hair fell into his eyes. "We both know my voice is kind of weird. He knows a lot about music. Maybe I should listen to him."

"Shut up, Wash," Ava said. "Shut up and sing something. If you're worried about him finding out, I'll keep your secret." Then she settled back into the pillow and closed her eyes and waited.

"And I'll keep yours?" Wash asked. "I won't tell anyone that you're not doing as good as you pretend to be?"

"Yeah," Ava said softly. Her eyes were still closed. "Don't tell anyone that I'm not going to keep doing this."

"What?"

"I'm tired," Ava said. "And I don't want any of this anymore."

Wash studied her face. He wished she would open her eyes and look at him as he spoke. But she did not. "Why did you do the thing with the dog? Why not tell your dad you want to stop?"

"Are you going to sing me a song or what?" Ava asked. She opened her eyes and looked at the boy and, in that moment, they both knew that, for now, the discussion was over. She squeezed his hand. "Thanks," she said.

It took a moment, but Wash managed a grin. "What about 'The Ballad of John Henry'?" he asked.

"Great," Ava said wryly. "Another song about somebody dying."

"It's part of my charm," Wash said. "Now hush and let me get ready." He cleared his throat and tilted his head the way he always did and his thumb and forefinger touched and made the familiar "okay" sign and the song rose up from his throat and filled the room and Ava simply lay there and listened and the pain drifted away until sleep came, softly drifting from the boughs of Wash's voice.

Reverend Isaiah Brown's church had secured itself in the center of Stone Temple. It was Wednesday evening and cold out but that would not stop the congregation. They came in cars and vans and buses and, once they had found accommodations among the townspeople—there was no hotel in Stone Temple, but its inhabitants were quickly learning the

art of renting rooms and converting wasted space to profit-
able acreage for tents and RVs—the members of Reverend
Brown's church, who had pulled Macon away from Carmen
on the day of her examination because they were erecting
their tent, had built a small community around the oak tree
at the center of town.

A few years back the town had gotten a grant from the
state and used the money to build a small park. They said
that it would help with the tourist season on account of the
fact that at the center of the park was one of the oldest and
grandest oak trees most folks had ever seen in their entire
lives. It swept up out of the earth like a great green flame
licking at the sky. Its branches burst out in all directions.
Even in the winter the tree still had a great deal to offer,
the way its naked branches connected and ran from one another like veins.

The town had set up a type of artists' retreat in one of
the old houses nearby that no one was living in. The house
opened up directly onto the newly created park with the
beautiful oak tree, and the artists would come to marvel at
the tree. They painted and sketched the tree, wrote poetry
and penned plays about it.

But then, as with nearly all things in Stone Temple, the
oak tree lost its luster. The artists came in fewer and fewer
waves each year until, finally, they stopped coming altogether and only the townspeople were left.

And now Reverend Brown's congregation was planted
beneath the bare boughs of the tree. They existed by the
grace of heated tents with a large, grand stage on the far side
of the park, beset on three sides by the small buildings and

houses of the town that held the thin population of people and failed businesses.

Reverend Isaiah Brown stood in the center of the stage, microphone in one hand, Bible in the other, and started into his sermon for the evening. It was a sermon on the miracles that Jesus performed and how, more than anything, it was the duty of the church—and, by association, members of the church—to seek to emulate, even more than anything else, the kindness and selflessness of Jesus's acts.

"It's easy to believe that we are different than Jesus was," the reverend began, "because we are, and yet, we are very much the same. Jesus lived, and we live. Jesus bled, and we bleed. Jesus died, and so do we. And in his lifetime he was able to perform amazing things, impossible things, things that you and I, in our failures, could only ever hope to achieve." He walked back and forth across the stage slowly as he spoke, taking in the entirety of the audience when he could, making eye contact, ensuring that his words were received as well as they could be. Reverend Brown had always believed that conversation—whether it be something as large as a sermon or something as small as a thank-you— was an attempt to pass, from one person to another, a flame of empathy. It was an attempt for one soul, trapped inside a body, to pass their thoughts and feelings, the essence of who they are, on to another person. And a sermon to a congregation was the highest form of that, Reverend Isaiah Brown believed, because it carried with it the task and turmoil of trying to connect people to something they oftentimes struggled to believe in, something they often felt unworthy of. It was like bridging the gap between the earth and the sun— both glorious in their own right, both caught in the gravity of each other, but with thousands upon thousands of miles of distance between them.

"But we cannot use our belief that Jesus was more than we were," Reverend Brown continued, "as an excuse to be remiss in our duty to be kind, to be compassionate, to be forgiving, to help others and to try to make the world around us a better place than it was before we arrived." He stopped pacing. "I mention all of this because, dear church, we all know what happened in this small town of Stone Temple. The whole world is talking about the girl at the center of it, and everyone is trying to understand its meaning, trying, perhaps, to assign their own meaning to it. We're all guilty of it, myself included. I won't pretend that I'm not as fascinated and intrigued as all of you by what has happened here. That was why I came, and I believe that is why so many of you followed me here.

"But as time marches forward, and as we begin to express our opinion about these events, as the world begins to converge upon this town and those people within it, I ask you all to remember that, more than anything else, this is about a child. And we need to stay away from hanging too much of our hopes, too many of our expectations, upon her. We need to remember that we are all as blessed and loved by God as she is. That we all have within us the ability to do good things, to save people—not through miracles, but through action. Free will allowing us to help others is the greatest blessing God ever gave us."

The applause began slowly. This was a very different sermon than much of the crowd had expected. A great many of them had followed Reverend Brown to this town expecting to hear him talk of how the girl was sent by God, sent to remind them of His existence and His ability to create miracles. And now, the reverend they had believed in so deeply was stepping away from that message. There were those who understood and agreed with what Reverend Brown had said. But there were also those who were left questioning.

But because the congregation was loyal to their leader, they all applauded. They all stood and raised their hands in reverence and when he concluded the sermon with the Lord's Prayer—as he always did—they spoke the words and their belief in him was reassembled.

"I thank you," he said solemnly. "I thank you, church, for everything that you do. Thank you so much," he said.

Macon watched from the front row. The reverend had invited him to come and hear the sermon, and he had accepted. There was something in the reverend that reminded Macon of his father—a stern but fair man that passed away months before Ava was born. There was a part of Macon that lamented how his daughter never got to know her grandfather. And Macon was cognizant enough to know that there was a small degree of transference happening with Reverend Brown. But he accepted it and moved forward.

When the sermon was over, Macon was asked to join the reverend in private.

"What do you think of all this?" Reverend Brown asked. He offered Macon coffee, but the sheriff declined, having never quite learned the intimacies of the drink. The two of them sat in one of the many large rooms of the Andrews House.

"It's quite a production," Macon said, choosing his words carefully.

The library room was large and the walls paneled with

wood that looked warm and expensive. It was the house of one of the wealthiest men in Stone Temple, Benjamin Andrews, a well-to-do investor that had made a career creating mergers and profits. He was often quoted by the townspeople as saying that his youth had "gone to mammon." Now that he was older, he had converted his large, sweeping home into an inn for travelers. Rooms could be rented at low rates for anyone in need of a break from the world. Travelers frequented the inn and admired the grandness and pomp of the house's architecture. It would make most people feel awestruck and small, but also inspire a spark of an idea that the world, as cruel as it could be, could be a warm and inviting place at times. Benjamin Andrews took great pride in this.

So when word was sent—earlier on than most people suspected—that Reverend Brown would be coming to town, accommodations were made for the great man and his church. Rooms that had otherwise been rented were held in wait, because the reverend was someone who people could believe in.

"Too much showmanship for you?" Reverend Brown asked.

"I was never really the church-going type," Macon replied. "So whatever people enjoy, showmanship or not, it's their own business."

Reverend Brown nodded in agreement. "And can I assume that you're not being 'the church-going type' was only made worse by the untimely death of your wife?"

Macon's body tightened. "I'll never get used to how much a person can find out about someone else these days," he said.

"It doesn't take much work," Reverend Brown said. "Especially now. There's a microscope hanging over this entire town and everyone in it." He made a motion with his hands, forming a small circle, as though he could look through it and see into Macon. "More than that," he continued, breaking the illusion of the microscope, "one should always know as much as they can about people." He rubbed his hands together as if to warm them, then he made one hand into a fist and placed the other atop it. "So why did you decide to become sheriff?"

"Just sort of fell into it, I suppose."

Reverend Brown stood and went around to the far side of the desk. He sat with a sigh and leaned back in his chair. Then, after a brief pause, he sat forward again, as if suddenly becoming uncomfortable in his position. He placed his elbows on the desk and crouched forward and peered over the top of his clasped hands. "Can I ask you what you believe, Macon? Spiritually, I mean."

Macon had known the question was coming. His religious views were a large part of the conversation everyone seemed to want to have with him these days. There was an obvious parallel between what Ava had done and the miracles performed by Jesus, and that was something the world couldn't ignore. And so, naturally, people wanted to know precisely where Macon stood in regard to the topic. They wanted to know if he was Catholic, Baptist, Methodist, Jewish, Muslim, Buddhist, Taoist or other. They asked if he was atheist, deist or agnostic. Something else? Miracles were never things to be confined. For as long as people have acknowledged the mundane, they've believed in the miraculous. Did he attend church every week, or hardly at all? Did he pray? Did he believe in anything at all?

Ultimately, he knew that it didn't matter what he believed—

or didn't believe. If he said he was a religious man, those who weren't religious would try to pick him apart—saying it was a hoax orchestrated by a religious nut. If he said something to indicate that religion wasn't a big part of his life, then there would be those who would attack him on the very grounds of the fact that there was no word that could be used to describe what Ava had done other than *miracle*.

"I believe what I believe," Macon replied. It was the best reply he could come up with. It declared nothing and affronted no one.

"Fair enough," Reverend Brown replied, and there was sincerity in his voice. "All of us," he continued, "are entitled to stand upon our own spiritual ground, whatever it may be. And maybe, at this particular point in time, with everything going on around you and your daughter, maybe you deserve that right more than anyone else."

"Why do I get the feeling there's a 'but' coming?" Macon asked.

"There is something I would like from you."

"What?"

"In short," the reverend said, "I would like your help." He paused for a moment, as if to allow Macon to imagine the specifics of what he wanted. Then he continued, "I think that I can help you and your family. I think I've made that abundantly clear to you. But I can't do it unless you allow me. And I would like for you to allow me to help Ava. And the best way to do that is if the two of you will join my church."

"What did Reverend Brown say?" Carmen asked. They stood in the driveway, bundled up in the unseasonable cold.

It was late and Ava was sleeping in her bedroom so they'd chosen to have their argument in the yard. One of the benefits of living in the middle of the woods was that there were no neighbors within hearing distance, something they rarely took advantage of, but enjoyed when the time was appropriate.

Macon looked down the long driveway toward the bottom of the hill. Where he thought he would find the lights of the reporters that had been watching their house every day since all of this began, he saw only darkness.

"What happened to the piranhas?" Macon asked.

"You're avoiding my question." Carmen folded her arms across her chest and Macon knew she wouldn't be moved until they'd talked.

"Don't underestimate how much talent it takes to avoid your questions," Macon replied.

"And don't underestimate the ability of a pregnant woman to hit you with a frying pan if you don't answer her."

"Okay," Macon said, grinning. Then he took a deep breath and the grin fell away. "I don't think he's a bad man," Macon said.

"What does he want with Ava?" Carmen replied with a directness not unlike Macon's.

The air was cool and crisp. Off in the west the moon sat low on the horizon, half-secluded by the mountains and pines springing up shaggy and thick in the dimness. The crickets and cicadas were singing their various songs and the wind that came down off the mountain smelled of night-blooming jasmine. Though it seemed the winter would be early this year, life still clung to the earth.

"Well," Carmen said. "How bad is it?"

"He wants Ava to help someone."

"What do you mean?"

"It's the same thing Eldrich wanted, the same thing they all want. He thinks that Ava, if she really can do what she does, has a responsibility to help people. To do good things. Or, at least, to do the best that she can." He tightened his mouth, trying to force the words forward. "And I can't say I'm a hundred percent in disagreement with him."

"Well, that's easy enough," she replied. "No."

"Carmen."

"What? I don't see the need for a discussion here." She rubbed the side of her head. "Tell him the same thing you should have told Eldrich—to go to hell. Nobody knows what happened with Ava and Wash, let's just all go ahead and concede that. Nobody knows how she did it. Hell, half the world still doesn't believe she did it. And, honestly, I'm okay with that. Maybe that'll help this blow over a little quicker." She stepped forward and took Macon's hand in hers. She looked him in the eyes. "But the one thing that we do know is that, whatever she did, it hurt her to do it. She was unconscious for three days. And she still doesn't look like she's back to normal. You've seen the way she can never get warm."

"I know," Macon said, looking away. "It's just that…well, we can't really pretend that none of this happened. We can't act like we have the option of just forgetting what she did."

"Yes, we do," Carmen said. "We can just say no. When people ask to do tests or ask her to do it again, we can just say no. That is an option. We all have the right to say no."

"You've got to understand how big this is, Carmen." Macon squeezed her hand gently. "She did something unbelievable. And maybe with him," Macon said hesitantly, "there's a better chance to steer all of this. I don't know. It just…it just feels so big." He made a motion with his hands to show that he was encompassing something large and unwieldy with his statement. "People keep asking questions and I can't answer any of them. She's my child and I don't know what's going on with her." He sighed softly. "The doctors said she's getting better."

"The doctors don't know shit," Carmen said sharply. "Every time she does *it* she goes into a coma. Think about that, Macon. Think about what all of this is doing to her body. Have you seen how skinny she's getting? She eats but it's like it's all going into a black hole somewhere. Her clothes barely fit her anymore."

"Carmen," Macon said exhaustedly. "Can't we just talk about this instead of arguing about it?"

"This is killing her, Macon," Carmen said slowly. "Little by little, it's killing her."

"Please…" Macon said, pleading. He stood with his eyes closed, not seeing what was in front of him.

Carmen began to speak again, but stopped herself. She had grown up in a household with a mother and father whose arguments were not unlike the one she currently found herself caught in. And she had always promised that she would not become the woman her mother was—a woman who did not give her husband or children the chance to make a case for themselves but, instead, launched into soliloquies and called them arguments. Even though the person on the other side of the conversation was never allowed to get a word in edgewise. She paused and caught her breath. "Okay," she said eventually. "Let's hear it."

"This whole thing, the way everyone is responding to it, I'm lost in it," he said. "I'm just a sheriff—a decent one, but just a sheriff. I handle lost dogs and burning ordinances and the occasional drunk who can't find his way back to his farm. That's it. That's who I am. That's what I know. And now I don't know what the hell is going on. Every day this all just gets bigger and bigger. More people come to town, more news cameras, more people asking for interviews, more people trying to tell me what it all means. And since I haven't really got a clue what it all means, I don't know who to believe." Macon walked to Carmen and, finally, she unfolded her arms. He took her hands in his. "I'm scared," he said.

Carmen could blame the tears that came on the pregnancy. She was always crying about something, it seemed. But she wasn't crying because she wanted Macon to concede, nor was she crying because of her hormones. She wept because, like her husband, she was terrified—adrift in a strange, unsure world. And she knew he would not cry, so she cried for him.

"Isn't there any better way?" Carmen managed.

"If you can think of it," Macon said, "I'll listen."

She had no reply.

"Look at where we live, Carmen." He made a motion with his head to indicate the house behind her. She did not turn. She knew, as well as Macon did, where they lived. "We're not quite starving," Macon continued, "but we need money. You know that. We're just scraping by and now we're going to have another member of this crazy little family of ours. There aren't any teaching jobs around here and being the sheriff is a joke." He shook his head. "I spent my entire life living in this house, watching it fall apart, unable to do anything to change it. Unable to make a decent living.

And now, by some chance, we've got a chance to change that." He reached up and wiped a tear from Carmen's face. "I know we'll make this work. I believe that something special is happening in our lives right now. And I don't want to turn away from that."

Carmen had a thousand things she wanted to say. A dozen different arguments against Reverend Brown alone. But she loved her husband, and she was as afraid and uncertain as he was. At least now, they could be afraid and uncertain together. At least now, neither of them would be striking out alone at things. "Okay," she said finally.

Then she stood on her tiptoes and kissed him. Her stomach—holding the baby they had made together pressing between them—was the proof of her love for him and her willingness to follow him into the days ahead. "But if we're going to do this, I'm not wearing any of those god-awful flowered hats that women at his church wear."

And then they laughed and the night did not seem quite as cold and the days looming ahead less arduous.

The drive over to the Campbells' had been more of a headache than Tom expected. If things were bad before with Ava and all of the attention they were getting, they were worse now.

As he drove through the town, he found the streets of Stone Temple lined with people, all of them with their eyes on his car once they saw that it was Wash inside. They knew that, more than likely, he was going to see Ava. When Tom stopped at an intersection, one man—a young man with a heavy, thick beard swaddling his face—raced over and knocked on Tom's window and offered Tom a thousand dollars if he would simply let him come with them to see Ava.

The man's sudden rushing of the car startled both Tom and Wash, but once Tom understood what was happening he only looked at the man quizzically and laughed. "What a crazy bastard," he said, then he pressed the accelerator and continued on. For the rest of the drive to Ava's no one else charged the car. While there was never any lack of people watching Tom and Wash as they passed, they kept to the side of the road and only shouted things or waved their signs or simply applauded. "You'd think we were the kings of England," Tom said at one point. Then he whistled—a long, diminishing note—to further punctuate his disbelief. "I don't think I'd wish this on anybody," he said.

"We can't even leave the house," Wash said.

Tom nodded. "That's what her mother told me."

"Carmen's her stepmom," Wash corrected. He was wearing blue jeans and a light sweater and, just now, he noticed a stain on the front of it. He wondered how it had gotten past his grandmother.

"I know," Tom said. "I remember the day we all met at the fair. But just because she didn't give birth to Ava, that doesn't mean Carmen's not her mom. Parenting's what you do. It's a job. And Carmen took the job." And then it was his turn to take stock of his clothing. His pants were dirty and the blue flannel shirt he wore had a torn pocket and smelled of motor oil, but it was the best he had.

"She's great," Wash said. "But Ava doesn't like her."

"That happens," Tom said. "She probably figures Carmen is trying to replace her mom. But she can't expect her old man to hoe his row in this world all by himself." His face tightened. "It's tough," he added.

For the first time since his father had returned, Wash noticed that his father was wearing a wedding ring. A knot formed in his stomach. He hadn't really considered the notion of his father remarrying in the time that he had been out of his life. He remembered his mother's face—pale and round, her blue eyes sparkling, wrinkled at the corner from prolonged smiling and with a light dusting of freckles across her cheeks. And when he remembered his mother he remembered his mother and father together.

"Can I meet her?" Wash asked.

"Meet who?" Tom replied.

"Your wife."

Tom's brow furrowed. He was concentrating hard on the road—the people lining the narrow mountain road were beginning to grow in number again now that they were getting closer to Ava's house. "What are you talking about, son? I'm not married." Then, as if understanding, he looked down at his left hand. "This is the only wedding ring I'll ever wear," he said. And then they turned the final corner—waved through by the police blocking the road—and started up the steep hill to Ava's house.

Tom parked the car near the front door and as he and Wash got out of the car he whispered, "Not sure I'm built for this."

"You'll be okay," Wash replied.

Tom put his arm around the boy's shoulders and the two of them knocked on the door together. As soon as the door opened Wash greeted Carmen. Tom did the same, making sure that she saw him remove his hat in a gesture of courtesy.

"I'll be back around dark," Tom said to Carmen. "You'll let me know if he's any trouble. But I don't think he will be." Then he patted Wash on the head and tousled the boy's hair and steered him inside the house. Wash headed for Ava's room. The two of them had hoped to leave the house and go into the woods as they usually did, but there were too many people outside. Too many things that could go wrong.

"Have fun," Carmen said to Wash as he passed. Then she turned to Tom. "He's never any trouble," she said. "He's practically family."

Tom nodded. "That's what I hear," he said. "But it just sounded like the type of thing a parent's supposed to say when they drop off their kid." His hands fidgeted in his pockets. "I'm still getting the hang of all this," Tom said.

"We all are," Carmen replied, smiling. "Every single day. Would you like to come in and sit for a while, Tom?" Carmen asked. "That's the kind of thing parents do, too."

Finally, Tom looked up at her. His brow furrowed, growing the "thought trenches" that Ava often teased Wash about. "I guess they do," Tom said.

"Come on in and make yourself at home," Carmen said, leaving the living room and walking into the kitchen. "I'll fix us something to drink."

"Yes, ma'am," Tom said, but he only lingered in the doorway.

"I appreciate the manners," Carmen replied from the kitchen, "but don't ma'am me. Hell, I'm guessing we're about the same age."

"You're probably right," Tom said. Finally he took a few steps inside the doorway, and he remained there, just inside the house, looking around, feeling uncomfortable. "I'm not sure how to do any of this," he said to himself. "I feel like I'm wearing a costume."

"What's that?" Carmen said, waddling back from the kitchen. She carried two glasses of iced tea and smiled brightly.

"Nothing," Tom said. He took the glass and looked at it skeptically. "I don't suppose you have any beer, do you?"

Carmen shook her head. "Not since I got pregnant. We hardly drink, anyhow, but once I got pregnant and couldn't drink at all, Macon decided to give it up, too." She wanted to sit, but Tom was still standing near the door and she didn't want to be rude. "So how are you and Wash getting along?" she asked.

"Okay, I suppose," Tom said. "He's a smart kid. Smarter than me."

"I know the feeling," Carmen said. "He and Ava are two of the smartest kids I've ever known. Sometimes I feel like I'm just holding her back, you know?"

Tom nodded. Still he had not tasted his tea. The glass was ice-cold, forcing him to shift it from one hand to the other intermittently.

"We're all just doing the best we can, though," Carmen said. "Ava and I have some tough days. She's still warming up to the idea of me being married to her father." She couldn't bear to stand any longer. The night had been sleepless and her muscles were sore and her back ached and her ankles were swollen and there were a dozen other things that her body was doing to her in the throes of the pregnancy. So, finally, she sat. "You're welcome to sit down," she said.

"No, thank you," Tom said. "I...I should be going." He stepped forward and placed the glass of tea on the coffee table in the center of the room. When Carmen began preparations to stand, he motioned for her not to. "No, you sit," he said. "I'm okay."

"You don't have to leave, Tom," Carmen said. "This might sound strange, but it feels good to talk to someone who's new to this parenting thing, too."

Tom flinched.

"I don't mean it as an insult," Carmen said, keeping her eyes on her glass. "It's just that, well, Macon has been doing this for years and Brenda's been a mother and a grandmother. Me, I feel like I'm always playing catch-up. And, to make it worse, things between Ava and me are tense." Finally, she looked up. "I guess it's just good to meet someone else who's struggling."

Tom watched the woman for a while. His first thought had been that she was coming on to him, but looking at her now, listening to her, he realized that it was the exact opposite. She was just as frightened of being a parent as he was. The only difference between them was the fact that she was enduring the struggle, day after day, while he'd run off into the world after the death of Wash's mother. He'd abandoned his child.

"I'll be going now," he said. He turned to leave.

"Wait, Tom," Carmen called after him. She struggled to stand. It was a clumsy and ungainly maneuver, getting up from the chair in a rush—an awkward maneuvering of her hips and stomach, followed by a hard push into slow, vertical lurch—and if Tom had continued walking, she wouldn't have been able to catch up to him. But he stood, and he waited.

"Nobody's asking you to be perfect, Tom," Carmen said

when she had finally crossed the room. "You're allowed to get it wrong sometimes."

Tom nodded. He tightened his jaw, preparing his mouth for something. "Can I ask you something?" he said. "About Ava?"

"Sure, Tom," Carmen said. She did not know what Tom wanted to ask. And, yet, at the same time, she felt that she knew exactly what he wanted to ask. Everyone had their own version of the same question about Ava. And Carmen was getting adept at answering them. There was a balance that needed to be struck. A compromise between saying that she didn't know more than anyone else and reassuring people that, regardless of what she knew, there was a plan in place.

Now it was Tom's turn to phrase it how he wanted to. Tom's eyes were downcast when he spoke. "How, uh, how does it work?" Tom asked. He lifted his eyes from the floor and looked at Carmen. He seemed afraid and penitent all at once. "Could she fix somebody that's never done nothing but fuck up their life?" He laughed darkly and twisted the hat in his hands. "Does what she's able to do work like that?" he continued. "Can she fix mistakes?" He looked down at his wedding ring. "And if she can't fix things like that, can she make it so that a person doesn't remember? Can she make it so that a person doesn't dream about the moment when everything in their life fell apart?"

"I don't know," Carmen said. She had learned to answer quickly when people asked her impossible questions. To delay was to offer hope where she did not have hope to offer. Then she added, "However she's able to do it, I don't think it works like that."

Tom nodded. He cleared his throat. "I figured as much. I

just thought I'd ask," he said. "I'll be going now. I'm sorry for…well…'I'm sorry' about sums me up, I guess."

Without pausing, he turned and walked out of the house. Carmen stood in the doorway and watched him walk to his car and leave. She wanted to call out to him, but the words she would have said eluded her.

"Do you like having your dad around?" Ava asked. They sat on opposite ends of Ava's bed with their legs folded beneath them with Wash's copy of *Moby Dick* between them. Ava still didn't particularly care for the book, and Wash was still determined to sway her. Once or twice since the two of them had been sitting, she opened the book to the dog-eared page where they'd stopped last time. She stared down at the words, then closed the book with an exaggerated look of disgust on her face.

"Grandma hates him," Wash replied. "But he's not that bad. He's different than I thought he'd be, is all. I've been staying with him a couple of nights."

Ava folded her arms across her chest and shrugged. She rubbed her arms to generate warmth. Both she and Wash were beginning to get used to the way she was never able to feel warm anymore. She wore jeans with a layer of gym shorts underneath, along with an undershirt, T-shirt and sweater. While she waited for Wash to answer the question about his father, Ava grabbed a knitted hair sash from the bedside stand. She tucked it onto her head—wrestling with the thick black frizzy mass of her hair. It was a comical process, watching her puffy hair resist the sash. When she had finished, they resumed their conversation. "What did your grandma say about it?"

"She said, 'He's your daddy. You'll figure out the rest.'"
Wash looked down at the book in his hand. He considered
reading it, but did not. "It's not like my dad died," Wash said.
"He just left. And I think a part of me thought that maybe
he *had* died. But now suddenly he shows up again, which is
almost worse because I know that every day he's been gone
was a day that he woke up and decided not to come see me."
He paused for a moment, taking in the sight of Ava in all of
her swaddling. "Are you sure you're okay?" he asked.

She shrugged her shoulders. "New topic," she said. Ava sat
with her legs folded against her chest and her arms wrapped
around her knees. She looked down at the copy of *Moby
Dick*. "This book is pretty terrible," she said. She picked it
up and tossed it into Wash's lap.

"It's a classic," Wash replied. "Just ask anybody."

"Just because people say it's a classic, doesn't mean it is.
That's all I'm saying."

"It's an adventure book," Wash said. "But it's more than
that, too. It's a book about a whole lot of things." He took a
breath in preparation to continue, but could not find what
he wanted to say. He could see the words in his mind—
all the things he wanted to say—but they were like bees
buzzing about him in the air: just enough to catch sight of,
but impossible to contain. "It's hard to really get my head
around it all." Wash's face tightened, not unlike his father's
sometimes did. "You just don't get it," he said, frustrated at
himself much more than at Ava. "Even I don't really get it.
Not all of it, anyway. But I think that'll change when I get
older. Just think about all the stuff people have said about
this book." He held up the novel as evidence of both its ex-

istence and merit. "It wouldn't still be in print if it wasn't really doing something amazing, right?"

Ava gave him a sidelong glance. "Just shut up and keep reading," Ava said.

Wash snorted a laugh and opened the book. He searched for his place, but when he found it he immediately closed the book again, still keeping his finger in place to hold the page. "Why do you think he did it?"

"Who?"

"Ishmael?"

"Why do I think Ishmael did what?" She reached over and took the book from Wash's hand. "I swear, Wash, how many times are you going to start conversations halfway in the middle?"

"It's all part of my charm," Wash said quickly. He sat up straight and smoothed his hair the way people did on television.

"Who said you were charming?"

"People."

"Whatever," she giggled.

"Why do you think Ishmael left home?"

"I thought it was because he was tired of being on land. He's a sailor, right? And that's what sailors do—they sail."

"Yeah," Wash replied, "but what about the people in his life. He had family."

"He didn't have any kids, though. So he could really do what he wanted."

"I guess," Wash said, his face confessing his confusion. "But..."

"But why does someone do something like that?" Wash said. "He had to have people that cared about him. Friends, cousins, somebody. We've all got somebody, you know? We're all connected to somebody. What does it take to just pick up and leave like that?"

Ava turned and looked out the nearby window. Beyond the window there were trees and brush and, beyond that, the steeply rising mountain. Sliding over the mountain, like a narrow serpent, was a thin, discernible trail. Ava and Wash had walked that trail countless times. It led away. It led into the world. "Wouldn't it be something," Ava began, "to go off on your own like that? To get away from everyone?"

"Would you do it?" Wash asked.

"Maybe," Ava said.

"Why?"

"Why shouldn't I?" She rubbed her shoulders again, beating back the chill she felt. "Do you really think somebody could do it?" she asked.

"What?"

"Do what Ishmael did," Ava replied. "Run away."

Wash could see the seriousness in her eyes, even if he did not fully understand its genesis. "Maybe," Wash said.

"How would you do it?"

"I'd head north," Wash said definitively. Perhaps there was a part of him that had considered this, as well. "If you got past the radio tower you could really disappear for a while. Nothing but trees and mountains."

"There's Rutger's cabin," Ava inserted, and it was clear that she was thinking ahead of the boy. "Dad and I go hunting up there. And Mom took me there once."

"Oh, yeah," Wash replied. "Grandma told me about that place. Some guy and his wife lived up there a long time ago.

They didn't want to be around anybody. They only came into town once a year."

"Once every two years," Ava said. "Dad told me where it is. It's not too far from where we go hunting sometimes. I know almost exactly where it's supposed to be."

"We've got to go sometime," Wash said. "Grandma says the ridgeline takes you right there, but nobody goes that way because that part of the ridge is pretty rough." Wash's face tightened, as if a decision had been made. "Anyhow," he said, "if you keep going, you could make it up into Virginia. The Appalachian Trail runs up that way—once you get past the radio tower on the north side of town. And then you could really control just how much running away you wanted to do."

"What do you mean?"

"Well, there are always people up that way. But at the same time, when you're on the trail, you can really disappear. You could walk along the trail, just off to the side—that way you wouldn't get lost and, if you needed help of some kind, there would be people not too far away. It's the perfect place to run away…if such a thing exists." He smiled awkwardly.

"Would you do it?" Ava asked.

"Are you going to do it?" Wash replied.

In Ava's mind she saw a small cabin in the woods—silent and forgotten and waiting. Calling to her as the sirens called to Odysseus, full of promise and terror.

It was Macon's second time attending one of Reverend Brown's sermons. He had trouble explaining to Carmen exactly why he came back—knowing full well what reaction people would have to him attending the church. To the rest of the world, it appeared that he was choosing sides, making a statement about what he felt Ava's gift meant, where he felt it was rooted. And, after his first appearance at the church, there were already people formulating theories that he might someday take over Reverend Brown's church. Or that he might start one of his own. There were all manner of theories and ideas drifting around the internet and television about why Macon was coming to this particular church. But none of them struck at the truth of things: the simple fact that Macon felt adrift, and Reverend Brown, for better or worse, was something of a tether.

But Macon was smart enough to know that he didn't need to fan the flames of conjecture any more than he already was. So when people asked him why he came, he simply said, "Because I want to," and left it at that. He knew that regardless of what he said, it would be twisted to each person's own ends, so he chose simply to tell the truth. Yes, it was a manicured version of the truth, but it was the truth nonetheless.

So for the second time he stood and he listened to Reverend Brown talk to his congregation about Ava and about how, above all else, they needed to guide their desire for her to fulfill wishes that they had. "She is her own person," Reverend Brown said. "And we have to be willing to let her be that."

Reverend Brown's sermons were not quite as well-received as many of his others. While he spoke of Ava's right to be her own person, there were others in town—and around the world—who spoke of Ava's duty. They had begun calling it "Divine Compulsion," the idea that Ava had no choice in what happened next in her life now that the world knew about what she could do. Her fate had been determined by a higher power, and many people felt that she should use her gift, regardless of the cost to her.

And so with each sermon of tolerance, Reverend Brown lost a few members. Some of them began following other preachers and ministers. Others simply decided that they did not need guidance on this matter—having already come to their decision about what Ava's responsibilities were. And, day by day, Reverend Brown watched his congregation start down the slow path of dwindling.

The reverend was not yet sure how Macon felt about him. He was sure that there was a large part of Macon that did not trust him, that saw him as just another person trying to exploit Ava. But he wanted more than that. Regardless of appearances, he wanted to help. So it was with great reluctance that he would do what he was planning to do tonight. Likely as not, he knew, Macon would see it as a betrayal. But the reverend figured that the best way to control a storm was to grab the lightning.

"As you all know," he said, halfway through his sermon, "the local sheriff, Macon Campbell, is with us this evening." A round of applause went up and all eyes turned to Macon. He sat in the front row, flanked by the church's deacons. Reverend Brown looked down at him. "I have a wonderful announcement," Reverend Brown continued. "I'm pleased to announce that, after much discussion, the sheriff has agreed to become a part of our church. And he will be bringing his family with him."

The roar that went up from the crowd was deafening. Before Macon understood what was happening, Reverend Brown came down from the stage, microphone in hand, and

asked Macon to join him in front of the church. Macon resisted. His fists were clenched and his jaw locked in anger,
but he went, compelled by the thousands of eyes upon him.

"You son of a bitch," he whispered to the reverend as
they climbed the stairs to the stage. "What are you doing?"

"Everything I can to help you," Reverend Brown replied.

And then Macon was before the crowd. Eyes and cameras
loomed upon him. He couldn't remember another time in
his life when he had been so afraid. Reverend Brown stood
in the center of the stage, smiling and patting his shoulder.
He turned the microphone away. "This is the only way you'll
make it through this," he whispered into Macon's ear. "They
won't let you sit idly by. You'll have to take a position sooner
or later. At least, this way, you're not alone."

He stood with one hand extended toward Macon and
the other aimed at the crowd, in a gesture of introduction,
as if he could take Macon's hand and provide a living link
to every person who was now standing on their feet and
cheering.

Macon felt light-headed.

"Here is the man himself," Reverend Brown said, and
Macon could hear his voice echoing around the arena,
thrumming from the speakers positioned around the room.
The crowd responded to Reverend Brown's voice by applauding all the louder. "Amen," Reverend Brown said.
Then he raised Macon's hand up like a referee raising the
hand of a conquering fighter, and the people became louder
and more excited and Macon trembled.

"Don't be afraid," Reverend Brown said, leaning in and
whispering into Macon's ear. Then he sat in a small chair
on the far side of the stage and Macon was left to face the

people of the congregation on his own. Seconds passed like years. Macon cleared his throat and the microphone picked up the sound and broadcast it through the speakers.

"Don't be afraid," someone said.

"Excuse me," Macon said, clearing his throat once more. "I apologize for my nervousness," he said. His voice was gathering itself up. "This is all…very sudden."

"Amen," someone shouted.

"How did it happen?" someone in the audience shouted. Macon searched the crowd, trying to meet the eyes of whoever had posed the question, but all he saw was a sea of waiting faces.

"Through God's grace," Macon replied. Though he had not spent much time in church over the course of his life, he was born and raised in the South. He knew the words to say. "But like so many of you here," he continued, "I am still waiting to see what the future holds for me and Ava." Macon stopped then, expecting a round of applause, but all that returned to him was a resounding silence—occasionally broken up by the shuffling of someone's feet or the sporadic and distant sound of someone coughing.

"What about your daughter?" some asked.

"My daughter…" Macon began, his hesitation booming through the speakers.

"When will she be coming to the church?"

Macon looked over at Reverend Brown. He hated the man just then. And he hated himself for trusting him, for coming to the church, for sitting and talking with him, for believing that, among all of this that was happening, there was someone who might be willing to help him.

Still the crowd waited, and still Macon looked at the reverend. The crowd followed Macon's gaze. All eyes fell on the man of the cloth.

Reverend Isaiah Brown stood and walked over to Macon. His suit was sharp and clean. He was the perfect image of order among chaos. He placed one hand on Macon's shoulder and covered the microphone with the other. "It's your decision," he said to Macon in a low voice. "Everything that happens after this will be your decision," he said. "I promise you that."

Then he took his hand from over the microphone. "Well," he said, and his voice was carried over the speakers. "Will you be joining us?"

In that moment there were a thousand variations of "no" swirling through Macon's mind. He would simply walk away. He could denounce the reverend. He could go home to Carmen and Ava and tell everyone to go away. But would it solve anything? Or would it simply make things worse?

There was no end to this in sight. If he walked offstage, the church would still be here. And so would the other churches. So would the reporters, and people like Eldrich, who wanted to poke and prod and test Ava. No one was going to simply let her be the child she had been. No one was going to forget. So, Macon suddenly thought, when there was no way around it, maybe it was best to just tuck your chin and head straight into the storm.

"Yes," he said finally. "Yes, I'll be joining the church. *We'll* be joining."

Then Reverend Brown raised Macon's hand high again. "Wonderful," he whispered. And the applause boomed and continued and continued and Macon felt as though he were being washed away in it.

Even if Ava remembered what had happened with the deer, her mother would not have let her talk about it. In the days following their journey into the woods Heather treated her daughter like delicate glass. At bedtime, on that first night, she tucked her daughter in and knelt beside the bed and asked, "Do you remember?"

Ava closed her eyes and thought as hard as she could about their walk together, but she could not recall. She shook her head, and so her mother recounted the story to her.

"I've never seen anything like it," Heather said.

"Did I really help it?"

"You did," Heather said. "But you scared me, too."

"I didn't mean to," Ava replied. "Tell me again how it happened."

Then Heather would retell of their walk, of the deer with the arrow through its lung, of the two of them kneeling beside it, expect-

ing to share its last moments. This was the time when Ava would become excited. She would grip her bedcovers and squeeze them to her chest and a grin would spread across her face. "What happened next?" she would ask. And Heather would act out the way Ava pulled the arrow from the animal's chest. The two of them would fix their hands together and pull the imaginary arrow out together.

"And then I covered up the blood and closed my eyes?" Ava asked.

"That's right," Heather replied. "And you're sure you don't remember anything else? You're sure you don't remember what you did or what you thought?"

"No," Ava said. "I wish I did."

Over and over again the story was passed from mother to daughter, refined just a little more each time, until it had become as much of a tale as that of men who discover icebergs buried beneath mountains. They shaped it together, with no input from Macon because he did not know about it. It was a secret between a mother and daughter. Heather asked her daughter about how it happened. She wanted the answers, but she began to realize that Ava did not have them. And, eventually, she wondered how much of it she could even believe herself. At the end of the day, all that had happened was that her daughter pressed her hands on a wounded animal and, perhaps out of fear, the animal mustered up strength enough to stand and flee into the woods. For all she knew, it might have marched out of sight only to die the death it was already destined to have.

"He wouldn't believe us if we told him," Heather told her daughter when the child asked why she couldn't tell her father. "He's the type of man that understands what he can grab ahold of. Not like you and me. He'd never believe us, and if he did, he'd want to tell people about it."

"What's wrong with that?" Ava asked.

"You passed out afterward and I don't know why. I just know that I don't ever want that to happen to you again. And if other people found out about this—even your dad—they might want you to keep doing it. Can you understand that?"

The child nodded. She understood. She trusted that her mother loved her and was making the decision that was best for her.

"Have you ever seen anyone do anything like that before, Mom?"

"No," Heather replied. "Not ever."

"That makes me special, doesn't it?"

"It does, my sweet girl. More special than you can understand."

SEVEN

AVA WOKE TO a hand over her mouth. It was very late on the night after Macon's appearance before Reverend Brown's church. He had come home from the event full of energy and confusion. He paced back and forth in the living room, telling Ava and Carmen all the details of how it felt to stand in front of the church. "Scared the shit out of me," he said.

The two women of his life said very little; they only let him speak, let him sort out his own thoughts as he stood before them. "I can do this," he kept repeating. "I can manage all of this and make it better for all of us. I know that she's sick," he continued, "and it's terrifying. But this can all be okay. This can all work out." Then he looked at Carmen and Ava and his face was filled with a type of asking, a need to be told that he was doing the right thing.

"This can't keep going this way," Carmen said.

"It's okay," Ava replied. She tried to sound strong. She did not want her father to be afraid. "I'll be okay," she said. "You'll make it work out."

After Macon had talked himself into exhaustion, the three of them went to bed. Ava drifted to sleep to the low murmur of Macon and Carmen continuing the conversation in the neighboring bedroom. Perhaps Carmen was saying all of the things she did not want to say in front of Ava. But then sleep took her.

Now she was awake in the late hours of the night and there was a hand over her mouth.

"Shh," a voice said. It was low and frightened, almost like a child's. But the hand covering her mouth was not the hand of a child. It was large and rough, and with enough force that she could not lift her head from the pillow. "It's okay," the man said. "Please...don't yell. It's okay. I won't hurt you." The words came fast and low and, still, there was fear in his voice.

Ava's eyes adjusted to the low light of her bedroom until, finally, she was able to make out the face of the man sitting on the edge of her bed, holding his hand over her mouth. It was the man who had found her in the street behind Dr. Arnold's office. The one who had begged her to help him. The one she had left standing alone. "I just needed to talk to you," the man said. "I promise I won't hurt you."

Ava's heart pounded in her chest. Her breaths came fast and shallow.

"Please don't worry," the man said. "Calm down, okay?"

Ava took a deep breath. Her heart slowed. She nodded in affirmation, uncertain of what the man intended or what she could do to resist him. She thought of pounding against the wall, of kicking and fighting. Macon and Carmen were asleep in their bedroom, and Carmen was always up and down in the course of the night to go to the bathroom. They would hear her, Ava knew. But what might happen in the time between when they heard her and when they made it into the room? She could be killed.

"It's okay," the man said again softly. He was pleading with her, as he had in the street that day. "My name's Sam," he said as though he had not told her that before. "I just need you to listen, okay?"

Slowly, Ava nodded in agreement. But, still, Sam did not remove his hand from her mouth. He shifted his position so that he was no longer sitting on the edge of the bed, but kneeling beside it, almost as though he had come to pray.

"I just need help," Sam said. "That's all." Slowly, he took his hand away from Ava's mouth. The weight of it was like a large stone being lifted from her body. She slid across the bed and pressed her back against the wall—still not brave enough to yell, still not ready to call out. Sam watched silently as Ava tucked her knees to her chest and wrapped her arms around them and made herself as small as she could. Her heart was pounding.

Sam held his hands with his palms upward, as though surrendering. He did not wield a knife or gun, as Ava imagined he might.

"My name's Sam," he said again. "I'm sorry. I didn't mean to do this. I didn't mean to scare you. I just wanted to talk to you. I just wanted to say I was sorry."

Sam smiled, and there was nervousness in it. Perhaps there were tears in the corners of his eyes. "I'm broken," Sam said softly. "I've always been broken. But I try not to be. I do my best." He nodded, as if to agree with himself. "I mess things up a lot," he said. "I try not to. But I mess things up a lot."

Still Ava did not reply. She did not call out for her father. She was transfixed.

"I want you to help me," Sam said. "I've tried a lot of things for a long time. But I need you to help me." He sat back on his knees and put his hands together. "Please," he said, looking up at Ava. "Please help me. I won't hurt you. I wouldn't ever hurt you. But, please, you have to help me. Make me better so that I'm not an embarrassment anymore. Make it so that he'll be proud of me."

"He who?" Ava asked.

But Sam did not reply. He reached forward and grabbed both of her hands tightly and jerked her forward. He pressed her hands on the sides of his face—just as he had done in the street. "Please," he said, again and again. "Please help me." Finally, the fear and confusion was too much for Ava. She screamed for her father. Over and over she called and, as she did, Sam held her hands tightly and pleaded for her to help him.

Macon came through the bedroom door in a blur of motion and confusion. He tackled Sam and rolled the man onto his face and placed his knee on the man's neck. There was yelling and Sam cried and, mingled into it all, was the sound of Ava yelling to her father, "Don't hurt him."

It was almost dawn by the time Macon arrived at the police station with Sam. The state police, who had been stationed at the end of Macon's driveway at the base of the hill, wanted to take the man in—if only out of some misplaced feeling of guilt over the way Sam had gotten past him and made it onto the property and, ultimately, into the bedroom with Macon's daughter. But Macon refused and told the man that there was nothing to feel guilty about. "You can't guard the whole mountain," he said, easing Sam into the back of the squad car.

"I can only imagine how else this could have come out," the officer said.

"It's better not to even think about it," Macon said.

But, of course, Macon did think about it. He thought about it the entire way to the station house. He thought about it during the drive, each time he looked back in the mirror and saw Sam's face. There was a small line of blood coming from Sam's lip, a by-product of their scuffle. And whenever Macon saw it, a part of him thought that it was not enough. He imagined Ava waking up with the stranger on her bed, holding her down. And he wanted more blood from Sam.

When they arrived at the station, there were crowds of media awaiting them. They took photos as Macon drove into the station house parking lot and they yelled questions about who the man was and how he had gotten into Macon's house and if he had done anything to Ava. When Macon asked them how they knew so quickly what had happened, they did not answer. They only pelted him with more questions. And his reply was simply to lower his shoulder and force his way silently through them.

It was perhaps an hour later, once Sam was settled in his cell, that the front door of the station opened. The officers sitting out front stood and, even before he saw the man, Macon knew it had to be Reverend Brown. The man entered the office and Macon couldn't help but notice that there was meekness in his body language, as though he had made himself smaller in the time since Macon had seen him last.

That evening after the reverend had ambushed Macon into joining his church, the two of them spent nearly an hour arguing once they were away from the stage, away from the crowd and the eyes of the world. Macon had very nearly punched the man. But after the arguing, after the yelling and everything else, the fact was that the decision had been made. For better or worse, the two men were linked to each other now.

"Ava's fine," Macon said immediately, predicting why the reverend had come.

"I know," Reverend Brown said. He sat in the chair in front of Macon's desk and straightened his back. "I've actually come to inquire about the other side of the equation, the man who broke into your house."

"Oh," Macon said, surprised. He sat back in his chair. "Do you mind if I ask why you're curious? Do you know him?"

"He's a member of my church," Reverend Brown said.

The reverend wasn't holding eye contact the way he had in previous meetings. Before, whenever Reverend Brown had come to speak with Macon, the man was always very direct, never letting his gaze stray from Macon's. It was both slightly unsettling and oddly reassuring at once. He gave off the impression that, whoever he was talking to, they had his full attention. They were the center of his world and of great importance. It was a look that made a person want to trust him, and Macon had always thought it sincere. He was beginning to trust the reverend. That is, until he betrayed him.

But now the man was unsettled. He had trouble maintaining the eye contact that was such an important part of his presence. There was something on his mind. "So you know him?" Macon asked.

"Very well," Reverend Brown replied. "And I'd like to see what I can do on his behalf. If at all possible, I'd like to see about taking him out of here."

"Do you do that for all the members of your congregation?" Macon asked. He understood the suspicion in his own voice, and he wished it wasn't there, but old habits are slow to soften, and can rarely be broken.

"I don't do it for all of them," Reverend Brown replied.

"Well, what makes this one so special?" Macon asked.

Reverend Brown finally took the seat in front of Macon's desk. He looked down at his hands. "Because he's my brother," Reverend Brown said.

"Your brother?" Macon had trouble believing it. A part of him thought, only briefly, that the church leader was speaking in the figurative sense: "brothers in faith." But the more the sheriff studied the reverend, the more he saw the truth of it. Even though Sam was larger and more muscled, the lines of his face weren't far removed from Reverend Brown's. They both had strong jawlines and a softness around the corners of their eyes. They both had a skin tone that suggested long days in the sun during their youth, and there was a similarity in their smiles.

On the drive from the house to the station, as Sam sat handcuffed in the back of the car, he had smiled often at Macon. Macon watched him in the rearview mirror, unsure what to make of the smile. But there was a genuine innocence in it. Something that said the man did not fully understand the distances to which his actions could reach. He looked like a man who could only see the moment before him. Whatever existed beyond it did not seem to matter.

"He wasn't always like this," Reverend Brown replied. His voice was soft. "Once upon a time he was a star athlete. A football player, and a damned good one. Made it through half of high school and he was building a name for himself." He smiled at the memory of it. "And then he was in a car accident." Reverend Brown shrugged his shoulders. "Lots of talk about what the cause of it was but, in the end, none of that really matters, does it? It was almost two decades ago."

Macon leaned back in his chair and scratched his chin. He had a question he wanted to ask, but he decided to wait and see just how much Reverend Brown was willing to volunteer. He had been a sheriff long enough to know that the best way to have a question answered is simply to keep a person talking, and most times keeping a person talking was just a matter of not saying anything.

"He was with some friends and his car went off a bridge and into a river. He hit his head pretty hard and, try as they might, it took them a while to get him out of the seat belt. All the while, he was underwater, drowning." Reverend Brown sighed. "You know, to this day I sometimes dream about that moment. I have this dream that I'm buckled into my seat belt in a car and there's water rising up around me and I can't get out." He made a motion with his hands to indicate water rising around his head. "Absolutely terrifying," he said. "I'm sitting there, struggling for everything I'm worth, giving it everything I've got, and I can't do anything about it. I can't change anything. Next thing I know I'm underwater, sucking it into my lungs." He finished his story with a clearing of his throat. "And then I wake up gasping for air."

Reverend Brown looked down at his hands again for a moment, then he looked to Macon. "It's not his fault," he said.

"Has he ever done anything like this before?" Macon asked. He didn't want to believe the reverend and his story, if only because he already knew where it was ultimately leading.

Reverend Brown shook his head. "He's not violent," he said. "He has never hurt anyone and I can't believe he ever would."

"But has he done anything like this before?"

"He has never done this specific act," Reverend Brown said. "But he's made mistakes, just like the rest of us. But his mistakes get put under a finer microscope because of his mental state."

"And what exactly is his mental state?"

"He's not a danger," Reverend Brown said. "He's just impulsive sometimes. And he can get confused easily about certain things. But that doesn't make him a threat to anyone. It just makes him a man who will always make mistakes and who will always struggle to understand the world. Is that so terrible?"

"I appreciate you telling me all of this," Macon said. He sat forward and placed his elbows on the desk. "And I suppose we both know where this conversation is heading, don't we?"

"I've always taken care of him," Reverend Brown said. "I always will."

"So you're here to take care of him now."

"I'm here to take care of both of us."

Macon nodded, understanding. "I suppose your church doesn't know about him."

"They know about him, but they don't know about us. He uses our mother's maiden name, and few people know that. So he's just a member of my congregation, a member of my church, who comes with me whenever I travel." He looked Macon in the eyes. "I'm not asking you to do anything illegal," Reverend Brown said. "I'm just asking you not to press charges. I'm just asking you to let him come home."

"How can I know that this won't happen again? Ava told me that this was the second time he's done this. She says he caught her in the street when she and Carmen were at the doctor's. I've got a family here, Reverend."

"Of course you do," Reverend Brown said. "And so do I. And I'm trying to do right by him. He hangs upon my word. I'm everything to him. I'm all he has. All he ever does is try to do right by me, Sheriff. And do you want to know the worst thing about it all? Do you want to know what's worse than having someone believe in you that much?"

"What's that?"

"It's having someone believe that you won't help them because they must have done something wrong by you. Even when all they've ever done is make you proud. Sam thinks I'm angry with him, or ashamed of him, and that's why I won't help him." Reverend Brown's voice softened, like music being taken out of earshot. "I've done everything I can, Macon, and I haven't helped him. And he blames himself for it."

Macon considered the man before him. This was not the Reverend Brown that he had known: powerful, confident, intimidating. It was not the leader of one of the largest churches in the country. It was simply a man mourning the brother whom he had lost in a car crash all those years ago. It was a loss the reverend wept for daily, Macon thought to himself. Perhaps it was not too far removed from the feeling that Macon felt in the wake of Heather's suicide.

"Okay," Macon said.

Sam was brought into the house through the back, away from the reporters and the masses of people who were not as informed about Reverend Brown's church. The reverend was in the study of the Andrews House. It was a large, sprawling room with a high ceiling and several large leather chairs placed strategically around the room. On the north wall was a map of the old world—a map made when it was still believed that there were coiling monsters in the lengths of the ocean. It was a map that told of the way things could be when a world was still inclined to imagine. Perhaps that was why Reverend Brown was drawn to it the way he was.

While in Stone Temple, he spent his quiet time, what little there was, sitting in front of the map, staring up at it from the leather chair. More than once, since he had come to the Andrews House, when he was supposed to be working— crafting the next sermon, keeping things organized within his church—he would lose himself in the map. There was both simplicity and complexity to it.

Reverend Brown was seated in a leather chair, looking up at the map and the large serpent breaching the water in the northern part of the Atlantic Ocean. And although Reverend Brown thought of it as a serpent—because of its long, slender body—he also thought of it as something else. Not quite a dragon, but something more primal, something older and not yet crafted into the mundane angles of iconography. It was a raw, visceral image. Unpolished and flawed in its beauty.

And that was something the man could not look away from.

When Sam was brought in, it had been several hours since the reverend's visit with Macon, but the time was needed to be sure that there was little correlation between his visit to the sheriff and Sam's release. He trusted that Macon would not disclose why he had arrested the man or who the man's identity was.

"I'm sorry, Isaiah," Sam said. He had been brought in by one of the reverend's security men. The man was gentle with Sam, having helped him often over the years, and he left the room without a word. Sam stood by the door, looking down at the floor, with his hands at his waist, as though he could make himself small enough to disappear from the world. "I'm sorry," he repeated.

Reverend Brown stood and walked to his brother and wrapped his arms around him and hugged him warmly and sighed into his ear. "It's okay, Sam. It's okay."

"Really?" Sam replied sheepishly.

"Yes," Reverend Brown said. "There was no harm done to anyone, and that's all that matters."

"But you told me not to bother her again. You told me to leave her alone and I didn't. I'm sorry."

"No more talk about any of that," Reverend Brown said. He took a step back and held Sam's face in his hands and, gently, he kissed his brother's brow. "We don't have time machines here, so it's best to move forward. What have I always told you?"

"That you'll always take care of me," Sam said. Finally, he lifted his eyes from the floor.

"And what else?"

"That there isn't anything you can't fix."

"That's right," Isaiah said. "There's nothing I can't or won't fix for you, brother. And why is that?"

"Because we're all we've got."

"That's right," Reverend Brown said. Then he placed his arm around Sam and the two of them walked into the center of the library. Sam mumbled apologies, which Reverend Brown left unanswered. The man was always in a state of apology. It was simply his way.

"She really is wonderful," Sam said when they had reached the leather chair where Reverend Brown had been sitting.

"Sit here," Reverend Brown said, guiding him into the chair. "I'll get you something to drink and then I want to take a look at you."

Sam removed his jacket. "She's nice," he said. "And her father is nice, too. He didn't mean to do this," he said, pointing to the bruise on his lip. "I think he was just scared. Parents get scared sometimes."

"So do little big brothers," Reverend Brown said, returning with a carafe of water and a glass. He filled the glass and watched as Sam sipped it gingerly, wincing when the glass touched the bruise on his lip.

"And you're my little big brother," Sam said, grinning.

"Ad infinitum," Reverend Brown said with a flourish of his hand. "Now, let me have a look at you."

Sam removed his shirt. Apart from the wound on his lip, there was a large red mark on the back of his neck and his wrists were ringed with a bruise from when the handcuffs were placed there. But the skin was not broken and there was no indication of any serious injuries. "You're a tough one, aren't you?" Reverend Brown asked when the inspection was finished.

"The toughest," Sam said, and for a moment his voice was that of his youth, when he was a football star with a splendid life sprawled out before him.

"Of course you are," Reverend Brown said. He handed Sam back his shirt. The man dressed and sat again and looked at his brother. The moment of clarity, the moment of happiness that had brought back memories—for them both—of the way things had once been, passed.

"I wanted her to fix me," Sam said slowly. "So you wouldn't have to take care of me. So I could help you. So you wouldn't be ashamed of me."

"I'm not ashamed of you, Sam," Reverend Brown replied, sitting in the chair across from his brother. Above them both, the map of the world persisted.

"I try," Sam said. "I try to get things right."

"I know," Reverend Brown said. "I know you do. And she'll help you. I know she will. I'll see to it. Just be patient." He patted Sam's hand lightly. "But for the next couple of days, I'm going to have one of the security men stay with you. I'll make sure it's someone you like. Probably Gary. You like Gary, don't you?"

"Yeah," Sam said gently. "Gary's good. He's nice, too."

"Yeah," Isaiah said. "He's a good guy and he's going to help make sure you're safe for the next couple of days. Just until things settle down. He's going to stay with you, and the two of you are going to hang out here at the house, okay?" He turned away and gazed up at the map.

"I'm sorry," Sam said yet again, and his voice was more childlike than Isaiah Brown had ever heard before.

"You know I love you, don't you, Sam?"

"I know," Sam replied. "I know. And you know I try, don't you, Isaiah?"

"I know," Isaiah replied. "What do you think of this, Sam?" Reverend Brown asked. He pointed at the map.

Sam looked up at it. He thought for a moment. "It's the world."

"It is," Reverend Brown said patiently. "But what do you think of it?"

Sam looked again, and considered the map more closely. "I like it," he said. "But why is the dragon drowning?"

"What?"

Reverend Brown sat forward in his chair, then he stood and approached the map. It did, in fact, seem as though the dragon was not swimming the waters between continents, but drowning in them. The agape mouth—which, only seconds ago, had been one of power, ferocity and menace—was now somber and frightened, almost calling for help. Isaiah could almost hear the sound of the waters rising above the creature's head, and he wondered how he had ever seen anything else when he looked at the image.

Tom and his son sat at the dinner table loading food into their mouths by the forkful and listening to the sound of the wind pushing through the pines outside beneath the moonlight. Now and again there was the clatter of silverware against the plate. The low scraping sound of a small hill of rice being corralled in one corner. The entire house smelled of sage and thyme and onions and crushed red pep-

per. There was a cast-iron heater in the living room with a
fire burning gently inside, the flames flapping their wings.
The smoke went up and out into the cool, autumn night,
rose for a short distance, then flattened and crept out over
the yard.

Tom was staying in the barn at the Johnsons' place. For
years the barn had housed horses and other animals, but
when the farming became a more difficult means of making ends meet Robert Johnson got rid of the animals and,
for many years, the barn remained empty—save for the occasional sick cow or horse stabled at the behest of some
neighbor with no other place to put it. Then Robert's wife
had the idea of converting the barn into an apartment. "In
case of company," she said, even though the couple rarely
entertained anyone. Robert resisted, citing better uses for
the money and the couple's scarcity of guests. But his wife
wouldn't be swayed and so the top portion of the barn,
which once held hay and tools, was insulated and dry walled
and painted and filled with all of the other amenities of the
"civilized world"—as Robert's wife had put it. The only
niceties lacking were a television and internet—things the
hidebound couple both felt weren't particularly indicative
of civilized people.

Fortune smiled on the Johnsons. They finished the reno-
vations just two weeks before the air show tragedy in Stone
Temple. All of a sudden the town was filled with people
needing a place to stay, and all of them having good, old-
fashioned money to spend. There were plenty of people
they could have rented the apartment to but, when he was
a younger man, Tom had helped Robert on more than a
few occasions. And Stone Temple was still a place that fa-

vored familiar faces over well-heeled strangers. So when
Tom called and asked if they could put him up, the Johnsons were more than happy to get him squared away. Now
he and Wash were settled into the apartment together. It
smelled of fresh paint and old horses. The smell was in the
wood, cured into it after years of holding animals, but like
so many things in life, it was a condition that was not so op-
pressive that it couldn't be ignored.

Tom had been staying in the apartment for a week. Wash
had come to join him two days ago.

"This ain't so bad, is it?" Tom asked.

Wash finished the last of his food and placed his fork in
the center of the plate. He rubbed his palms back and forth
against his thighs. "No, sir."

"We get along okay, don't we?"

"Yes, sir."

Tom rose from the table, shaking his empty beer can. He
got a full one from the refrigerator and leaned against the
kitchen sink. "Tonight," he said, taking a sip, "tonight was
good. I'm glad Grandma finally changed her mind about
this. Maybe she's not quite as much of a hard old bird as I
remember."

Tom settled across the table and looked long and hard at
his son. Wash sat with his hands in his lap and his eyes down-
ward toward his dinner plate. Outside the breeze picked up
and there was a light flapping sound in the ceiling as a few
loose shingles caught in the chilly wind. Wash's father listened to the sound of the shingles and to the slow popping of
the fireplace in the other room. He heard the gentle hum of
the refrigerator and the low roar of the wind, the rhythmic
breathing of his son and the pale moon sweeping by above

the world. He heard the impossible sound of everything and, as he listened, he fiddled with the top of his beer can and that tinny, metallic sound of his fingers playing against the metal was the only sound that he could hear.

He took a sip. "Did I ever tell you how your mother and me met?"

Your mother and I, Wash wanted to say, but he only said, "No, sir."

"We met at church," Tom said, grinning nostalgically. "Not many folks would believe it, but I used to go. Anyway, we were very young. Around your age, maybe. I'm bad with dates and details and all that. But I wasn't much bigger than you and neither was she. Your grandma and grandpa had come to visit our church. It was normal back then for people from one church to visit another. I guess folks still do that, don't they?" He paused to reflect.

"Well, I kept noticing her all through the service. I don't really know why I kept noticing her, not then I didn't know, anyway. She wore this white dress—perfectly white. With little pink frills around the bottom and at the sleeves. She used to tell me that she hated that dress. She said it made her look like a doll."

Tom laughed.

"It did. It was a little goofy, I guess. All puffy and frilly. She wore these white shoes with white socks. My God, it must have been horrible to wear something like that, a girl at her age." He leaned back in his chair, laughing a little. "You wouldn't know it about your grandmother now, but she used to love seeing your mama in dresses like that." Tom took another sip of his beer. "It was years from the time I saw her in the church that day to our first date. Not until I moved here to work at the mill. Sometimes I wonder what would have happened if the two of us had grown up together. Maybe we would have been childhood friends. Maybe she wouldn't have been willing to go out with me when I finally did ask her. I don't know. Nobody can ever say what might have happened. 'If this' or 'if that.' Wondering about what might have been doesn't do anybody a lick of good. That's a fact."

He paused reflectively.

"Can't nothing be undone. It's all just ashes and missed opportunities."

Tom looked down at his hands, then glanced over the table at his son. "I've got an idea," he said. He stood and cleared the table and, after drinking down his beer and getting another, he motioned for Wash to follow him as he started down the stairs.

It was still early in the evening but already the countryside was dark and empty. Inside the Johnsons' house the blue glow of a television shimmered and danced. The porch light burned softly above the front door.

"Can you drive?" Tom asked.

"I'm thirteen."

"True," Tom said. "But that's not what I asked." He looked into his beer can for a moment and then, in one long draft, finished it. "Let's go," he said.

Tom's car was an old Chevy Nova. It was painted a deep, rich blue with two white racing stripes running down the center. It was a car meant for movies, Wash thought.

"Get behind the wheel," Tom said. "I'm a little past curfew, if you know what I mean. Can you drive stick?"

"No, but I know the basic idea," Wash said. Inside, the

car smelled of beer and cigarettes and grease and paint and leather—all the things that cars of that age were known for.

"There's nothing to it," Tom said, smiling. The long scar on his cheek did its familiar transformation into a single, long S. The two of them slammed the car doors closed. "Press the clutch in and start her up," he said.

Wash was tall for his age, even if he was thin, and so he was able to manage the clutch without much trouble. He fastened his seat belt, and when he turned the ignition the car started with a bark from the exhaust. It was a lumpy, metallic sound, like an animal waking from slumber.

"You'll have to take it easy," Tom said, slumping back into the seat.

"Are you going to put your seat belt on?" Wash asked.

"Never need one," Tom replied. "Now focus on the car. It can be a lot to handle if you're not careful."

Wash wrapped his hands around the steering wheel and, for a long moment, he sat and let the vibration of the car crackle through his fingers. He took in the sight of the old, circular gauges.

"Right foot on the brake," Tom said.

Wash nodded and complied. Immediately the car stalled.

Tom laughed. "I didn't say take your foot off the clutch, son."

Wash started the car again.

"Now, it's just a matter of being slow and easy. Don't be afraid of a clutch," Tom said. "You're not driving if you're not in a manual. It's what separates us from the animals."

Wash chuckled.

Tom held up his hands and used them to demonstrate how to work the clutch and the throttle. His explanation was long and sprawling, as Wash had expected. But he did not care. He listened to the sound of his father's voice and he felt the vibration of the car and he realized that this was a moment that he had spent his entire life dreaming about.

"Got all that?" Tom asked.

"I think so," Wash said. "It's like dancing."

"You dance, son?"

"No, but I've read about how clutches work. You're putting two things together, basically. They're both spinning at different speeds, doing their own work, and you have to ease them together so that they match. So that they can share the same space."

"Like dancing," Tom said softly.

On his third try, Wash got it right.

They rode in silence through the dark countryside. They took the road north, away from the town, away from the people and the noise of Stone Temple. The course was Wash's to choose, and he did not want to share his father with anyone.

After a while Tom, who was almost asleep, reached into the glove compartment and retrieved a silver flask. He took a sip. "You're a natural," he said, his words lazy and slurring.

Wash nodded, but kept his eyes on the road. Now that they were at speed, there was no more gear shifting to be done, but there was still the nighttime road to navigate. He had ridden along this stretch of highway more times than he could remember, but it was different now that he was driving it. It was exhilarating.

"Can I ask you something?" Wash said, almost calling Tom "Dad."

"Don't ask if you can ask a question," Tom said. His words

were more slurred as the alcohol seeped deeper into him. "Just ask your question. Be confident."

"Would you have stayed if Mom hadn't died?"

"I don't know," Tom replied quickly. He scratched the top of his head and coughed to clear his throat. "Have you ever flown anywhere, Wash?" he asked.

"I've never been so far away that I needed to fly," Wash replied. The road ahead was dark and smooth. It flattened out between a long valley and the car seemed to glide through the world.

Tom tilted his head back and closed his eyes. "At night, from high up in a plane," he began, "the world looks like the bottom of the ocean—the dark, deep parts, like you see on TV specials sometimes. It just stretches out forever. Now and then you see the lights of cities or houses. Only they aren't cities. They become something else—all light and curves, like those glowing jellyfish they say live at the bottom of the ocean. Just a blob of beautiful light. And a whole city passes by that way—all the people in it, everything, everyone— gliding past you in the darkness. And you wonder if there is anything real about it."

His breathing shifted for a moment, but still his eyes were closed, his body collapsed like a man worn out by life. "You can believe you might see anything outside your window, Wash. Kind of like all you have to do is believe it and wait for it and look hard enough into the darkness and, some- how, she'll come back." Finally, his eyes opened. He gazed out the window into the night. "Sometimes I really believe it," Tom said.

"Why don't you play music anymore?" Wash asked. The moment the question left his lips, he regretted it.

"Because I'm a fuckup," Tom said directly.

Wash didn't know how to reply to his father. All he could think to say was, "Am I doing okay?"

"I'm bad at everything," Tom said. "The thing I do best is quit. And I know I'm not a good dad, but I love you, Wash. I loved you every day of my life, from before you were born. And I loved your mom. I just wish I was better at it. Better at everything." His voice shook and he looked down at his wedding ring. Then, slowly, and with a tone of sorrow, he said, "Too bad that girlfriend of yours can't do anything for me. Can't do anything with the type of brokenness I've got. I'm sorry that this fuckup is all you get as a father, Wash." Then Tom was asleep and there was only the sound of the engine, the tires upon the pavement, the wind beyond the windows.

The road became something Wash had never known it could be. It was liquid, smooth, sliding beneath the car. But there was no fear, no uneasiness. The car moved over the road with grace and ease, and it made Wash believe that he could go anywhere in this world, do anything he wanted. It made him believe, if only for a little while, in the possibility of grand and sweeping things. It made him remember that there was a life to be had in this world.

Then he downshifted to negotiate a turn and, when he went to find the next gear, the gearshift shuddered in his hand and there was a loud pop from the bowels of the car and the engine revved, but it felt connected to nothing. The steering wheel lurched in the boy's hands, but he held it. He called for his father, but the man was too drunk to hear. The car eased off the road just as it was reaching the bottom of a hill. It was only luck that they were driving along a field.

The car bucked and bounded into the grass, all the while with Wash clutching the steering wheel with both hands, hoping and praying that nothing would suddenly leap out in front of him. In the headlights he saw only grass and brambles and the light layer of fog that was draping over the field.

Eventually, the car squealed to a stop.

Wash's heart beat in his ears. "Dad?" he called. "Dad!" He shook Tom, but it was to no effect. Wash unbuckled his seat belt and got out of the car. Around him there was open field and the sound of the insects and above him there were stars. He walked around the car, using the glare from the headlights to help him see the car as best he could. There were some small dents in the front of the car, and one of the tires was flat, but that was the worst of it.

Wash placed his hands on his head and sighed and thought about what might have been if he'd lost control of the car up on the mountain. He stood there in the night and looked in the window and watched as the man that was his father slept, oblivious to it all. He went back and sat inside the car. The glove compartment had come open in the tumult. When Wash went to close it the registration fell out. The name on the registration was not Tom's name. Wash considered this, then he considered his father. Of course the car wasn't his, Wash thought. But he had tried, hadn't he?

Then he heard the low, hissing sound of a car driving over the fog-soaked pavement. In the rearview mirror he saw the glare of headlights. He could just make out the silhouette of the car descending the hill. "Shit," Wash said. He shook his father. "Dad! Dad, wake up! Wake up now!"

It did nothing to wake the man.

It was then that the blue glow of police lights glittered

in the night, off and on, illuminating the thirteen-year-old boy and the stone-drunk father who had put him behind the wheel.

"It's the kind of a thing that a child gets taken away for," Macon said. He paced back and forth in front of the jail cell. Inside, seated on a cot, was Tom. He held his head in his hands and there was a cup of coffee placed on the floor in front of him. "Brenda's on her way over to pick up Wash," Macon said. "What happens next will be decided between the two of you, I suppose."

Tom rubbed the sides of his head. "I just want to thank you, Sheriff."

"For what?" Macon asked.

"For whatever," Tom said. "For everything."

Macon stopped pacing. He and Tom were alone in the holding area. And he'd made sure to keep it that way. These days, with all the new officers on the force in the wake of the air show tragedy, he didn't know who he could trust. Already, one of his men had gone on television to tell his story about how the boy Ava saved was almost killed when his drunken father let him get behind the wheel of a muscle car. He even went so far as to volunteer information about Tom's police record—drunk driving, drunk in public, drunken and disorderly. Always drunk. That was Tom.

"Drink the coffee, Tom," Macon said. Tom looked down at the mug on the floor between his feet. "Brenda will be here any minute, and you're going to need every bit of your wits when she comes through that door."

Tom picked up the coffee and sipped it. "She never did like me," he said.

"And you're giving her all the reasons she needs to keep not liking you, aren't you?"

"I gave it a try, though," Tom said, cupping the mug between his hands. He leaned back on the cot, resting against the concrete wall of the jail cell. He rubbed the scar on his cheek and looked at Macon. "I guess we can't all be parent of the year, can we?" Tom said.

"Nobody's asking you to be, Tom," Macon said. He placed one hand on the bars of Tom's cell. "But there's got to be something in you that's better than this. Maybe not parent of the year, but how about parent of the week? Parent of the day? How about spending more than a week with your son without getting locked up?"

Tom laughed darkly. "You know me, huh?"

"No," Macon said sharply. "I don't. But I know Wash. And, hell, I know Brenda. And the sad part is that neither one of them hates you, not even Brenda."

"I was never cut out for this shit," Tom said, lifting the coffee mug to his lips, drinking hard and fast. It was still steaming hot and it burned, but he did not stop.

"You can learn," Macon said.

"Why?" Tom asked. "Why the hell does it matter to you?"

"Why the hell doesn't it matter to you?" Macon replied sharply.

"Yeah, well," Tom began, "take a long look at yourself before you start lecturing me."

"And what's that supposed to mean?" Macon asked. He looked through the bars at Tom.

"How's that girl of yours doing?" Tom replied. He stood slowly and walked closer to the door of his cell where Macon stood. "I saw her on the TV the other day," Tom said. "She's looking sick. Looking thinner than she did when all of this started." Macon flinched. "Wash thinks she's not getting any better. She looks like shit," Tom said. "And I wonder if you, being the fine, upstanding father and sheriff that you are, I wonder if you can see it? I wonder if you want to see it."

Macon felt his hands tighten their grip on the bars of Tom's cell. He held on to the cold-wrought steel as though his life depended on it. "Is that all?" Macon asked.

"More coffee," Tom said, and looked at the coffee mug in his hand. "Nice mug," he said. Then he threw it against the concrete wall, shattering it.

Macon let go of the prison bars. "Don't worry, Tom," he said, "someone will clean up what you break when you leave. Just like when you left your son." And then he left without looking back.

Upon exiting the holding area, Macon found Wash waiting for him. "What happens now?" Wash asked. But before Macon could answer, the door of the police station opened and Brenda barreled through. "Where is he?" she called.

"Wash is right here," Macon said quickly. "He's fine."

"I can see that," Brenda said. "I'm talking about Tom."

"He's in the back," Macon replied.

Brenda did not wait for permission to go through the door leading to the cells. She opened the door and marched forward, letting it slam behind her like thunder.

"I think we should go find someplace else to be," Macon said to Wash.

"What are they talking about?" Wash asked. He stood where he could see through the glass partition in the door. He and Macon watched Brenda as she talked to Tom. Both of them had expected yelling, cursing. They'd expected to see

Brenda's arm flailing. Maybe even she would throw something at the prison bars, they'd thought. But, instead, they saw the old woman standing before the prison cell speaking calmly, almost solemnly, as though making a confession. And on the other side of the bars, Tom only listened, growing more and more attentive with each moment. "What's she saying to him?" Wash asked.

"I don't know," Macon said. But he knew perfectly well what Brenda was saying to Tom. She was telling him about Wash's cancer.

"Let's go take care of some paperwork," Macon said. "Then you and your dad can get out of here." He placed his arm on the boy's shoulders and pulled him gently. After a moment of resistance, the boy went with him.

"Macon?" Wash said.

"Yeah?"

"You'd tell me if there was something going on, wouldn't you?"

Macon laughed stiffly. "If I knew something that I felt you needed to know, Wash, I'd tell you."

"Okay," Wash said.

"Can I ask you something, Wash?"

Wash nodded.

"Is Ava okay? The two of you keep your secrets sometimes, like all kids do. And I don't mind that. But if you knew something about Ava, something that maybe she wouldn't come out and tell me, but something that was really important, you'd tell me, wouldn't you?"

"Yes, sir," Wash said.

"Good," Macon said. And then he and the boy walked together into his office, and for the rest of the evening there was a truce held between them. They talked about sports. They talked about movies. They talked about how cold the pending winter would be. But they asked no more questions of each other that would warrant lies.

The ride from the police station was a quiet one. Brenda revved her old station wagon and nearly took out a crowd of reporters that tried to stop them as they pulled out of the parking lot. She pressed the gas pedal and the engine roared and the cameraman that was standing in front of the car leaped out of the way, breaking his camera in the process. They did not follow.

Wash and Tom sat in the backseat, saying nothing as Brenda steered them through the town. It was early morning, and the town was slowly coming to life. Here and there a few cars passed. People who were camped out in empty lots were just beginning to come out of their tents. Each and every day, Wash was surprised by the fact that they were still there. He wondered about their lives before any of this. Didn't they have homes to go to? Family? Jobs? How could they simply relocate the way they had? Was Ava that important to them?

They passed a woman standing on the corner of downtown. She held a sign that said Please Heal My Child. Then the car moved onward, and she was gone.

From time to time Wash looked over at his father. But Tom only gazed out of the window, full of thought. Up front, Brenda wrestled the old, tired car through the streets to the road leading out of town. It was then that Wash realized they weren't heading toward home.

"Gonna be a cold winter," Tom said, still looking out the window. He smelled of coffee and alcohol.

Wash knew that his father was trying to tell him something, but he wasn't sure what. It did not take long for them to reach the place where Tom's car had run off the road. There was a tow truck there, already in the process of pulling the car out of the ditch.

Brenda eased the station wagon to a stop.

"Okay," Tom said. Then he opened the car door and stepped out. When Wash opened his own door, Tom turned and said, "No. You hang here with your grandmother." He glanced forward at the woman who scowled at him in the rearview mirror.

"Are we going to meet you at the Johnsons'?"

"No," Tom said. He squatted on his haunches, resting one hand on the still-open door. "You're gonna go back home with your grandma. I'm gonna see about getting this car straightened out."

"And then you'll come get me?" Wash asked. He looked at the rearview mirror, hoping to catch Brenda's eye, hoping to get an indication of what was happening, even though he knew perfectly well what was happening.

"I've got some things to tend to once I get this car fixed," Tom said. "But I'll be back before too long." Tom looked over at his car, then up at the sky, then down at the ground. "I'll be back before too long," he said again.

"Don't say that," Wash said. His voice was hard and even, like a door slowly closing home. "You don't have to say that."

"Wash," Tom said.

"I won't make you do it," Wash said. "I won't make you say something you don't want to say." Then he turned to

Brenda. "Can we go, Grandma?" Their eyes met in the rearview mirror, and there was sadness in her. She turned around in her seat, looking back at her grandson. "I won't make you say anything, either," Wash said. "I just want to go. I just want to see how Ava is."

Tom lingered for a moment, watching the son he was losing for the second time in his life. Then he closed the car door and Brenda clunked the station wagon into gear, pressed the gas pedal and let the distance open between Wash and his father.

Saturday was yard sale day and Ava spent most of her week waiting for it. The Saturday morning cartoons that she missed out on seemed like a fair exchange for the time that she and her mother spent cruising from yard to yard, town to town, sometimes even county to county, in search of trinkets and worn pieces of splendor.

They started out before sunup, leaving Macon snoring on his pillow. Heather and Ava sat at the kitchen table with a map of the local area with certain houses and streets highlighted. Those houses were the ones they knew were having yard sales. They also marked the "possibles"—those places that had promised nothing, but who had yard sales on such a regular basis that it could almost be depended on them to do something special.

Today their plan would take them over the length and breadth of three counties. They packed a picnic basket of food and bottles of Gatorade that they could drink through the course of the day,

and they stashed away small amounts of chocolate and hard can-
dies in the places in the basket where they would fit.

"We can't eat just candy," Heather said, stuffing more and
more into the basket.

"When have we ever eaten just candy?" Ava asked.

"That time about two months ago."

"Oh, yeah." Ava laughed.

"Don't tell your father," Heather added. "Did you remember
to get the Toblerone bars?"

They rode through darkness for half an hour before coming to
the first yard sale just as the sun was brightening the sky. An old
man and woman stood out front wearing thin jackets and smoking
cigarettes and they smiled and said hello and asked if there was
anything in particular Ava and Heather were looking for.

"Everything special," Heather said. It was what she always told
the yard sale people when they asked what they were looking for.
And it was the truth. In the years since Ava and her mother had
begun their yard sale hunting they had found many things that
Ava felt were special. A very old broach with the face of a woman
carved in it. A piece from a rifle that they had not been able to
identify, but it was thick and square and made of brass and adorned
with carvings that Ava had never seen. She had promised that she
would one day find out where it had come from. And, even if she
didn't, it was still something beautiful to look at.

Ava liked finding pieces of things more than she cared for finding
something whole and complete. A person couldn't really understand
a fully formed thing, she thought. Not unless they understood how
it was before it was finished.

When someone came across a piece of something—just an ele-
ment of the whole—then they were able to see the mechanics of
it. They were able to put together, in their head, all the other pos-

sible ways that a thing could be. All the other paths a thing could take. It was like a ribbon unraveled into simply a smooth, even line of glimmering silk.

They rode half the day and came across little of importance or interest. There were T-shirts and chairs and tables and old records and toys that no one had played with in a very long time and movies that no one wanted to watch anymore and paintings that weren't very impressive.

But then, when they had traveled two counties away and were about to start their journey toward home, they came upon a yard sale and a woman who stood out front wearing a large coat even though the sun was high and it was very warm that day. The woman smiled when she saw Ava coming, as though she had been waiting for her all the while.

"I've got just what you're looking for," the woman said as she saw Ava and Heather approaching. Ava couldn't tell exactly which of them she was talking to. Then the woman reached down onto a small table in front of her and retrieved a large wooden box. She handed it to Ava.

"Can you open it?" the woman asked.

Ava looked the box over. It seemed as though it had been made of a dozen smaller boxes. It was perfectly sealed, and the wood smelled fresh and was perfectly cut. She searched and searched, but could not find a way to open it.

"It's a puzzle box," Heather said.

"How do I open it?" Ava asked.

"You have to figure that out," the woman said.

Ava's eyes went wide. Suddenly the container was filled with mystery and splendor. She imagined all the things it could hold inside: old coins, arrowheads, jewelry, treasure maps, secret letters from famous or infamous individuals, lost books and on and on. *Her imagination began to push even further, in the way that only a child's can, and suddenly the box contained people, entire cities—miniaturized and perfectly preserved—and she handled the item gingerly and with great reverence. She imagined that the very stars of heaven were held within that space, waiting to be released and returned to the sky.*

She imagined that there were parts of her mother contained within the box. All of the parts of the woman that Ava could not understand. The parts of her that were sometimes sad. The parts that woke her in the late hours of the night when she would wake and walk outside of the house thinking that her husband and daughter were asleep and could not hear her as she wept. The parts of the woman that, when the morning came, would give her the strength to smile and laugh as though the sadness that Ava heard the night before had never occurred.

On the ride home, Ava could believe that all of these things were inside the intricate folds of the box. It was several days later that she finally discovered the secret to opening it. And when she opened it, she found only dust and air inside.

Her mother was more than that, Ava knew. She placed the box aside, tucked away in a chest filled with the rest of the toys Ava had once adored and had long since forgotten.

EIGHT

SINCE MACON HAD officially announced that he would be joining the reverend's church, the attention that he'd been trying to avoid had only gotten worse. A group of people had taken to camping out at the base of their driveway with a large banner that read Ava Belongs to Everyone. Macon was never able to discern whether the people were religious zealots, hard-line atheists or something in between. And, in the end, it didn't matter.

All the while, Reverend Brown was doing a good job of helping Macon navigate the chaos. He advised him about whose phone calls to take and which to ignore. He told Macon how to be interviewed and how to avoid saying anything at all. And, throughout it all, the reverend never asked anything of Macon. As he had promised, he let Macon do the steering. He did everything in his power to make the sheriff and his daughter feel that they had a say in their lives.

So when the reverend told Macon that he wanted to speak to Ava personally, to speak to the whole family, and that it would look better if it took place at their house, Macon agreed.

Now the reverend stood in the doorway wearing a dark suit and a thin overcoat. Behind him the policemen who had escorted him past the crowds and up the driveway waved politely to Macon before heading back down the road.

"Come on in," Macon said, ushering the reverend into the living room.

"Thank you," the man said, fixing his hair—which had become slightly tousled in the stiff, chilly breeze blowing outside.

Carmen and Ava sat in the living room on the couch together. Regardless of how Ava felt about Carmen, there was a solidarity beginning to form between them. Perhaps it came from the prolonged amount of time the two of them spent trapped in the house together lately. While familiarity can sometimes breed contempt, it can more often breed understanding.

Ava was beginning to understand that Carmen truly did not want to replace her mother. She simply wanted to love Macon, to have a healthy baby and to make a family with Ava. And since neither Carmen nor Ava had actually met the reverend in person before, they were unified in their leeriness of the man—regardless of how much Macon proclaimed that he was only trying to help them.

"It's wonderful to finally meet you both," Reverend Brown said as he crossed the room. He shook Carmen's hand first, and then Ava's. He shook Ava's hand slowly. "Ah, yes," he said. "The child herself." Then he took a seat in a chair Macon had placed in the living room for him.

Macon, Carmen and Ava sat on the couch together, all three of them aimed at the reverend. "It's such a pleasure to be here," he said brightly. "I apologize for insisting that we do this here, but I do feel that it will help people understand that all four of us are in this together."

There was suspicion in Carmen's eyes and Reverend Brown saw it. "I know what you're thinking," he said. "But I really am here to help."

"And what is it you'd like for Ava to do for you?" Carmen said. She rubbed the top of her stomach, then adjusted her dress. The dress was dark blue and it was tight and uncomfortable. She'd bought it months ago halfway through her pregnancy, but it was never intended to be worn at this late stage, with the extra girth of the third trimester.

"You're very direct," Reverend Brown said. "Much like your husband."

"I'm a bit curious myself," Macon added.

"I'm sure you all are," Reverend Brown replied. "So I'll get straight to the point. I'd like to facilitate a healing at my church."

"No," Carmen said immediately.

"Please," Reverend Brown said, "hear me out." His gaze shifted from Carmen to Ava. "Only once. That's all. Just one time, that's all that we'll need."

"What's the point of it?" Ava asked. Then all eyes were upon her.

"The point is to help," Reverend Brown said. "The world knows who you are. They know what you can do. And

there are people out there who want your help, people who
need your help. And I'm not asking you to help everyone,"
he continued. "It's clear that doing this is taxing on you.
But that's why I feel that we should get out in front of it.
By helping someone—not an animal, but a person—and by
doing it publically, you might be able to get some type of
reprieve from all of this."

Ava's mind was swirling. She wasn't sure exactly what
Reverend Brown meant. Mostly, she remembered how it
felt to wake up blind in the hospital. And there was a part
of her that knew, should she heal someone again, it would
only be the beginning. And she might not be able to come
back from it the way she had before. She was still having
trouble maintaining her weight. Carmen had been forced
to purchase new clothes for her because of how poorly her
others fit. And then there was the cold, the hollowness she
felt most days. She felt as though the wind could carry her
off into the world.

"How does helping someone in front of your church help
her?" Carmen asked.

"Because then people will understand that she's not trying *not* to help people." He sat back in his chair. "I know
it sounds confusing, but there are a lot of people out there
who believe your daughter is being selfish. When all of this
started, I heard that there was a pair of men who broke into
the hospital asking Ava for help. Is that true?"

"Yeah," Macon said. "A couple of crazies."

"They weren't anomalies," Reverend Brown said. "There
are many more like them in this world. And they're gaining a voice. But if you can show them that you do intend to
help, that you really are trying to use this talent of yours in a

selfless way, then we can control the time and place of it all. We can make sure people understand that none of this comes without a cost, and that Ava wants to help, but she can't help everyone. And then you're in charge of your lives again."

The family considered the man's words. Even Carmen found a certain degree of logic to them. Maybe there was a way to get control of all of this, as Macon had suggested, and maybe the reverend really was there to help.

Once the reverend left, Macon, Carmen and Ava discussed his offer throughout the day and into the night. There was talk of responsibility, talk of duty, talk of selflessness, talk of religion, talk of the general notion that people should help those they can. There was even talk of money. Publishers offered book deals and television personalities offered to pay a premium for exclusive interviews. Everyone wanted a piece of the Miracle Child.

Their talking went into the late hours of the night until, finally, Ava was drowsy from exhaustion and went to bed, leaving Carmen and Macon in the kitchen, still talking.

It was a little after 2:00 a.m. when Ava woke to the sound of Carmen crying in the bedroom next door. She was sobbing gently, obviously trying to mask the sound of it. She heard her father's voice. She spoke in a low tone. There was something between them that they did not want Ava to hear. But with the small, frail nature of their old house, secrets were impossible to keep.

"Brenda says they're still trying to decide how to treat it," Macon said.

"Why won't they tell him?" Carmen replied. She sobbed.

"It's Brenda," Macon said. "In her mind, she wants to let

him have a little bit more of his childhood. Cancer is a hard road. Even if he responds to the treatment, Wash has got some miserable days ahead. I think she just…well, I think she just wants to let him have a few more days of sunlight."

Ava trembled. Her stomach tightened and she thought she might vomit. It made sense now—the testing that Wash has been going through since the event. She'd thought that they were testing him to find out more about how Ava had healed him, but what they were actually doing was trying to find out more about his cancer.

Wash. Cancer.

The two words spun in her head. Without a sound, Ava turned and buried her head in the pillow. The tears came heavily. How had it happened? And why wouldn't they tell her? She had healed him, hadn't she? So why did he have cancer? Had she caused it somehow?

The questions swirled in her mind, and still she wept. She cried until she could not keep it silent anymore and her sorrow rolled out of her in a long, painful wail. And when Macon and Carmen came rushing into her room, asking what was wrong, she could not even say the boy's name. When they finally calmed her, she said to them, "I'll do it."

"Do what?" Macon asked.

"What the reverend said. Heal somebody in front of his church."

"You don't have to," Carmen said. "You don't have to put yourself through that. You almost died the last time. Who knows what will happen if you do it again?"

"I need to know if I can do it again," she said. "And maybe, like the reverend said, if there's a big enough crowd, maybe people will understand."

"Understand what?" Macon asked.

Ava only shook her head. "I want to do it," she said. "I want to show everyone."

Finally, at last, Ava had discovered a plan to stop all of this. She knew what she had to do, once and for all, in front of everyone, in full view of the world, for as many people as she possibly could, no matter what the cost. If she could only heal once more in her life, she knew who it would be. And she knew how to make it happen in a way that everyone would leave their family alone when it was over.

"I'm the worst father in the world for what I'm about to do," Macon said. He and Ava were backstage, waiting for the time when they would be called out front so that Ava could perform the act that so many people had come to see. He and Carmen were still not in agreement on whether or not they should allow Ava to do this. "It's killing her," Carmen had told him whenever they were alone in the days leading up to now. She repeated it whenever she could, like a chisel working against stone.

"She only has to do it one time," was Macon's defense. In his mind, one more time, one more miracle, would be enough. Then they would get enough attention, enough notoriety, to really make ends meet. The money would come. He never said it directly, and he didn't have to. Carmen knew just as well as he did what was really motivating him. It was the weight of poverty combined with the notion that, if a person could endure one painful decision, they could be liberated from the worry, from the day-to-day toil of dreaming of one life while living another. "Just once." It was his mantra of justification.

But regardless of how they felt, this had become Ava's decision.

"I can't believe I'm going to do this," Macon said. He was seated in a small, steel-framed chair and Ava sat in a similar one beside him. Around them there was a buzz of people, all of them affiliated with Reverend Brown's church—deacons and assistants and more. For the most part, they kept their distance, treating Macon and Ava with reverence from afar, like movie stars that, out of respect, they pretended not to recognize.

"It's okay," Ava said. She took his hand and squeezed it.

"How do you know?" Macon asked. He wanted to laugh; he wanted to turn the question into a joke, as if he had the answer and was only teasing her. But there was no humor in his voice.

"I don't," Ava said. And somehow she achieved the humor that Macon had been attempting. They both smiled and she squeezed his hand tighter.

"We're ready for you both," a man said, walking over at a lope. And, just like that, their time alone together was at an end, though neither of them could know it.

Reverend Brown's sermon had gone on for almost two hours before the time finally came when Ava was brought out before the church. The reverend had spoken on the topic of "Willingness to Believe."

He stood in the center of the stage—the choir and his deacons behind him, the tent above him and the twilight sky above it—and he was dressed in a suit so fine and so sharp that it seemed to be a part of him, something that he had been born into and had spent his lifetime in. The night air was crisp and, now and again, Reverend Brown would draw a handkerchief from his pocket and dab the sweat from his brow. He was full of a vigor and excitement his church had not seen from him in a very long time.

When the time was near, the reverend removed his suit jacket and passed it to one of his helpers who took it away. "And now," he said solemnly from the center of the church, "we will all be witness to something amazing."

Then there was a commotion at the rear of the church and the entirety of the congregation turned to witness it. A young couple was led by the ushers through the aisle. Walking between them was a boy. His hair was thin and dark, a striking contrast to the pale skin on his face. There were circles around his eyes and a stiffness in his gait as if, for each day of this child's life, sickness had shadowed him.

"How long has your child been afflicted?" he asked when they had finally reached the stage. He pointed a microphone toward the boy's father.

"Since he was born," the man said.

"And what have the doctors had to say about his illness?"

"They're hopeful," he replied. "But they've been hopeful for a long time and my son has been sick all the while."

Reverend Brown squatted slowly, as if to show that he was an old man and tired from the day's sermon. "And what is your name, child?" Reverend Brown asked the boy.

"Ronald," the boy said. "Ronald Williams."

"And how old are you, Ronald?"

"Eight."

"Eight years old," Reverend Brown repeated—a slight tremble in his voice. "Eight years old and stricken with this terrible illness."

"Yes, sir," the boy said.

"Such a terrible thing," Reverend Brown said. "Come now, child," he said, and he reached down and lifted the boy and turned toward the rear of the church and there, in the doorway, being led by Macon, was Ava.

She clutched Macon's hand and looked up at him. "I don't think I should have said I'd do this," she said, but Macon was already moving forward, leading her out from backstage and into the middle of everything. The crowd held their breath. The silence was such that footfalls and the flutter of clothing could be heard as Macon and Ava marched through the aisle. A wall of deacons in matching blue suits stood at each of the pews, blocking anyone that might decide to step out or reach for the father and daughter.

Toward the end of the aisle, just as they reached the main stage, Ava heard someone call her. She turned and saw Wash standing there. He was dressed in a black suit with a white shirt and black tie. He looked taller than he ever had before, and his hair was combed and smoothed down. He waved timidly.

She waved back.

Beside Wash was Brenda. She was dressed in her Sunday gown with her hair hanging down to her shoulders. She looked regal and proper, but still with a hint of iron about her, like royalty in its twilight. Next to Brenda was Carmen, draped in a loose-fitting dress. She held her hands on her round belly and waved as Ava saw her. She mouthed the words *You'll be okay.*

Ava looked for Tom, but didn't see him, which didn't completely surprise her. In the end, it was only Wash who she had wanted to be there, anyway. Seeing him gave her courage and strength, even knowing what she knew about him, knowing that he was sick and that he did not know it.

"It'll be okay," Macon whispered, and there was a hint of fear in his voice. He gently tugged Ava forward. She didn't realize that she had stopped walking and was fixated on Wash.

"There she is, brothers and sisters," Reverend Brown said. His voice boomed through the speakers. It shook with the words and his face was, all at once, an expression of pain and sadness and wonder and hope. "Come forth, child," he said to Ava.

It could not be stopped now, she knew that. Everything that had been building had come to this. Macon led her to the center of the stage where Reverend Brown and the Williams family were waiting. All the eyes of the crowd and the cameras and the television screens and computer screens, and cell phones—all of them trained on her.

Reverend Brown, still holding the sick boy in his arms, nodded at the choir and they sang. The words of their song were nothing more than guttural moans and wailing to Ava. Her heart beat in her ears and her legs were weak, but her father was there with her, holding her hand, almost holding her up. "It'll be okay," he repeated.

"Hello, child," Reverend Brown said.

"Hello," she replied.

And someone in the audience said, "Amen."

"Do you know why you're here?"

Ava looked at Macon.

"Yes," Ava replied.

"This child needs your help," Reverend Brown said. Another round of "Amens" came from the crowd. The young boy looked at Ava. He reminded her of Wash. "He has a ter-rible condition called ATRT," Reverend Brown said. "It's a kind of brain cancer."

Macon released Ava's hand, like releasing a paper boat into a fast-moving river. She walked over to the boy. His par-ents looked at her with a strange mixture of skepticism and yearning. As if she were everything they feared and hoped for all at once.

"You'll be wonderful," Reverend Brown said, placing his hands on Ava's shoulders. She reached forward and took Ronald's hand. It was cold, clammy. He trembled slightly, as if he expected to be stung.

"How does this work?" the boy asked.

"I don't really know," Ava said slowly. There was a thought in her mind, something that she knew she needed to say. Something she knew she needed to do. But she was afraid. And looking into Ronald's eyes just now, having the entire church, the entire world, watching, it did nothing to make what she would do any easier.

She glanced up at Macon, as if she could convey to him what she was about to do. He stared back at her, not mov-ing from where he stood and, slowly, understanding spread across his face. He opened his mouth to speak.

"It's okay," Reverend Brown said. He kneeled beside Ava and Ronald. He took both of their hands and wrapped his around theirs, as if binding them together. He squeezed their hands. "It's going to be okay," he said. "Just do what you did before."

And then all the breaths of the church were held. Everyone watched and waited. Some people wept silently. Others fidg-eted as they stood before their seats. No one spoke, no one moved, no one committed any action that might break the solemnness and the magic of what they knew would happen next. They waited; they listened as the speakers piped in the dull, electric hiss of microphones awaiting voices. Everyone wanted to hear what Ava might say when she performed the healing, what the boy might say once he was healed, what his parents might say when, finally, their son was saved, what Reverend Brown might say when it was all over.

The silence was a bell jar, smothering them all. Until, finally, Ava broke the silence.

"No," Ava said. She looked up into Ronald's eyes as she said it. "I'm sorry," she said, crying a little. "But no, I'm not going to do this." And the microphone caught her words, amplified them and the mountains echoed.

"She wouldn't do it," Reverend Brown said. He paced back and forth in Macon's office, clenching his jaw. "She utterly and flatly refused to do it. That's all this comes down to."

"Settle down," Macon said. He peeked out through the window blinds and was immediately met with the flashing of cameras. If things were bad before, when Ava had done her healings, they were worse now that she'd gone before Reverend Brown's church and refused their pleas.

"Why?" Reverend Brown growled. "Then again, I don't really care why. I don't really care how." He stopped pacing, but still his jaw tightened and released, as though chewing through his anger, piece by piece.

"Does that help?" Macon asked, stepping away from the window and closing the blinds.

"Does what help?"

"The jaw thing," Macon said. He made a motion with his hand to indicate Reverend Brown's jaw. "Does that help you keep a handle on things when you get angry?"

"It helps with all manner of things," Reverend Brown replied coldly. He took a deep breath, considering Macon as he held the air in his lungs. Then he sighed, long and slow, and when he was done, his jaw did not clench anymore. "Okay," he said. "Where is she?"

"They're safe. While the reporters were all chasing our car toward the house, Carmen, Ava and Wash were able to sneak into another one and slip out. Carmen has been having more problems with the baby and all of us would feel better if she stayed at Dr. Arnold's house for a little while. All of us are going to stay at the Doc's. They should be there by now."

Reverend Brown nodded approvingly. He took a seat in the chair in front of Macon's desk. "Let's talk this out. All is not lost here."

"Personally," Macon said, "I don't think anything is lost."

"Nonsense."

"I feel like I dodged a bullet tonight," Macon said. "And I don't think I'm going to step in front of it again. Maybe she just can't do it anymore. Maybe whatever it is, whatever it was, it's over."

Reverend Brown laughed. "Like a planetary alignment? Like a summer cold that stuffs up the sinuses for a few weeks in the most prime and vibrant time of the year? Like a coincidence, you mean?" He crossed his legs and rested his hands in his lap. "She chose," Reverend Brown said. "That's the crux of it. You saw it, the whole damned world saw it. They heard her. She said no. She refused to help that boy."

"I don't think it's that simple," Macon said. He continued to stand, even though the reverend was now sitting.

"Whatever happened, whatever her reason," Macon said, "I'm sure she had a good one. Why else would she choose not to help?" He tucked his thumbs into the belt of the suit Reverend Brown had bought for him for the night's event.

"A powerful question," Reverend Brown replied. "I wonder if she wasn't told not to help that boy. I wonder if maybe her father sat her down just before coming into the church tonight—or even before that. Maybe this has been something you've had up your sleeve all along. Maybe you told her that, if she failed this time—'threw the fight,' if you will—then you all could create enough to make a little more money from someone else." He looked down at the floor and released a hard chuckle. "Honestly, I can't believe I didn't see it coming. I can't believe I didn't think of it myself."

"You're more paranoid than I thought," Macon said. He stepped away from the window and walked behind his desk. Still he did not sit. Reverend Brown was a different man now and it made him uneasy. He took off his suit jacket and readied his muscles.

"Paranoia takes a man far in this world," Reverend Brown said, lifting his eyes from the floor and back to Macon.

"Nobody planned anything," Macon said. "She said she wanted to do it. She wanted to help."

"If only I could believe that," Reverend Brown said.

"Why is it impossible to believe that whatever this is, whatever it was that let her do those things, has ended?"

"Because nothing ever ends," the reverend said. He straightened his back slightly. "Everything we do in this life is as permanent and eternal as God's very grace. You want things to go back to the way they were, don't you?" he asked. "You want your town, your life, to return to that invisible, sleeping state that it once was." He shook his head. "That'll never happen. The best thing you, your daughter and your family can do is embrace it, control it, before it gets too far out of hand. No one will ever believe that your daughter can't do those things, not really. There are too many tapes, too many videos. They'll always come around, always show up in your lives, asking for help. Asking for guidance. There's no stopping this," he said.

Then the reverend stood and adjusted his suit and flashed a smile that could have stopped the progression of a hurricane. "Now," he said, "I'm going out to talk to those reporters. We'll get another chance at this. And it'll all work out just fine. Go and talk with your daughter."

"About what?" Macon asked.

"About whatever it is you need to talk with her about," Reverend Brown said. "There's a schedule we need to keep. I'll handle the reporters, Sheriff. And let's not forget that, regardless of what you think of me and my church, we're both trying to achieve something."

"I don't have anything against you or your church," Macon said. "I've got a family to think about, simple as that."

"Then do your part," Reverend Brown said, his voice hard and even. "Your daughter, she has a responsibility. No matter the cost." He clenched his jaw one final time. "She has a responsibility," he said once more. "We all do. Every single day." Then he exited the office toward the waiting reporters. On his way out, he waved at the other police officers as though his conversation with Macon had never happened.

It was then that the weight was lifted from Macon's shoulders. He relaxed into the chair behind his desk and rubbed the sides of his head. Try as he might, he could not escape the image of Ronald's parents when their boy was taken to the back of the church and the examination that followed revealed that nothing had changed.

Nor could he drown out the sound of the weeping. The way Ronald's father moaned like a wounded animal. The way his mother whimpered, over and over again. And the thought that would not leave him: *What if it were my child?*

Though he did not want to, he heard Reverend Brown's words: "She has a responsibility. We all do."

It was then that he heard the explosion.

He had been in the audience that evening, like so many others. Watching and waiting, trembling with anticipation as the girl that had come to them, to the whole world, would perform the miracle they had all been waiting for. And, this time, it would happen before a congregation, where it was always destined to happen. Wasn't that what his brother believed?

Sam watched and he was as patient as he could manage as his brother performed an extended sermon on willingness to believe and Sam felt that he understood everything his brother was trying to say—which was not always the case. When Isaiah spoke before the church or in front of cameras, he was a different person than Sam knew. He was harder to understand. His words were like fast-moving rivers, and they cut a path through the air that Sam could not follow, no matter how hard he tried.

Sometimes he wondered if, when he was younger, he would have been able to follow his brother's words. But those memories of who he once was were more dream than recollections. They were simply feelings that came to him sometimes, like small birds that fluttered into view inside his mind, but darted away before he could ever really take sight of them.

But the news of Ava and her ability had brought a new hope to him. It was a hope that he could not define, and it welled up inside of him.

She could fix things, Sam knew.

She could fix people.

She could even fix him.

There needed to be another air show, Sam decided. Another chance for the girl to do what she had done. Another chance for her to become what she was meant to be. And, maybe then, she would help him. Maybe then she would fix him and he would not be such a burden to his brother. He had been a hardship in his brother's life for too long, he felt.

Sam was rarely alone anymore after his second incident with Ava. He now had a caregiver named Gary, a tall, white-haired older man who Sam liked because he was kind and understanding and liked to talk about football and took stock in Sam's opinions as few others did. He never seemed frustrated or irritated when Sam wanted to talk. So when Sam came out of his bedroom in the Andrews House and found Gary sitting alone at a small desk at the end of the hallway reading a newspaper, it was not out of the ordinary when Sam sparked up a conversation.

"Redskins again?" Sam said.

"Always," Gary replied without looking up from his newspaper. "Though I still don't get all of the fuss people are making about their name. Maybe I'm just old," he said, and he seemed to be pleased with himself.

"I don't want to do this," Sam said when he was standing close enough to Gary.

"Do what?" Gary replied. "What's the matter, Sammy? You sound vexed."

"I just want to help," Sam said.

"Don't we all?" Gary replied. He turned to the next page of his newspaper, still not looking up. "Now who do you like for the playoffs?"

Sam did not answer. He tightened his grip on the object in his hand, and he wondered if he would have the courage to do what he believed he needed to do. He liked Gary, and did not want to hurt him, but something had to be done.

"I'm not sure," Sam said.

"Same here," Gary said. "Lots of trades in the off-season. I can hardly keep up with who's playing for what team anymore, you know what I mean?"

"I guess," Sam replied.

"Ah, well," Gary said. "It'll sort out. It's not like I'm actually playing on the team, is it? I'm just another face in the crowd." He paused. "Man," he said, "if only you could have made it out there, Sam. I can only imagine what you would have done if you'd gotten your chance to play in the NFL. You would have been one of the best running backs anybody's ever seen, wouldn't you?"

"I…"

"Of course you would have," Gary said.

"I'm sorry," Sam said, and, finally, Gary looked up from his newspaper. He saw the conflict in Sam's face, the weight of what was going on inside of him.

"What's the matter, Sammy?" Gary asked. "What's wrong?"

Gary did not see the bedpost descend upon him as Sam hit him with it. He only fell to the floor with a thud.

"I'm sorry, I'm sorry, I'm sorry," Sam repeated, even as the bedpost clattered to the floor next to Gary's body. He reached into the man's pocket and retrieved a pack of matches—Gary always enjoyed cigars. Then Sam made his way hurriedly through the house and out into the bustle of the city.

The thought raging in his mind was simply that he needed to help. Over and over again, it came to him: help. There were so many people caught up in what was happening within the confines of Stone Temple, so many people around the world, watching and waiting and, in their souls, hoping. Hoping that what they had heard about the girl and her ability to help people was true. Wasn't there, in a lifetime, a thousand moments that people needed something to believe in?

And Sam knew that he would help them, that he would give them something to believe in.

The town of Stone Temple was up late that night, and buzzing with the news that Ava had failed to help the boy. There were arguments of faith, arguments of responsibility. Answers were all that people wanted.

Sam knew that he was not smart enough to have the answers. No, at best, Isaiah might have them, but Sam was not as smart as his brother, which was one of the reasons he loved him as much as he did. He loved him enough to do whatever it took to compel Ava to help people, even if that meant something unimaginable. It was the only way people would believe again. It was the only way he could help his brother.

He had seen it done in a movie once, and it seemed like something he could manage.

He had trouble finding a metal clothes hanger as he made his way through the town. He would search in garbage cans, but never long enough to draw attention. When he could not find the hanger he ducked into a small alley behind a building and thought. It took a long time but the idea of what to do finally came to him. So he returned to sorting through a small trash can behind the building and he did, in fact, manage to find a small length of wire—roughly the length of his forearm—and he decided that it would be enough.

He could not be sure, but he was confident and proud of himself.

When he came out of the alleyway he was surprised to find that there were even more people in the center of town. They were gathered together, not far from where Isaiah's church was set up, and they bustled about in a small circle surrounding a person Sam could not make out. Whoever it was, they were important, or famous or both. They were flanked on all sides by photographers. And where they went, the crowd followed, chattering and gawking, holding up phones for photographs.

Sam did not know it, not expressly, anyhow, but he could not have asked for a better distraction as he approached the service truck that was parked at the edge of the town square.

Without pausing to see if he was noticed, Sam opened the gas cap on the truck. He grabbed the bottom of his shirt between his fingers and, after a little effort, managed to rip a sizeable strip out of it. He then tied it to the electrical wire. When he tried feeding the wire into the gas tank of the truck, the wire turned back on him, lacking the stiffness he needed.

But Sam did not panic. He paused and looked around and, after a moment, found a small stick that did the job of helping to feed the wire, and the strip of shirt that was attached to it, into the gas tank. Then he removed the stick and tugged at the wire and, after some effort, it came out of the tank, bringing with it the strip of his shirt, soaked with gasoline. He made sure that the other end of the gasoline-soaked cloth remained inside the tank

Without hesitating, he reached into his pocket, took out the pack of matches, struck one and lit the shirt.

In the movie from which Sam got the idea, the car had taken a few moments to explode. It was enough time for a person to get away. But Sam did not remember that just now, in the milliseconds between the time when the car exploded and the time when his life was snuffed out.

In that final glimmer of time Sam also did not remember the childhood he spent in Georgia chasing after his big brother, Isaiah. He did not remember the nights he and his brother spent lying atop the roof of the barn, dreaming about who they would one day become. Sam was to become a football star. Isaiah was to become a veterinarian. The younger brother and his football career would pay for the slightly older brother and his love of animals. They would be a pair that took pieces of the world and held them in the palms of their hands and crafted them into something they could love.

Sam also did not remember the way their father used to get drunk and yell at them. The way he would hit them and their mother. The way he and Isaiah would take turns defending each other, as well as their mother, on the nights when their father so hated the world that he needed to sink the teeth of his anger into it. Nor did Sam remember the time after their father died, when Isaiah had only just finished high school and, rather than go to college as he had planned, went to work in order to help support his mother. And Sam did not remember the hope that was pinned to his football career, how it would be the way that all three of them would carve their path in the world, how they believed that it was the destiny they had long suffered for.

Sam did not remember the crash.

He did not remember the water rising above his head, taking away his boyhood dreams with it.

He did not remember his brother becoming a minster, his mother's death in the years later, just as success and wealth came to their family.

The only thing that Sam remembered in that final moment of life, in that instant of time between existence and whatever follows, was the sound of his brother's voice, a memory of Isaiah, playing in the synapses of his mind, like a lullaby: "I'll take care of you, Sam."

"Why?"

"Because that's what little big brothers do."

"One day I'll repay you, Isaiah."

"Love doesn't ask for repayment."

"One day," Sam said. "One day I'll make it better."

Over and over he heard the words, until they rose up around him like a tide, washing over him, taking him under, never to let him go.

There was heat and light and a sudden deafening. And, for some, an ending. For others, there followed a ringing of the ears, a long moment lacking in understanding as they watched the fireball roll upward into the night sky.

Inside Dr. Arnold's house, it sounded like fireworks. Just a thunder in the distance. But there came with it a rattling of the house, like the shock wave from when the dynamite exploded in the old mine a few years back. Carmen's head was buried in the toilet—yet another bout of vomiting, but worse than the others—when the sound of the explosion swept through the house. "What was that?" she called out.

"Hell if I know," Brenda said, standing in the doorway. "Sounded like the damned Soviets attacking." She looked at the vomit in the toilet.

"I'm fine," Carmen said, even though she knew that was not the truth. She thought she felt a contraction. Whatever it was that was going on with her body just now was not normal. "There's something wrong," she said. "It sounded like an explosion."

"You're sure you're okay?" Brenda asked. She had her hand on Carmen's back. "Dear Lord, girl," she said. "You're anything but okay. Just look at you." Carmen was pale and trembling. She swayed back and forth above the toilet. "Call Doc Arnold!" Brenda yelled.

Ava and Wash raced into the bathroom. They'd come to ask about the sound of the explosion, and instead they'd come upon Carmen kneeling on the floor in heap of sweat, tears and vomit, repeating, over and over again, "I'm fine… I'm fine…."

Ava ran upstairs to get Dr. Arnold while Wash stayed in the room with his grandmother, watching.

"It's going to be okay," Brenda said to both Wash and Carmen.

"You think it was some kind of car crash?" Carmen asked. "Do you think Macon's okay?"

"I'm sure he is," Brenda said. "Now you just hush up and let me help you get into the bed. Wash, come help me." Together the two of them helped Carmen up off the floor. She held her stomach and trembled when they got her to her feet. They looked down to find a puddle at her feet.

"No," Carmen said. "It can't happen now. Not yet. It's too soon. Just like last time, it's too soon."

"Hush," Brenda said, and she and Wash forced Carmen down onto the bed. She pushed against them, resisting them as though it meant resisting the fate that she most feared. "Doc Arnold's going to come in here and he's going to make it all okay," she said. She sat down on the edge of the bed and stroked Carmen's hair just as another contraction came. "I promise you that it's going to be okay," Brenda said. "I promise."

Wash stepped back from the bed. He stood and watched, understanding, but afraid. "I'm going to find Ava and Dr. Arnold."

"Okay," Brenda said, not looking back.

"Where's Ava?" Carmen asked. "She can help, can't she?"

Wash left the room and met Dr. Arnold and his wife in the hallway. The doctor moved briskly, rolling up the sleeves of his shirt as he walked. His wife was at his heels, her face full of worry. Dr. Arnold patted Wash on the shoulder as he passed wordlessly and, in the same motion, indicated that the boy should leave the room.

"Where's Ava?" Wash asked. He had expected to find her behind the doctor and his wife, but she was not there. He moved off into the house, stepping faster and faster as he did. Outside, in the street, he could hear the sound of people yelling and screaming. Far inside the house the phone began to ring. Dr. Arnold was the only person Wash knew who still owned a landline phone, and a part of him sometimes enjoyed hearing the heavy, dense sound it made when a call came in. But just now, at this moment, he knew that the ringing of the phone was something to be dreaded.

As he passed the window before the stairs he saw a glow swelling up from the center of town, almost like a sunrise. It looked like it was only a few streets over. The reporters that had been parked outside of Dr. Arnold's were gone. Whatever was happening was enough to draw them away, which made a knot form in the pit of Wash's stomach. Whatever it was, it was terrible.

"Ava?" Wash called as he reached the top of the stairs. He could hear her in a bedroom—her footsteps moving back and forth hurriedly. "Ava?"

When he entered the bedroom, he found her loading a small satchel with clothes. "I'm leaving," she said. "I'm leaving and I want you to come with me. Right now."

On the floor below, in the bed Dr. Arnold had given her for the night, Carmen's pain had not lessened. "Just let me get through this," she said to Dr. Arnold as he examined her. "Just promise me the baby and I will be okay."

She rolled onto her side and held her stomach and closed her eyes as Dr. Arnold said the same thing that Brenda had said, over and over again: "It'll be okay."

Her imagination got the better of her as she lay there in bed praying that her child would live through the night. She saw herself standing next to the grave of two dead children. It was a bright and sunny day, and there was no one there with her. Not Macon. Not her first husband. No one.

There was only her and the two children she had failed to give life to.

The image hung before her like a ghost, as she imagined herself sitting on the end of the bed with Macon's gun in her hand. She imagined the heft of it in her fingers. She had always been fascinated by just how heavy guns really were, their density made greater by the weight of what they could do to the world. She imagined turning the muzzle toward herself. She imagined trying to look down the black pit of the barrel. She wondered if she might actually be able to see a glimmer of the bullet just before it exited the chamber and entered her skull, taking away all of her pain, all of her memories, all of the hopes that life had taken away from her. It would be quick and painless, she knew that. Not even a flash. Not even a pinprick. Just a sudden nothingness—a place without fear or pain or memory. And then she imagined Ava standing near the headstones of Carmen's two dead children and she looked at her with accusing eyes and said, "You could have saved him."

She did not know exactly when she had fallen asleep, but she was jarred by the sensation of waking. She was afraid of how much time might have passed and how the world might have changed. "Ava?" she called out. "Ava, where are you?"

"Settle down," Dr. Arnold said. He motioned for Delores and Brenda to help hold Carmen down. She was sweating heavily, and the bed beneath her legs was drenched with blood.

Brenda had come out of the room to get water for Carmen when she passed the window and first caught sight of the people. There was a small crowd, perhaps only seven or eight of them as best she could make out in the dimness of the streetlights lining the road. But, behind them, she could see that there were more on the way. "Delores?" Brenda called. "Delores, come here. Come quick."

Brenda could hear the shuffling of Delores's feet as she rushed to the front door. "Lord, Brenda. What's so important that you'd pull me away?"

Brenda nodded to the window. The group of people were coming across the front lawn now, looking up at the house. She could see that some of them were hurt. Behind them, down the street, she could see more coming. The fire department of Stone Temple only had one ambulance, and it could take up to a half hour for the paramedics to show up from one of the nearby towns—and that was before the roads were crowded with people hoping to get a glimpse of the Miracle Child. So, now, the people came, with more following, to where the doctor lived and where the healing girl was being kept.

"Goodness," Delores said. "I'll get my husband."

"I don't think they came for your husband," Brenda said.

"Of course they did," Delores replied. "What else could they have come here for?" She walked past Brenda and opened the door. "Come in," she said, waving her hands. "Come in and we'll get you taken care of." Her hands flapped in front of her, motioning for people to come inside. "I'll get my husband," she said. "We'll get you all taken care of until we can find some more help here."

"Is Ava in there?" someone asked.

"What?" Delores asked. Her hands stopped moving.

"I told you," Brenda said, backing away from the door. "Shut the door," she said.

"I'll do no such thing," Delores said. Then she turned back to the crowd. "Well, yes, Ava is in here. But I don't see what that's got to do with anything. You folks need medical attention. I'm a nurse and my husband is a doctor. What's that girl got to do with anything?"

"Shut the door," Brenda repeated. She backed to the stairs, blocking them and, at the same time, listening upstairs for Ava and Wash, but not hearing them.

"It's okay," Delores said, her voice thin.

There was still the sound of the fire burning in the center of town. There was the glow of the fire and the glimmer of the lights from the fire trucks. There was the sound of people yelling, giving orders. Perhaps one of those voices was Macon's. Then a woman standing in the crowd before Dr. Arnold's house stepped forward, holding a child in her arms. "Please," a woman said, holding her child. "You've got to do something." Her child was young, no more than four or five, and his shirt was covered in blood. There was a large gash on the child's head and the blood was running down his face and onto his clothes in spite of the way his mother held a cloth against the wound. "You've got to do something," the woman said.

"Oh, Lord," Delores said. "Come inside, quick!"

"Not you," the woman said. "Not the doctor. The girl. Ava."

"Ava can't help you," Brenda said, stepping forward into the doorway. "But there's a nurse and a doctor here who'll do everything they can, every single thing possible. Now get in here."

"Yes," Delores agreed. "Your boy needs help."

"I want Ava to help him," the woman said. "I want to know that he's healed. I want to know that he'll be okay. She's the only one who can do that."

"She can't help everyone," Brenda said. She looked over the crowd as she said it, hoping that they would somehow understand, but knowing full well that they would not.

"Just help my child," the woman said.

"We'll get your son to a hospital as soon as we can," Delores said. "My husband will do everything he can."

"I don't want a hospital," the woman yelled. "I want her help!"

"She can't help you," Brenda said.

"Who are you to decide?" a man said. He pressed forward and stood beside the woman with the injured child. "Who are you to say? What gives you the right?"

"Settle down," Brenda said.

"We deserve help," someone yelled. "She needs to help us."

"This will all be sorted out properly," Reverend Brown said, his voice booming. He raced up the front yard, his voice booming ahead of him as he spoke. The crowd parted to let him through. His coming impressed upon the crowd that they should behave as best they could, a sense that there was a judgment that might be passed upon them. But the lull it created did not last.

The arguing began quickly. The man standing in the front of the crowd bolted forward, past Brenda and Delores, and into the house. "Where is she?" he yelled. "Where is she?"

"Get the hell out of here," Brenda yelled. The man dashed from room to room, calling Ava's name. "There's help here if you need it," Brenda said, "but the girl will stay out of it." She stood at the bottom of the stairs, planted and firm as an oak.

After he was done checking the rest of the house, the man looked at her thoughtfully, his mind adding things up. "She's upstairs," the man said, as if both creating and confirming the theory at the same time.

"And to hell with you if you think you're getting past me," Brenda said. She made her hands into fists at her side.

"You've got to stop this," Delores said. She spoke with her hands flapping around her. Her nerves had always been weak, and the way things were turning was doing nothing to help that. "My husband and I can help everyone," she said. "Or, if we can't, we'll make sure you're okay until we can get you over to the hospital."

Still Brenda and the man locked eyes on each other. He walked over to the old woman. Brenda was tall, but the man was taller. He looked down at her with a hard, angry face. "Move," he growled.

"You'll have to kill me," Brenda said. "And even God Almighty ain't figured out how to do that one yet."

The moment stretched out. The man stood firmly and stared down at the old, red-haired matriarch. And like the mountains themselves, Brenda waited, and did not move until, finally, the man turned and walked out of the house.

Brenda sat on the bottom stair as the people entered the house and Delores and Dr. Arnold began hustling to take care of them. She would protect the children at any cost.

But it was not until sometime later, when she finally had a moment to check on them, that she would find them missing.

Ava and Wash were already half a mile way—escaped through the upstairs window, dipping between the houses, disappearing into the night, into the loneliness of the mountains.

They woke in the short hours before dawn and her mother had breakfast ready even though the day was still far off. Ava's eyes burned with drowsiness but her mother had made cocoa and the house was thick with the smell of pancakes and the television in the living room was turned on to a low murmur that was warm and welcoming.

"How long until sunrise?" Ava asked.

"About an hour," her mother said. "But we're going to have to make it on up the mountain soon. So don't dawdle with breakfast."

They ate quickly and left the house into the cool darkness with the smell of maple syrup and coffee clinging to the collars of their jackets. The crickets trilled and the wind was still and it seemed that they could make out the sound of the dew falling through the leaves of the trees—a gentle tapping, like a small question being asked again and again by the earth.

They made their way in silence up the mountain. Heather carried a small flashlight and swung the beam of it back and forth on the path even though her legs knew the way well enough. Ava held her hand as they walked and the morning dew wet her shoes and dampened the bottom of her pants. She liked the smell of the grass and the loamy stench of the earth they left behind them as they trekked up the mountain.

When they had crested the mountain, Ava's mother turned eastward and led the child into a small clearing with a stone outcropping that looked out over the entire mountain range—a shaggy band of blue-black beneath the moonless night sky.

"Come sit," Heather said. She settled upon a large slab of stone and folded her legs and stared off to the east. Then she reached into the pockets of her large jacket and waited.

"How much longer?" Ava asked, settling onto the stone beside her mother. The rock was cold and slightly wet beneath her. It was a detail that she knew would stay with her.

"Not long," Heather said. "Look." And then she pointed off to the east and, with a quickness that Ava could not have imagined, the sky was already casting off its darkness, the stars receding gently.

"Look through this," Heather said, handing Ava a dark piece of square glass from her jacket pocket.

"Why do I need this?"

"Because you'll go blind otherwise. That's how the sun works, kiddo."

And then there was fire in the east. A bright torch from behind the trees that grew into a well of light that swelled and swelled— perfectly circular—and when Ava looked, her mother was holding the smoked glass in front of her, staring into the sun, and Ava did the same.

"The sun gets smaller when I look through the glass. What happened?" Ava asked.

"That's what the sun really looks like from this far away."

Ava took the glass away from her eyes and the sun was a huge glowing ball of fire that sent pinpricks of pain into the backs of her eyes. And then, with the glass, it was smaller than a dime again.

"Magic," Ava said softly.

The two of them sat and watched the sun clear the horizon and then they saw when the moon rose up and conquered a third of the sun, and Ava was torn between watching the eclipse through the smoked glass that would protect her eyes and staring headlong into the brightness. She felt that there was something being lost in the transition between the glass and the naked eye.

"Is that really the moon?" Ava asked.

"It's the moon," Heather replied.

"Is it going to block out the sun?"

"Not completely. Today it's only a partial eclipse. There won't be another full eclipse for a few more years."

"And that's when the moon completely blocks out the sun?"

"That's right."

Ava continued to watch the sun and moon dance with each other through the smoky glass. Already the moon was receding, the dark spot of ink slowly marching out of view. Ava pictured the sun and moon and the earth in her mind. She had trouble giving them scope and distance. They were simply three large orbs—one yellow, one blue and one white. In her mind, the sun changed size, going from large and blindingly bright, to the small yellow dot she saw through the smoky glass.

It was a universe difficult to contain in her mind, but she did her best.

"Nothing lasts forever," Heather said finally. And when Ava

looked she saw that the moon had completely passed from the sun. It had returned to being simply a small, perfect dot of yellow in front of her.

Ava stopped looking through the glass and suddenly she could feel the warmth of the sun pouring over her. The world looked different from anything she had ever remembered seeing. The bushy green rug of trees and brush and rocks and earth stretched out before her. Suddenly the world felt small and large at the same time. It seemed to breathe.

"It's something, isn't it?" Heather said.

It was only two days later—when the echo of this time together still reverberated in her daughter's mind—that Heather would hang herself.

NINE

THEY COULD JUST make out the radio tower blinking in the distance above the trees and above the mountain. Ava pointed and told Wash that was where they had to go. "Why?" Wash asked, huffing from the effort. He had not yet thought of how they would achieve this escape.

"Trust me," she said, and then she pulled him forward.

When they first got out of town and into the woods she gave him one of her sweaters to wear so that he had some layers of his own. It smelled of her, and he liked wearing it beneath his jacket more than he cared to admit. "I'm sorry we couldn't get some of your clothes," Ava said. "I didn't really plan this."

"I can't believe we're doing this," Wash said.

Ava trudged onward and, as if pulled by gravity, Wash followed. They treaded through darkness and underbrush, moving as fast as either of them could manage. Sweat beaded up on Ava's brow. Her head lolled. She stumbled now and then.

"Maybe we should stop," Wash said. He could not ignore the way her clothes hung loosely from her body. They swallowed her up, even with the layers she wore. She seemed to be disappearing, even as she stood in front of him.

"We can't stop," Ava huffed. But she had already come to a standstill. Her body swayed in the cold wind racing up the mountain. She closed her eyes and held her breath and Wash watched her, not knowing what to do or what to say to bring back the Ava he used to know.

"We've got to stop," Wash said. He found a fallen log that would hold them. "Come sit." He tucked his hands into his pockets and waited. After a moment Ava walked slowly toward Wash and sat on the tree beside him. "What's going on, Ava? I mean, what's really happening?"

"I wonder what happened in town," Ava said. She looked in the direction of home, but the mountain blocked her view. She rubbed her temples to push away the headache that was growing steadily inside her. "You think Dad and Carmen are okay?" she asked.

"I'm sure your dad's fine," Wash answered. "I'm not sure we should have left Carmen, though."

"I know," Ava replied. She prepared to add to the statement, but she chose to swallow the words instead.

"I wonder if they're taking her to the hospital." Wash stood and, as Ava had done, looked in the direction of Stone Temple. He knew there was no way to see the town from where they were. There was too much distance between them—too much stone and earth, too many decisions they probably shouldn't have made. But regardless of whether or not he thought they should have run away, there was never any question as to whether or not he should have followed Ava. They were caught in the gravity of each other, just as they always had been.

If he had stayed, she would have stayed. But since she left, he left.

"We should go," Ava said. She stood slowly. Her body swayed and she stumbled a little, but finally she caught her balance. After a few deep breaths, she gathered herself. "I'm okay," she said preemptively, looking at Wash. He was worried enough about her that it would not take much for him to turn back, and that was not part of her plan.

"They'll catch up to us eventually," Wash said. "You know they're not going to just let us run off like this."

"I know," Ava said. She tucked her hands into her pockets and shrugged away the cold. Her teeth had begun chattering and she tightened her jaw to stop them.

"Then what are we doing?" Wash asked.

"Just trust me, Wash," she replied.

"When haven't I?"

And off they went.

The two of them high-stepped over the underbrush and rocks and fallen branches and mysterious things that reach out from the darkness of a nighttime mountain and hinder progress. Wash had always been a little clumsy, and not being able to see much of where he was going now did not help things. He tripped over rocks, stumbled at dips in the path and generally had a tough time of things. His legs quickly grew tired and his ankles were sore from being rolled. There were a dozen things he wished he and Ava had done differently. They should have brought flashlights. They should have brought food. They should have brought more clothes. They should have chosen another path.

The fact that Ava was taking them north was of particular concern to Wash. The mountains around Stone Temple were formed so that, of all the cardinal directions a person could choose, north was the most difficult. The mountain rose and fell with both swiftness and suddenness. There were jagged patches where a bad stumble meant landing on the point of a rock. And there were places where the rocks were smooth and flat and, as the night brought dew, it was easy to slide and tumble down a long, unforgiving slope.

And to worsen matters there was no moon to see by. Over time Wash's and Ava's eyes adjusted to the dimness, but it was only the fact that they had traveled upon this land before that they made any headway and were not yet injured.

All of the worry about the mountain, all of the thoughts of the town, all of the stress over what they were doing, all of it swirled around in Wash's mind. He needed a distraction to keep himself from taking Ava by the hand and screaming for her to go back to town. Whatever it was she was leading them to, he wanted to let her have it. There are times in a life when one person follows another, regardless of where it leads. But that didn't mean he wasn't afraid.

"I wish I'd brought my copy of *Moby Dick*," he said. He decided not to call attention to the fact that it was night and the sky was moonless and, even if he had brought his book, he would have no way of seeing the words. "We need something to talk about," he added.

"I want to go back to that house," Ava said. She was ahead

of him on the trail and marching slowly, but in the stillness of the night, her voice carried. It was full of fatigue.

Wash was surprised by the topic. He didn't want to think about houses because that meant thinking about being indoors and warm and not alone in the middle of the woods. He tried to think of a joke, any joke at all, to lighten the mood, to further distract them. But nothing came to mind. "What house?" he asked.

"The one behind Dr. Arnold's. The big one with the tall fencing."

"The one where you're going to try to hide from everybody?" He meant it as a joke, but his tone missed the mark.

"Yeah," Ava said heavily. Then: "Maybe I wouldn't keep everyone out, though. Maybe, if you didn't bring in that damned book—and you know which one I'm talking about—maybe I'd let you in. Just you and me. Nobody else."

"You'd get tired of me," Wash said.

"That wouldn't happen," Ava said.

"Plus I'd still bring the book. So you'd have to deal with that."

"Jerk."

"Whatever," Wash said. "Besides, how do you know that you wouldn't get tired of me?"

"Because it's going to be you and me in the end, Wash." Ava was still huffing, but the conversation was making her forget just how tired she actually was.

"Like Beowulf and Wiglaf?"

"Like Lucy and Ricky."

"Okay," Wash said, smiling. "I think I could get behind that."

For a very long time after that the two of them were silent. They simply walked. And when Ava's breathing became labored again they stopped and looked at the path ahead.

The two of them stood there in the darkness with only the sound of the wind and of their own breathing and of their beating hearts to be heard. They would, now and again, prepare to speak, to say something that would take away the silence that had settled between them. But there was never anything that either of them felt needed saying and so they only stood within the gravity of each other. There was foreboding and splendor in those moments, adventure and fear. As if each of these moments were the last. Every moment was a breath that would not return.

Wash remembered moments in movies like this. Times when the guy and girl were alone just before they were destined to part ways. Sometimes they seemed completely oblivious to the fact that, for them, this was their final quiet moment of happiness. The fact that, from this point on, all things would get worse. Become more difficult. Completely fall apart in their hands.

But Wash knew what this moment was. And he wondered if Ava suspected.

It was then that Ava took Wash's face in her hands and kissed him. It was a clumsy kiss at first, the way first kisses often are. But the longer she held him the better it felt. Everything that was not Ava…faded away. It was a kiss that made him feel whole and alone all at once.

The possibilities of what life could be like for them swam through his mind as he became heady and slow from the feeling of Ava's lips pressed against his. He saw them living a life together, just as he saw the two of them dying in some horrible tragedy. He wondered where she was leading him, since she knew that they would not escape her father, the reverend and the town that would come looking for them.

"We've got to go," Wash said, pulling his lips away from Ava. When he finally opened his eyes and looked at her, there was something that, in the moonlight, looked like blood coming from her lip.

"Okay," Ava said, wiping her nose. She sniffled.

"Is that blood?" Wash asked.

"Let's go," Ava said.

Wash took her hand and pulled her close. He wiped her nose with the sleeve of his jacket. "I don't have any tissues," he said apologetically.

"It's okay, Mom," Ava said, half smiling.

"It's going to be okay," Wash said.

"I know," Ava replied.

"Ava's gone," Brenda said through the phone.

Macon could barely hear her over what was going on in the town around him. There was still a fire burning and people were crying and, where there wasn't crying, there was yelling and shouting—people barking orders, calling for help or yelling the name of someone they were not yet able to find. In the middle of it all was Brenda's voice, buzzing through cell phone static, telling him that his daughter was gone. "What are you talking about, Brenda?"

"Run off somewhere," she said. She spoke matter-of-factly, the way she always did. "She and Wash both. There were people here—must have been hurt from the explosion. They came here to Doc Arnold's wanting Ava to help them—demanding it is a better version. I got into yelling at them and whatnot. Anyhow, when it was all over, I went to find the kids and they were gone. Slipped out the back of the house in all of the commotion, I suppose."

"Jesus, Brenda!" Macon said. He turned around, looking in all directions, as if he might suddenly see them. "Where did they go? How did you let them leave? How long ago was it?" He rattled off the questions without giving her enough time to answer, even if she had the answers. "Where are you?" he added. "Are you out looking for them? Let me know where you are and I'll come meet you."

"I'm still at Doc Arnold's," she said.

"What the hell are you still doing there?" Macon barked.

"Doing what I can to help your wife," Brenda said flatly.

The words were like a bell being rung inside Macon. He froze and let the sudden fear he felt wash over him. "Brenda," he said slowly. "What's wrong?"

"The baby's coming early," Brenda said. "Doc Arnold says we need to get her Asheville, to the hospital. We're leaving soon. Don't know what the road out of town is going to be like with all of those people, but a couple of the policemen are driving us. Maybe that'll get us out of here faster."

"Put Carmen on the phone," Macon said.

There was the muffled sound of the phone being exchanged.

"Macon?" Carmen said. Her voice trembled slightly as she spoke. She cleared her throat and, when she spoke next, she had better masked the fear she felt. "I'm sorry," she said. "I don't know how Ava and Wash got away."

"Let me worry about that," Macon replied. "How are you feeling?" He walked over to a small bench that he happened to be standing by. He sat. In this moment, all of the commotion—the yelling, the people running by around him in a blur—all of it went away. There was only Carmen.

"I'm not good," Carmen said, almost crying. She made an awkward, clucking sound as she choked back the tears welling up inside of her. "You find Ava," she said. "I'll... we'll be okay. I can do this."

"I'm coming over there," Macon said.

"Don't be stupid," Carmen replied. "You've got to find Ava and Wash. You know that. You can't let them be out there on their own like that. There's no telling what will happen if someone else finds them first." She cleared her throat again. "Everything's so crazy," she added. "And, besides, we'll be on the way to the hospital before you get here. The baby's coming. It's too soon and everything hurts, but the baby's coming." Then she added, "I'm scared, Macon."

"I know," Macon said. He looked off in the direction of Dr. Arnold's. He could not see the house, but he knew where it was—just a few streets over, tall and old, waiting for him to come running. But what about Ava and Wash? "I'm scared, too," he said.

Carmen gasped in pain and there came the sound of several people talking at once in the background. "Carmen?" Macon called. "Carmen?"

"Hello?" a voice called through the phone. "Macon? That you?" It was Brenda.

"Brenda, what's happening?"

"We're going," Brenda said. Macon could hear her moving as she spoke. "We're going to the hospital. I'll stay with her. I'll take care of her."

"Thank you," Macon said. There was a powerlessness in him at that moment. It was the way he felt when he could not reach Ava and Wash to help them at the air show. It was the way he felt when she fell unconscious after healing the boy. It was the way he felt when the world came calling, taking over their small corner of life, pressuring him to make one questionable decision after another—all for the sake of trying to prevent what he felt was impossible to prevent: the moment when Ava would be taken away from him. Either by doctors or churches or simply by all of the people who wanted her to do something for them, to be something for them.

And, even more than all of that, he felt powerless the way he had on the day when he came home and found his wife hanging from the rafters of the barn, and his daughter on her knees, sobbing, becoming broken in a way that could never be healed.

"Just take care of her," Macon told Brenda. "I'll find the kids."

It was all he had left inside of him to say.

The search party swept out from Stone Temple like a great, calamitous fog. Their number was difficult to count. They were town locals, people from Reverend Brown's church, newshounds, the curious, the confused, the hopeful and they were even those simply concerned about a pair of young teenagers who had disappeared in the midst of horror and tragedy. It did not matter to them that they were strangers to the town, unaware of the intricacies of the mountains into which it was believed the children had fled. All that mattered to them was the return of the boy and girl.

Seeing that he would be the only one able to stem the tide of people heading off into the mountains on their own to search for the children, it was Macon who came up with the idea of pairing one local with a group of visitors. At least then the groups would have some means of navigation and, when the night ended, there would be fewer people lost among the trees and rocks and bracken and deep places of the mountains. If they were lucky, they wouldn't have to send out search parties to find the search parties.

Heading south, the country was harsh and the last thing he needed were strangers unfamiliar with the mountain stumbling through the darkness. There were pitfalls and precipices enough on the mountain to guarantee a tragic outcome. So he sent the majority of the searchers off to the south. The mountains were smoother there and it was the direction that led, soonest, to civilization. If the children were heading toward another town, hoping to catch a bus or to hitchhike away, that was the direction they would most likely go. He still wasn't sure exactly why they had disappeared. There was still the possibility that they had been taken by someone, but he doubted that.

With so many searchers combing the south, Macon took the more treacherous stretch of forest and headed north. He had a feeling that, if his daughter had escaped to the woods, she would probably have gone in this direction.

Ava was headstrong, and if she truly had it in her mind to run away, it would not be impossible for her. But she was sick, too. Sicker than he wanted to admit to himself. She had been dying, little by little, with each healing she performed. And he had pushed her into it.

This was the thought that haunted Macon, even as he watched the town burn around him. There were still fires to be put out, still people that needed tending to, and no help or emergency support had arrived yet. The fire department was doing what it could, but they were few and most of them too old and out of shape to be doing the work of putting out the massive blaze. This was the problem with being in a town where the worst emergency was a brawl at a barbecue. When you really needed help, it was hard to come by.

"Macon!" someone shouted. "Sheriff!"

Macon turned to see Reverend Brown racing over to him. The man's clothes were dirty and his face was riddled with worry. "Have you seen Sam?" Reverend Brown asked. His jaw was clenching and releasing and he was sweating. His breaths came fast and haggard. "Have you seen him? They found the man that takes care of Sam unconscious. Sam must have hit him and then ran off somewhere. Have you seen him?"

"No," Macon said, "but we will. If he's out here somewhere, we'll find him."

"You don't understand," Reverend Brown said. "He wanted to help. He wanted to help me." His voice trembled.

Finally, Macon was beginning to understand. "Jesus," he said.

"I don't want to believe it," Reverend Brown said. He placed his hand on the window of Macon's car. His hand was red with the force of it, as if he were holding to a life raft in the middle of the ocean.

"Just stay calm, Reverend," Macon said. "We'll find your brother. But, right now, I've got to find Ava. She and Wash have disappeared."

"Disappeared?"

"Ran away, from what I can gather," Macon replied.

"Where might they go?" Reverend Brown asked. The

confidence came back into his voice. "I'll take some people and I'll go," he said.

"You find your brother," Macon replied. "I'll find the children."

The ridgeline led the children to Rutger's cabin. It was nestled in the grip of dense pines and overgrowth, on a flattened section of the mountain. The cabin was hidden, but it was there, the imprint of the life left behind, enduring through all the years of neglect. The yard surrounding the cabin was wild and overgrown, but not impenetrable. There was a sense about it that it was being maintained by someone.

In the center of a stump near a small stack of old firewood, a rusty ax sprouted and pointed toward the sky. There was an old, rotted plow propped against the base of a tree as if someone had placed it there in a rush a long, long time ago. On another tree dangled what looked like animal traps. Wash studied them as he and Ava passed. She walked sure-footed and confidently through the yard, hardly noticing so many of the things that fascinated Wash.

He wanted to walk up beside her and take her hand, like a couple. It felt like the correct thing to do. But the thought of holding her hand that way was electric to him. It made his lungs tighten and created a buzzing in his ears like the hum of a thousand songs all playing at once: an infinite loop of tinny words and crescendos. It was enough to make him slightly dizzy, enough to make his stomach clench as if he had not eaten in years.

But maybe that's what love was.

There was a sprawling, almost feral growth of mint near the front of the cabin. Mingled in, somehow—straining and nearly choked to death—he could see sprigs of sage and what was, perhaps, thyme peeking up from among the mint. The mixture of the smells was hypnotic and he closed his eyes and inhaled deeply and imagined how the world would be if this one moment, this one aroma, covered it all.

"Watch your step," Ava said.

But already Wash was in the process of tripping over a tree root and tumbling to the ground.

"Smooth," Ava said with a grin.

Wash stood and brushed off his clothes and followed Ava as she went to the front door and opened it without hesitation. "Shouldn't we knock?" Wash asked.

Ava chuckled. "There's no one here but us," Ava said.

The old cabin smelled of dust and mildew. Inside, it was even smaller than it seemed from the outside. It was only four walls placed far enough to contain a bed and a wood-burning stove and a small table that sat beneath a broken window, covered in leaves and debris that the wind had deposited there over the years. On one of the walls, near an empty bed frame, there was a large hole in the wall through which the wind came. It was large enough for an animal—or a small adult—to slip through and Wash wondered how it came to be.

The place seemed built for a single person. It was never meant to hold more than one. It was, in many ways, the house that Ava had always wanted, somewhere where she might live alone and have her dogs and her silence. He wondered if this was where the idea had found its roots. And he wondered why she had never told him about this place before.

They went directly to the stove and opened it. Inside were

a few small logs—old and burned through. "We could find wood," Wash said.

"But we don't have any matches," Ava said. "And I'm cold."

"I can make the fire," Wash said. "My dad taught me."

His father's lesson had not fallen on deaf ears. Just as Tom had done, Wash walked around outside of the cabin and collected the smallest twigs and kindling he could find. It was difficult and slow work, and there was always, in his mind, the thought of how long this was all taking. There was a persistent feeling that time was not on his side. Every now and again he would hear the sound of Ava coughing from the cabin. The sound was a spur in his side.

He folded the bottom of his shirt up into a pouch and collected the kindling there. He picked up what rocks he could find, hoping that he might have good enough fortune to find some that he could strike together to make sparks. It was a foolish thought. It would take luck and fortune to have it happen, but he had hope.

When he came back inside Ava was curled up on the floor in front of the stove, shivering. She opened her eyes to look at him as he entered and she did not seem to recognize him. She closed her eyes again and seemed to tighten in on herself, like a frightened child. Wash emptied his collected items onto the floor and sifted through them. There was wood enough for his purposes, but the rocks were still uncertain. So he took his time and tried out different rock combinations he thought would work. After several failed attempts, there came a spark.

"It's gonna work!" he shouted. He turned to see if Ava had heard him, but she did not stir. Her eyes were closed and her breathing was slow—slower than he had ever seen before. "It's gonna work," he said again to himself.

Starting the fire took longer than he had expected. The kindling was easy enough to organize into the small stack that his father had demonstrated, but lighting it with the spark made by the rocks seemed a matter of luck more than planning. Again and again the sparks glimmered and darted through the air and landed atop the kindling and, again and again, nothing else happened. With each clap of the stones the frustration grew inside Wash. He noticed the cold more and more. Ava coughed, as if to remind him of what was at stake.

But he was relentless. Relentless until it finally produced results.

When the small thread of smoke began to rise from the kindling Wash held his breath. It was like watching a life being born, and the thought of all the ways it could be ended overcame him. His hands shook, but he forced them to form a wind barrier around the kindling—the way his father had that day—and he whispered, softly, into the ember, "She'll die if I don't make this work." Then he pursed his lips and blew as gently as he could manage and he prayed.

The fire caught.

The boy wanted to scream. He wanted to stand and dance and to pick Ava up and spin her around the way people did in movies. But, instead, he gently lifted the kindling from the floor and placed it into the stove where he had already stacked the wood. Now was not the time to get carried away.

For the next few minutes he sat in front of the stove and watched the fire grow. It danced at the occasional draft, and the fear that it might be extinguished rose up inside the boy each time, but the flame continued to grow until, finally, it was a steady, crackling fire in the belly of the cast-iron stove.

He laughed then—deep and heartily. "I did it, Ava," he said. She was still asleep on the floor, unaware of what he had done. For a while, Wash watched her sleep. Her breathing was slow and deep, but still she shivered. So he went over to lie down on the floor behind her and placed his arm around her and pressed his body against her and held the girl tightly. Almost immediately, the trembling stopped.

"I hope you're okay," Wash said, his words brushing against the back of Ava's neck. And, even though she did not reply, Wash decided that he had done the right thing. He decided that she would be okay. And the knowledge of it was enough that he could fall asleep.

Beneath the roof of the old cabin, among the dust and the cold night wind that came in through the broken window, carried on the legs of the moonlight, beneath the gentle crackling of the fire and the warmth that was filling the cabin more and more, beneath it all a boy held tightly to the girl he loved and a girl slept in the arms of the boy she loved and the rest of the world did not exist.

Brenda sat on the edge of Carmen's bed and held her hand and refused to leave her side. She was surprised by how quickly they made it to the hospital. She thought back to the day she brought Wash home after Ava's first healing. There had been so many people and reporters and cars lined up along the road with no way for a person to get through. Her fear, for Carmen's sake, was that the crowds would be far worse now, and they would not make it to the hospital. But the roads were mostly clear—only a few other cars, and very nearly all of them heading into town rather than out of it. Police cars, ambulances, news vans, all of them racing into the town as Carmen and Brenda raced out of it. But even though she was thankful on Carmen's behalf, she still worried about her grandson.

Yes, she trusted that he was old enough and smart enough to survive a night in the mountains. But she also knew that nothing was the way it had been. The worry formed a ball in her chest that made it difficult to breathe at times. It was only because of Carmen that she did not give in. "How would it look if I went to pieces now," Brenda said to herself as they reached the hospital.

"Any word on the children?" Carmen said as they brought her in.

"Macon'll sort that out," Brenda replied. "You got other things you need to see to." Then she squeezed Carmen's hand and walked beside her as the pregnant woman was rolled through the corridors of the hospital.

For Carmen, it was difficult keeping up with what was going on around her. The pain came quickly and it lingered, exhausting and terrifying her. She drifted in and out of consciousness. She could remember being placed on the stretcher at Dr. Arnold's, but the time when they loaded her into the ambulance was an empty place in her mind. She remembered Brenda talking to her about Wash and Ava as they rode to the hospital, but what was actually said was foggy.

Carmen smiled and nodded when the nurses came for blood samples and ran back and forth from doctor to doctor with the results. They medicated her and it made everything seem far away and woven from cotton. She lay in bed, holding her belly, sweating and breathing at an uneven pace and thinking to herself about Ava. She pitied the girl. She pitied everything that her life would become from this point forward. Whatever chance there may have been for Ava to have even a modicum of normalcy, it was gone.

Then someone took her hand. She hadn't heard anyone come into the room. The medicine had made her vision blurry and he appeared distorted to her.

"Carmen?" Dr. Arnold said. "Carmen, I just wanted to let you know that I'm here. Everything's going to be okay. There's a proper obstetrician here. I've discussed your pregnancy with him many times, and he's going to make sure everything is okay."

She tried to read the man's expression, mining it to discern whether or not he was telling the truth. It was all very foggy and uncertain for Carmen. She could see his face, but it was as if he were far away and gaining distance. She thought for a moment that it was Macon, but she knew that could not be true because he was off trying to find Ava and Wash. And that was where he was supposed to be, she knew—even as she resented him for it. Even as she resented the fact that he had left her here to bring this child into the world or to lose it. The entirety of the decision and responsibility was hers to contend with. She covered her belly and held her baby, as if he had come to take it away. "Is my baby going to be okay?" she asked.

Then she was asleep and dreaming, and Dr. Arnold was gone, though she could still hear the sound of his voice asking where her husband was.

And then her husband was there, only it was not Macon; it was Charles, her first husband, the first man she had loved and believed would be by her side for the rest of her life. He looked older than she remembered. But he had aged well, and she hated him for that. She hated the way her heart stirred at the sight of him even though she had grown to hate him over the years. Why would he come to her now, at a time when she was moving on with her life, about to bring into the world the child she had always wanted? That *they* had always wanted.

"It wasn't my fault," she said to her husband. "I did everything I was supposed to," she continued.

"I know," he replied. His voice was warm and even, the way he always spoke. He had never been an excitable man.

"It would have been easier if you had died," she said. "You didn't have to leave," she said. "It wasn't my fault."

"You did everything you could," he said.

"I tried to make you stay," she said.

"You never let go," he replied.

"You shouldn't have run out," she said.

"You shouldn't have sent me away," he replied.

And then he was gone and there was only darkness and something swirling about her that felt like wind and she thought she could hear the sound of someone screaming, far off in the distance. Her body tightened and she waited, though she did not know exactly what she was waiting for. It was as if she was waiting for the world to be created, waiting for the mountains to rise up out of the darkness of her mind.

But again there was the sound of someone screaming in the distance. She could not tell if it was a man or woman, child or adult, boy or girl.

But she was not alone. There was another life here.

"You shouldn't have left," she said to no one. "And I should have let you go."

★ ★ ★

The fire department was finally getting a handle on the blaze. The trucks had doused the flames for long enough and they were receding. It was the people that were the concern now. Everywhere there were injured and dead.

The firefighters were doing what they could and, mingled among them, were townspeople and strangers and other Samaritans lending aid. They raced from person to person, tending wounds and, sometimes, simply checking for signs of life. It was when the fire near the center of the event was all but extinguished that Isaiah Brown came across Sam's body. It was torn and broken, but Isaiah could still recognize the childish face of the man. Somehow it had eluded being burned. Though there was blood upon him, Sam looked asleep, caught in a perpetual dream.

Isaiah lifted his brother and moved him onto the grass in the center of the park. It was a place that the rescue staff decided was centralized enough and far enough away from the dying fire that they could take care of the injured and, when necessary, serve as a place for the bodies of the dead to be identified. He kneeled beside the covered body of the brother that he could not save, that he could only love over the years, and he pulled back the sheet that covered him. He reached down and stroked his brother's face. Already the man was cold, the color of his face ashen.

"I did everything I could, Sam," Isaiah said. The thought came to him that there were Bible verses appropriate to this moment. Final words of solace that he often gave at funerals.

But eulogies and epitaphs are not for the dead, but for the living. Sam would not hear his words. He was gone, to make a place for him on the other side, and to await the day when they would be able to speak to each other again—the day when the apology that Reverend Isaiah Brown felt he needed to give his brother would be heard, understood and, he hoped, accepted.

So for now he only leaned down and kissed his brother's forehead and tried to keep from crying. "All the broken things will be made whole," he said softly. Perhaps he said the words out of habit. Perhaps he said them because he hoped that, even though he was dead, Sam was there with him still, watching, listening, able to hear that his brother still loved him enough to say such things.

Or perhaps the words were intended for his own ears. Perhaps it was his way of letting go: of both the brother he lost in the car crash long ago, and the brother that had come into his life after, the one who wanted nothing more than to have things go back to the way they were, the brother who heard Isaiah say, "Nothing is ever healed," and who took the words to heart and, because of it, would not forgive himself.

"You were never broken, Sam," Isaiah whispered. "Never."

Ava and Wash had spent the day playing Commando, slogging through the creek and the bushes and briar. The logging company owned most of the mountain on which they were adventuring and the ditches were six feet deep and nearly twice as wide and they were always filled with water—stagnant and brackish in some places, running and almost clear in others.

The shadows grew at the base of the trees like spikes. The air cooled and the clouds came up out of the west—gray and heavy—promising the evening's shower that always came at this time of year. The crickets would soon sing.

"What'll we do tomorrow?" Wash asked.

"I say we go pick briar berries," Ava replied.

"They're called blackberries," Wash said.

"That's not what my mom calls them. And she says that things can be whatever we call them."

Wash thought on this for a moment. "Well," he said finally, "I don't know if I want to."

"That's just because you fell into that bush last time," Ava replied, giggling a little.

Wash blushed.

They walked in silence for the rest of the way. The mud and water caked upon their clothes hardened with each step. Their skin itched and they wished the rain would come sooner rather than later. The clouds were scraping their shaggy bellies over the peaks of the mountains, but remaining stingy.

When they reached Peterson's Fork, they parted ways. They waved goodbye to each other and set off for home. Wash's grandmother lived on the north end of town, near where the mountains had yet to be much affected by the imposition of humanity. Where the trees were old and rooted deeply into the earth. It was a place where generations of Stone Temple children found themselves and their place in this world—among the shadows of pine and cedar and white oak.

Ava had heard that Wash's grandmother owned much of the forest and, for reasons many in the town could not understand, would not let the logging companies have their hands at it. There was money to be made in the selling of the timber, after all. And if Stone Temple lacked anything, it was money.

When Ava arrived home, she was nervous approaching the house. Her clothes were caked with mud and, no doubt, her mother would have a great deal to say about it.

When she reached the house, she found it empty and silent. There was only the low hum of the refrigerator and the sound of the wind fluttering the curtains now and again. She called for her mother.

No reply.

On the kitchen table she found a letter, the contents of which led her to the barn. It was in the barn that Ava found her mother hanging from the rafters, a length of rope coiled around her neck. An overturned chair at her feet. The only sound was the buzzing of carpenter bees in the bones of the wood and, now and again, a gentle creak of the wooden beam as it struggled to bear the weight it had been given.

TEN

WASH COULD NOT tell how long he had been sleeping, but it could not have been very long because the fire was still burning. The cabin was warm and comfortable, in spite of all of the gaps in the walls through which the wind crept. He could smell the sweat from Ava's skin along with the scent of the pine logs burning. He lingered there on the floor of the cabin, his body cradling Ava's. All he could think of was the kiss that she had given him and he wondered what he should do next. He closed his eyes and could feel her lips against his: the tenderness of the skin, the cold air washing over them both. The moment grew into hours in his mind, one that he could live in for an eternity.

But there was a fire that needed tending to. He decided that he should check on it. When he went to lift the arm that was draped across Ava he found her fingers intertwined with his. She held him there.

"Ava?" he called softly.

"I'm awake," she answered in a low voice.

He sighed. "Good. You had me worried." He felt her squeeze his hand.

"I remember her," Ava said.

"Remember who?"

"I remember my mom," Ava said. "Every time I help somebody, I remember her, the details about her, I mean. The way she smelled, the sound of her voice, the softness of her hands. I didn't really know how much I had forgotten about her until now." Her voice shook. "I couldn't remember the sound of her voice before all of this. I couldn't remember the color of her eyes. How does that happen?"

Wash was thankful that Ava had her back to him, that she could not see the despair in his eyes. More than anything, he wanted to say the right thing. But, in the end, he said nothing. The only sound in the small cabin was the fire burning.

"But I can't remember all of it," Ava said. "I just get pieces, glimpses. And I try to talk to her. I try to ask her why she did it, why she killed herself. But she never answers me. It's like she's in a play and can't change her lines. It's like she can't stop what's going to happen to her."

"I'm sorry," Wash replied. It was the only thing that he could think to say.

"It's okay," Ava said, her voice soft, like a secret told in a cathedral. "I'm okay with it all now," she said.

It was then that Wash could smell it: the scent of vomit. He sat up and there, on the floor in front of Ava, was a pool of bile and blood. "Jesus," he said, bolting up from the floor.

"Oh, my God, Ava," he said. He took her arm and helped her sit up. She swayed drunkenly back and forth. He waved his hand in front of her and it took her a moment to focus on him. "We've got to go back," Wash said.

"I know," Ava replied. "I just wanted more time with you. I just wanted to—"

"You can't save me," Wash said suddenly. His voice was so low that Ava hardly heard him. But she did hear him. "I'm smarter than the average Pomeranian," he continued, trying, unsuccessfully, to lighten the mood. "I may not know a lot of things, Ava Campbell. But I know you. I know what you're thinking." He took a deep breath and held it. And when he released it, he spoke slowly and there was fear and resignation in his voice. "I know about the leukemia. Everybody thinks that I don't. Nobody wants to talk to me about it, like that'll make it go away. But I know about it. I heard one of the nurses talking about it when I was at the hospital. I don't think she meant for me to hear, but I did. People are rarely as good at keeping secrets as they think they are." He looked around. "I guess not telling me about it was everybody's way of helping me. And I guess my pretending that I didn't know about it was my way of helping everybody else." He laughed. "That doesn't make any sense, does it?"

"Wash," Ava began.

"It's okay," he said, holding up a hand to stop her from speaking. "I'll be okay. I've researched it and I've got a chance. The survival rate is low, but not impossible. It's like spotting a white whale, and that's happened before, right?" He tried to laugh at the joke, but the comedy was not there. "You can't save me, Ava," Wash said slowly. "It'll kill you. We both know it. And I won't let you try."

"You're something else," Ava said. Suddenly the shivering began again.

Wash sat on the floor beside her and placed his arm around her and pulled her close. "You can't even save yourself," he said. "But I'll take care of you. I'll sing badly and read books you don't like so you'll get better, if only to make me shut up."

Then he reached over and took her earlobe between his fingers and tugged it, the way she had done to him in the hospital. "I'll always take care of you."

It was the dim glow of their firelight that caught Macon's attention. He could just make out the small cabin planted in the elbow of the mountain, the light from it flickering like a candle in a difficult wind. From outside the cabin he could see a glimmer through the cracks in the broken wood and he could see the silhouette of someone sitting by a dim light of what looked like a wood-burning stove. He could see that it was a child, and he could tell arms were wrapped around their legs, but he couldn't discern exactly whether it was Ava or Wash.

He did not hesitate any longer.

"Ava," Macon called as he came through the door.

She looked up at him with an expression on her face of fatigued expectation, as if she were finally waking from a moment she knew, all along, was nothing more than a dream.

"Hey, Dad," she said softly.

Macon crossed the room at a lope and placed his arms around her. He hugged her and, simultaneously, began checking to see if she was injured. "Are you okay?" he asked, then he turned to Wash. "Are the both of you okay?"

"We're fine," Wash said.

"Ava," Macon said, taking his daughter's face in his hands. "Ava, what were you thinking? You could have been killed. You have to know that."

"I needed to get away," Ava replied. "Even if it was just for a little while."

"Where did you think you were going?"

"Nowhere. Just here. Just away from everyone."

"Jesus," Macon said, and he hugged her again. He held her tightly and kissed the top of her head. "You could have been killed," he said. "I could have lost you." He took a moment and studied her face, and it was as though he were seeing her for the first time in years. Finally, more clearly than he had before, he saw the thinness of her face, the way the skin seemed stretched too tightly over the bones. He saw circles of exhaustion around her eyes. He felt the texture of her hair—dry and brittle, as if it, too, were worn too thin. "I'm sorry," he said. "I'm sorry for all of this. But running away isn't the answer."

"I don't want to go back," Ava said.

"I know," Macon replied. "I know you don't." He sat beside her. Wash eased down onto the other side of the girl. "I know you want to get away, you want for all of this to end, but I'm sure you also know that we can't sit here and pretend that the two of you running away into the night is something that we can just let happen." He sighed and looked down at his hands, as if laying blame upon them. "We'll go back and things will be different," he said.

"No, they won't," Ava replied. She leaned against Wash. "They'll never leave me alone. This will never stop."

"That's not true," Macon said, though he wasn't sure if

he believed it. "I'll find some way to make all of this better, to make everyone go away and leave us alone. I can fix all of this. I can get our lives back to the way they were, back to normal."

"She's not going to do it anymore," Wash said. "Not for you, not for anyone." He looked into Macon's eyes as he said it. Even though he was still a child, and a Southern child—raised with all the rules of formality between adults and children, indoctrinated with the belief that parents knew what was best and it was a child's position to do as they were told—regardless of all of that, he still cared for Ava and he had promised to take care of her. "I won't let anything happen to her."

"I know you won't, Wash," Macon said. "And neither will I. I promise it'll be different. It'll be like it was. It'll just take some time to sort out, is all. I'll admit, people won't forget quickly or easily." Macon sighed. "You're able to help people, Ava," he said, taking his daughter's face in her hands. "You're able to help people and give them hope and do things that no one else in this world is able to do."

"She deserves her own life," Wash said.

"And she'll have it," Macon said.

"They're always going to want something," Ava said. "There's always going to be someone who wants me to help them. And I'll have to tell them no—over and over again. I'll have to say no like I did to the boy at the church and I'll have to see that look he had in his eyes." She shook her head. "I don't want to have to do that," she said. Her voice began to tremble. "But I can't keep doing this, either," she said.

Both Macon and Wash searched for the words to comfort the girl. They knew what they wanted to say, how they

wanted to reassure her that there was another possible outcome to all of this. But when they both imagined all the ways
that the future might unfold for Ava from this point forward,
the consequences of her gift upon a world that longed for
such things was irrevocable and undeniable.

She would never be allowed to rest. Never be allowed to
live a normal life. She would always be imposed upon, always hounded, pulled in a million and one directions.

"I'm sorry," Macon said.

"I want to help people," Ava replied. She looked up at
her father. "If it was just that I got tired or sick after I did
it, I could handle that. I'd get through it. I'd keep doing
it. But every time I do it, I remember Mom. Every single
time, something that I had forgotten about her comes back
to me. And that wouldn't be so bad, but I wonder...I wonder if I could have helped her. I wonder if I had it in me to
heal her before she killed herself and I missed it." She was
crying now. "I can't help but think it was my fault."

Macon pulled her close and hugged her tightly. "It wasn't
your fault," he said. "It wasn't your fault." He repeated the
sentence again and again. Saying it to Ava, but also saying
it to himself.

"Why did she do it, Dad?" Ava asked. Her voice was full
of years of pain and longing, full of too long spent not understanding how it could be that a mother, a wife, could end
it all, step off into the darkness of eternity, leaving a family
adrift in the world behind her.

"I don't know why she did it," Macon said. His voice
shook, and he was crying, as well, though he did not know
when it had begun. "I wish I could say why she did it, but
the truth is that I don't know. I'm not sure one person can

ever truly know or understand why someone does something like that. But I do know that it doesn't mean she loved you any less. It doesn't mean you missed something or failed to do something. It doesn't mean it was your fault," he said.

And then the two of them wept together, and Macon rocked back and forth slowly and squeezed his daughter more tightly and he wished that he, finally, started to believe for himself that his wife's death had not been his own fault. He had carried inside himself, over the years, just as much guilt about Heather's death as Ava had. Likely as not, he carried more, because Ava had only been a child at the time when, if Heather had given any signals about what she was about to do, they might have been noticed. But he was the one who had missed the signs. He was the one who had been too busy or too distracted or whatever it was that made a person not realize when something so terrible was on the verge of happening.

He had blamed himself for his wife's death. Each and every day he blamed himself, though he did not realize it until now, when his daughter wept in his arms, begging to be forgiven for something that was not her fault.

"It was nobody's fault," he repeated. "We both loved her. And she knew that we loved her and she loved us back. That's all we can ever hope for in life."

The march back to town was long and winding. Macon carried Ava in his arms. She was limp, drifting in and out consciousness. Eventually they emerged from the forest with Macon, and a crowd raced to them, cheering.

Macon called for an ambulance and, maybe because he was the sheriff but more likely because the Miracle Child was sick and needed help, the paramedics came immediately and they began the long drive to the hospital.

Wash would not let Ava out of his sight. "We'll get her to the doctor," everyone said. She was placed on a stretcher in back of the ambulance and she, Macon and Wash started off over the mountain. There was a crowd of people and cars along the road, but they parted when they heard that the ambulance was carrying Ava.

"You kids gave everyone a good scare," the paramedic in the ambulance said. He monitored Ava's vitals as he spoke. "I can't believe I'm the one who gets to save you," he said to Ava. Outside the van, as they passed alongside the mountain, they could see the flashing of camera lights as they zoomed over the two-lane road out of Stone Temple. The world would not let her go. They would be there in Asheville, she knew, waiting, snapping photographs, waiting for her to tell her story.

But she would disappoint them all. For now, she simply had to hold on.

"Has anyone heard anything about my wife?" Macon asked the man in the back of the ambulance.

"Who's your wife?" he responded, though his attention was still focused on Ava

"Shit," Macon said. He took out his phone and called Carmen. No answer. When he tried Brenda, the result was the same.

"Is Carmen okay?" Ava asked.

"I'm sure she is," Macon replied quickly. "She's at the hospital with Brenda. We'll check on them when we get there and get you squared away."

"Did she have the baby?" Wash asked.

"I don't know," Macon replied. "I don't know anything," he added.

When they had finally made their way through the sediment of people and were starting down the mountain properly, the paramedic driving reached into his pocket and took out his phone and started a conversation with someone. "She's right here," he said proudly. "I get to bring her back. Can you believe that?"

Macon reached out and snatched the phone from the man's hand. He dropped it to the floor and stepped on it without explanation or apology.

Wash hated the man driving just then. He hated whoever it was the man was talking to. He hated all of the people who had been there when they had emerged from the forest, watching them pull away and start down the mountain. He hated everyone who had come to Stone Temple looking for some kind of salvation, and everyone sitting at home watching television and surfing the internet, waiting to hear that Ava had been found. He hated the world.

"I wish we could have done it," he whispered. "I wish we could have gotten away."

"We weren't supposed to," Ava whispered back, low and soft, her head rocking back and forth gently on the stretcher. Her thick dark hair formed a crown and framed her dark skin. She looked like a painting.

Wash flinched. "I thought you were asleep."

"I was," Ava said, "but I heard your voice."

"I'm sorry."

"Don't be," Ava replied. "That wasn't how I meant it." She coughed, and it was a wet, hacking cough. "I heard your voice the way I heard it that day in the hospital. You've got a good voice."

Ava shivered. Wash asked the paramedic for another blanket. Behind the ambulance there were the bright lights of others driving down the mountain, following the Miracle Child.

"Don't worry about it," Ava said softly.

"Are you doing any better?" Wash asked.

"No," Ava said. Then: "You smell like pine needles." She laughed softly.

Wash looked out the window. The mountain fell away and, up ahead, he could see the lights of the town rising up from the darkness. Now and again they passed people parked along the edge of the road. Already the news that Ava was being brought back to town had spread and everyone was preparing. Some of the people held up signs. Others cheered and clapped as the police car passed. "I'm sorry," Wash said.

"For what?" Ava replied.

"For being excited about all of this when it first started. For, I don't know, for everything."

"Do you want to know something?" Ava asked.

"Sure," Wash replied.

"I actually don't mind *Moby Dick*. It's not as bad as I always say it is."

Wash smiled, but with his face turned away, Ava could not see it. "That's good to know," he said. "It's one of the best books in the world, you know."

"That's what I keep hearing," she replied. "Thank you for coming with me tonight. Thank you for making that fire."

"We had to stay warm," Wash said.

"I wasn't asleep when you were making it," Ava answered.

"Not completely. I saw you. I could see your face in the light of the fire. You looked scared, but you kept going."

"You could have helped out," Wash joked.

"I liked watching you," Ava said. "I liked the way your face looked."

Wash giggled. "First I smell like pine needles. And now you're all obsessed with how my face looked. What happened to the Ava who told me I reminded her of the marshmallow man from *Ghostbusters?*"

"They're the same person," Ava replied.

Then there was a moment of silence in which Wash's mind began to ponder the nature of their conversation. In all of his life, he had never heard Ava speak in the tone she had now. There was a quiet reservation in it, a type of "giving up." As though, finally, she had stopped resisting something that she had been fighting against for a very long time. All of the talk of smells and how he had looked, as though she had been trying to capture images of him.

It was then that the thought came into his mind. "Ava," he said sharply. "Ava, open your eyes."

She hesitated. She grinned, but her expression was full of fear.

"Please, Ava," he said. He squeezed her hand and, slowly, she opened her eyes. Then, in the passing glare of the street-lights as they entered Asheville, he saw it: her eyes were filled with gray. It was as if she had captured the winter sky within them.

"Ava," Wash said slowly, "you can't see, can you?"

When they reached the hospital Ava had vomited in the back of the ambulance. Hordes of people had gathered and were there to see it all when the doors were opened. But even the sight of it was not enough to quiet them. They still called her name, still yelled for her to turn and look at them so that they could better frame their photographs.

The nurses raced her down the hall and into an examination room. Wash chased after, and when they told him he could not come with her, Macon told them simply, "He's coming."

Then the onlookers became nothing more than a wall of flashing light and sound. The cameras flashed in brightness and everyone clamored. It took a line of policemen standing with arms interlinked to keep them all back.

Though Ava could not see the lights and the people, she could feel their fervor. It was like the crashing of the ocean against the shore. But through it all, there was the sound of Wash's voice—constant and familiar as a cone of light reaching out from a lighthouse—just as it had been that day in the hospital.

"We'll get you fixed," Macon said.

"Okay," Ava said.

The darkness in which Ava existed was not as terrifying as she had expected it to be. She was thankful that neither Wash nor her father could see the pain she felt. It was the same pain that she had felt every day since the beginning of all this: a constant type of hollowness, an emptiness in her bones and blood, as though certain parts of her did not exist anymore. The pain was rising, slowly. Filling her up like sand. She was better at controlling it than before. She was finally understanding how to navigate it, how to take it in small doses rather than to have it wash over her all at once.

"Here we go," Macon said as they finally placed her on the mattress. He stroked her head.

Macon looked around for a doctor but there was none nearby. There were too many other patients with serious injuries that had been arriving from Stone Temple. The explosion and the fire that followed had injured more people than Macon expected. So the doctors did what they could, helping who they could. People were shouting for nurses and being rushed into surgery. The room was a maelstrom of people.

Macon needed help for his daughter, and he also needed to find his wife.

"Damned doctors," he said in frustration.

"Where's Carmen?" Ava asked.

"I'm going to find out," Macon asked. "I just need you to stay here for a minute. I'll be back," he said, and he kissed Ava's brow. "Just…just let me see that they're okay." A nurse came over and began checking Ava's vitals. Macon said something to the woman, then raced off to find Carmen. In that one moment, he felt like a horrible father and husband. Nothing was going the way it should have gone. He did not want to leave Ava, but he had left Carmen for too long already. If things turned a certain way, he could lose a wife and two children tonight.

There were no right decisions anymore. There were only the consequences of the decisions he made.

"Where's Carmen?" Ava asked after Macon was gone.

"I don't know," Wash replied. He looked around, just as Macon had done, but he saw nothing.

"I wasn't asking you," Ava said softly. "I was asking the nurse."

The woman had been checking Ava's blood pressure. She stopped. "Excuse me?"

"Do you know who I am?" Ava asked. Though she could not see the nurse, she imagined her with a kind face, not unlike her mother's and, at the same time, not unlike Carmen's.

"Of course I know who you are," the woman replied. There was a small degree of reverence in her voice. To be sure, she knew who the Miracle Child was.

"I need to find my stepmom," Ava said. "Can you help me?"

"You're in no condition to go anywhere," the woman said. The awe in her tone was lessened as her training as a nurse began finding its footing again. She was used to people trying to get up in the middle of an examination. People were stubborn when they were hurt, no matter if you were simply trying to help them.

"Please," Ava said. "I'm worried about her. Please."

Ava heard the clicking of camera shutters. "Get out of here!" the woman shouted. Then there came the sound of people shouting Ava's name followed by more camera shutters. The reporters had made their way into the hospital. But still the nurse would not allow Ava off the examination table.

It was Wash who ended the standoff.

"She just wants to see her mother," Wash said in a loud, pleading voice. Ava could only imagine the reaction on the woman's face. Suddenly the sound of the cameras was louder than before. "She wants to see her mother and father and this woman won't take her to them!" he shouted. Since the start of all this, the boy had learned, like Macon, that being the center of attention could be turned to one's benefit when they needed it.

The nurse protested, but Wash repeated it over and over again until it became an accusation that, with all of the cameras watching and recording it, the nurse could not ignore.

"Okay," the woman said finally.

Ava was helped into a wheelchair and rolled down the corridors of the hospital. Wash walked beside her. She was tired and cold and hurting and there were people shouting her name, asking for help, asking for healing. But all she thought of was Carmen.

"What are you doing here?" Macon asked when they entered the room. "What are you doing bringing her here?" he asked the nurse. His voice was bitter and hard. "Has she seen a doctor?"

"It's not her fault," Wash said. "I made her bring us. Ava wanted to come."

"I'm sorry," the nurse said. "I just didn't know what else to do. She kept demanding to be brought in to see her stepmother. I tried to stop her, but the two of them...they—"

"Get out," Macon snapped. "Go get a doctor."

The woman left without a word.

"Where's the baby?" Ava asked. She was still in the wheelchair, with her arms folded across her stomach. Because of her blindness, Ava could not see the incubator in front of which Macon was standing. She could not see the way his face was streaked with tears. And she could not see the small, fragile child inside the incubator—attached to hoses and tubes, struggling to breathe each breath.

"She's here," Macon replied. The hardness was gone from his voice, replaced by the weakness of a frightened father. "You've got a sister now. Her name's Elizabeth. She's beautiful—just like you, just like Carmen." He paused. "But the baby's struggling. She's got blood in her lungs."

"Let me help her," Ava said.

The statement floated in the air. It expanded until it filled the entire room and pushed into Macon's chest and made his lungs tighten. "No," he said. Ava could not see the way he trembled when he said the word. "You'll die," he continued. "I've already lost your mother. I won't lose you, too." He looked at the baby. "I won't lose anyone else. I won't."

"Dad," Ava called. She sat up straight and tried to look as strong and confident as she could. She needed to convince her father to let her do the thing that he was afraid to. She needed him to believe that she could survive helping the child, that everything would be okay, that the entire family would survive the night.

She needed him to hold to that truth, even if she was not certain of it herself.

"Dad," Ava repeated when Macon did not answer. "I'll be okay. You won't lose me. Let me help my sister. Let me help Elizabeth." Then, with Wash's help, she stood and followed as the boy led her across the room to where Elizabeth lay.

Macon made a move to stop her, but he did not follow it through. A part of him knew that she would not be okay, no matter how much his daughter wanted him to believe it. But what about his other daughter? What about Elizabeth? If Ava could help the child, shouldn't she be allowed to try? He could no more bear the thought of losing one of them than he could bear the thought of losing them both.

He was trapped between two horrors, and they paralyzed him into inaction.

"She's right in front of you," Wash whispered into Ava's

ear when they reached the incubator. There were latches that sealed it, and the boy released them. "Here," he said, and guided Ava's hand.

Ava reached forward into the darkness until her hand touched the edge of the bassinet. It was cool to the touch. Then her hand felt the softness of a blanket. She slid her hand forward slowly, afraid that she could hurt the baby, but knowing that her intentions were just the opposite. The baby was impossibly soft when she finally touched her. With skin like cloth itself. And her mind marveled at how small she was, how tender. Anything in the world could break her, she thought.

"Ava…" Wash said.

"It's okay, Wash," Ava replied. Then she placed her hand atop the child's.

What came next was like falling—a lifting off and a pulling down all at once. Memory upon memory rose up in her mind. Everything that she had lost of her mother after the woman's death came back to her, as though a door had been unlocked in her mind. She remembered the night a bear came to their house. She remembered the clanging pots and pans, all the ways the family hoped to keep the outside world at bay. She remembered going to the fair, being carried on her father's shoulders, the way her mother smiled that night. She also remembered the way the smile faded at the end of the evening, and how that change was the beginning of her understanding of her mother. The day the two of them spent digging in the backyard, the day they went off and found a puzzle box at a yard sale…all of it came back to her and, for the first time ever, she saw the entirety of her mother—all of her mother's grandness, all of her terror, the ebb and flow of her mother's emotions, the shifts between happiness and joy. All of it Ava could see and understand suddenly.

An entire lifetime came and went and, in the scope of understanding its entirety, Ava could finally see the long, winding road that led her mother to the rafters of the barn that day. And she could see that, upon that road, there was no guilt. She had loved her mother. And her mother had loved her. And, sometimes in life, love and loving can still lead to an ending that we would otherwise choose. A fate with no blame to be taken. She understood that, in this world, there are unexplained wonders and faultless horrors both.

"We're going to get you help, Ava," Wash said. His voice was low and far away, like the calling of a bird in the deep of the night. He squeezed her hand and she squeezed his in reply. She could not tell how long he had been speaking to her. "You did it," he said, his voice heavy with sadness. "You healed the baby."

"Good," Ava said, slowly waking. Before her eyes she still saw only darkness, but at least the pain was gone. Replacing it there was simply a numbness, a type of drifting off that her body seemed to be doing, getting farther and farther away from the girl. She wished she could have seen Wash's face.

"Don't go drifting off," Wash said, and Ava could hear the tears in his voice just as clearly as if she had been able to see them on his face.

Somewhere far away Macon was yelling, calling for help. Screaming for people to rush from whatever they were doing. But then the sound of his voice drifted away into the darkness, the way her body was doing. She could not feel her feet or her legs. And her arms were little more than imaginings—like constructs of dust and air.

But she could not let go of Wash's voice.

"Talk to me, Wash," Ava said.

"Talk about what?" he replied.

"Read to me," she said. She could feel a weight on her chest, rising up and down slowly. She could count by the rhythm of it. Up, down…up, down… The weight continued. But it was slowing, ever so slightly, as time marched forward. "Where's your copy of *Moby Dick?*"

She heard Wash laugh. Or perhaps it was a sob hidden within a laugh.

"I don't want to," he said. "The truth is I hate that book. I always have." His voice was confessional and apologetic—as if he had held the words within himself for too long. "Honestly, I don't understand it. It's a mess. But I always wanted you to think I was smart and it's a book that smart people like."

Ava laughed, and she hoped that it did not sound mocking. It was not meant to. Again, she wished that she could see Wash's face. "I know," she said.

"Then why didn't you say anything?" He laughed now, and it was genuine. "Why'd you suffer through it?"

"Because I can't think of a single time when I didn't want to hear the sound of your voice," Ava replied. The up-and-down sensation she felt in her chest was still fading. She understood now that the feeling was that of her lungs, slowing. "Just talk to me, Wash," Ava said. "Sing something to me. I just want to hear your voice a little more."

"All the songs I know are about people dying," Wash said. He spoke slowly, as if each word were an anvil falling upon his heart. Then, after a moment, Ava heard the boy clear his throat. The song he sang then was one that she had never heard before. It was a ballad, soft and somber. It spoke of a man and a woman, of love, of loss, of the moment between the loving and the losing, of the starlight that shined down upon her body as she lay by a slow-moving river and he held her and wished that things could be different than they had been.

He sang beautifully. His voice was rich and deep. It did not falter the way it always had. He did not stagger, he did not pause. She could see the story of his song. She could see the words themselves in the darkness of her mind. They shined like a sea of fireflies.

The song broke off halfway through. She could hear him crying. "Don't cry, Wash," Ava said.

"I'm not crying," he sobbed. She heard his sniffle. "You're going to be okay," he said.

"You are, too," Ava replied softly.

The boy paused. He put together the pieces of their time together that night, and the terrible truth of it washed over him. Then, after a moment, he said, "It was up on the mountain, wasn't it? You did something when you kissed me." His voice found its footing. "That's when you started getting sick. You healed me when you kissed me, didn't you? And that's why you got sick, isn't it?" He swallowed. "You shouldn't have done that," he said, sorrow clouding his words.

"How does the song end?" Ava asked.

"What?"

"Your song," she said slowly. "How does it end?"

"It ends the way all those songs end," Wash said after a moment.

To Ava, his voice became heavy and old, as though all of the years of his future life had come to settle inside of him all at once. As if he would never again be a child from this point forward.

"But it doesn't have to end that way," Wash said. Then, without pausing, he cleared the sadness from his throat and, after a moment, resumed the song that he had been singing for Ava. There was still death and sorrow in the tale, but it began to turn. It became a song of love, a ballad of renewal, a story that, at the end of which, just when the two lovers were farthest apart, they found each other, and lived.

They both lived.

Then the faraway feeling in Ava's legs and arms, the numbness, disappeared. The darkness created by her blindness became deeper and she felt as if she were moving through it at an impossible speed, flying, free and liberated. There was no fear in this moment, in this letting go that was happening, because behind it all—soft and warm and almost calling to her—was the sound of Wash's voice. It was everything: that sound, that cadence, that piece of the boy that she would never let go of, not even in death. And his voice pulled her toward it. It became a beacon, a mixture of light and sound at the end of a tunnel walled in by darkness. She raced toward it, toward the light, toward the voice of the boy she loved.

It was October, the time of the Fall Festival. Stone Temple's final celebration before the snow and the hard, cold nights—that long, lethargic continuity of winter—would come and settle upon the town and its inhabitants. Each year the townspeople assembled at the sweeping, open field that sat in the bowl of the mountains. They set up bleachers and sheltered them around the old grain silo that was no longer used and vendors came and there was popcorn and cotton candy and funnel cakes and pies and exotic decorations, the likes of which the children of small towns are seldom to find in their portion of this world.

Each year everyone in the town attended, and when Ava was six years old her mother and father bundled her up for the cold wind that would come sweeping down off the northern mountains once the sun set and the lights of the festival began to glow and they took her to the festival, hoping that she would finally be old enough that the memory of it would stay with her.

She spent most of the evening in a dream of amazement. The sights and sounds and the smell of sweet, candied fruit that her parents rarely allowed her was intoxicating. She rode the Ferris wheel for the first time just before sunset and craned her neck to look up into the sky as a man in a small airplane performed stunts in the fading light. He rose and fell through the sky as it slid from blue to gold to purple and the blackness of night encroached. And then the announcer in the grain silo made a remark about the pending darkness. The man in the airplane landed in the far end of the field and the crowd cheered. Ava asked her father how it was that planes were able to fly and he smiled at her and said, simply, "All things are possible in this world."

It was after the Ferris wheel—when the night was fully stretched across the earth—that Ava met the boy. She was standing in line for cotton candy with her parents when she saw him in front of her looking back at her with an expression of great curiosity. He was small for his age and very pale, with brown hair and a sharp nose and he sucked his thumb.

Around the two of them there was the buzz of people talking and vendors shouting for patrons to test their luck and calls for people to buy tickets to the haunted house at the far end of the festival and on and on. It was an ocean of sound that could become so loud at times it made Ava's ears hurt. But in spite of all this, she heard very clearly when the boy in front of her took his thumb out of his mouth and waved at her and said in a polite voice, "Hi. I'm Wash."

"I'm Ava," she said.

And then he stepped forward and took her hand in that gentle way that children do and said, "Do you want to come over to my house and play?"

Ava nodded happily.

Ava's parents and the boy's parents looked down at the children and they laughed. And the laughter was light and full of joy and free of worry. "Instant friends," Wash's father said, and the adults laughed again.

The children stood and looked at each other and they could not help but smile at the exuberance of their parents. They shared the cotton candy they had both been waiting in line for and, for the rest of the night, they would not be parted from each other. They walked among the lights and glitter of the evening, talking and holding hands, and creating the future that they would share together.

Ava held Wash's hand for as long as she could that night. In her heart, she made the childish promise to never let him go.

★ ★ ★ ★ ★

ACKNOWLEDGMENTS

DEEPEST GRATITUDE TO Michelle Brower and Erika Imranyi, the best agent and the best editor I could have ever asked for. And let me give a particularly huge verbal hug to Erika for everything she's done for me as an editor. Too many good deeds to recount, but they are all remembered and appreciated.

A huge round of high fives to the usual rogue's gallery of friends and family who continue to love, support and encourage me. There are too many to list here, but I pray that you all know how much I love you and how grateful I am to have you in my life.

Lastly, I would like to especially thank my readers and fans. I've discovered many wonderful, warm and loving people in the past year, and I cannot thank you enough for the kindness you have all shown me.

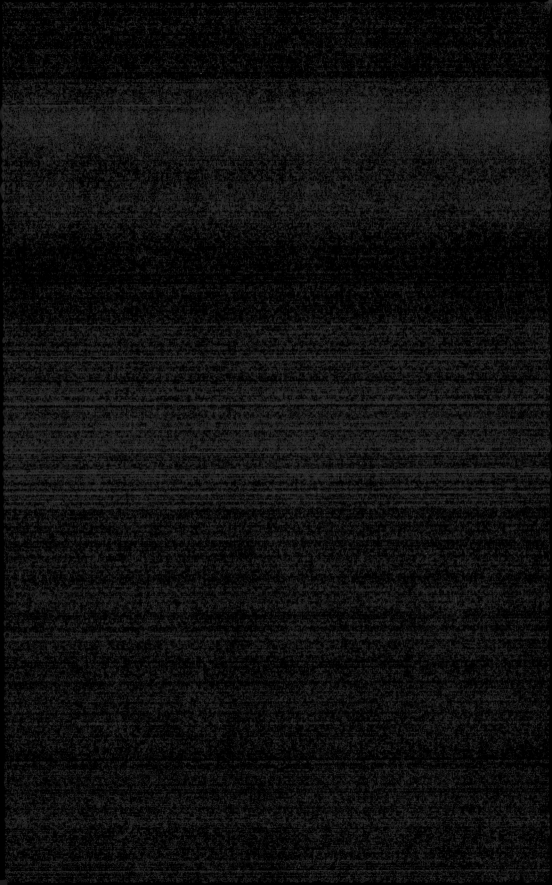